Producer & International Distributor
eBookPro Publishing
www.ebook-pro.com

Mission Patriot
Charlie Wolfe

Copyright © 2019 Charlie Wolfe

Contact: Charlie.Wolfe.Author@gmail.com
ISBN

MISSION
PATRIOT

CHARLIE WOLFE

PROLOGUE

September 11, Houseboat on Dal Lake, Srinagar, Kashmir, India

The slim girl was swimming as fast as she could in an attempt to outpace the muscular man chasing her. She was trying to get to the houseboat that was just fifty feet ahead.

He was rapidly closing the distance between them with long, powerful strokes. She squealed with joy and excitement as she reached the wooden stairs leading from the tranquil, clear water to the deck of the houseboat and mounted the first step. Less than a second later, he also mounted the same step and managed to grab her ankle before she could get to the third step.

She fell into his arms and in Hebrew told him she loved him, although he swam like a whale while she could swim like a dolphin. They were too engrossed in each other to notice the two gunmen that were just stepping out of the door that led to the small kitchen of the houseboat. One of the gunmen pointed his AK47 at them and while shouting something in Urdu, motioned them to get into the kitchen. The other gunman removed a long curved knife from the folds of his robe and wielded it in an arc that would have severed the girl's head had she not moved away fast enough.

The muscular man spoke English and said they had some money they would gladly give them if they left them alone. The gunman with the knife pulled the man by his hair and pushed him into a flimsy rattan kitchen chair, pulled four strong nylon cable ties and secured his feet to the legs of the chair and his arms to the armrests. The girl, who at a closer look appeared to be in her mid-twenties got the same treatment, with some unnecessary pawing by the gunman. Her man, who was in his late-twenties, just grunted and swore under his breath but stopped when the gunman whipped him with the butt of his AK47.

The first gunman looked at the handiwork of his mate and smiled and said in British--accented English that they were not after small change when a real prize awaited them. He asked the young man what his name was and when he refused to answer he just smiled again, showing a set of perfect teeth that obviously were not his own, and waved a blue covered Israeli passport and simply read out the name—Zohar (Zorik) Shemesh. He then opened the second passport that belonged to the girl and pronounced her name—Inbal Sabatani. He said that if they behaved well and followed his orders no harm would become them but if they caused problems then he would inflict upon them so much pain they would wish they had not been born.

Zorik looked at Inbal and in English so their captors could understand he meant no mischief, told her to keep quiet and cooperate. They both hoped the gunmen caught them in a random act against Israelis and were not aware of the fact that

Inbal was the granddaughter of the Israeli Prime Minister from his first marriage and that her surname was that of her father who was married to the PM's daughter.

CHAPTER 1

One year earlier, Late November, Vienna, Austria

Dr. Ali Abdul Abadi emerged from the St. Stephen metro station in the center of Vienna. The first thing he saw was the famous St. Stephen cathedral all lit up and decorated with Christmas trees and surrounded by stands selling alcoholic punch, beer, and spiced wine in ornamental cups and a few stands that displayed souvenirs for tourists.

There was a pervasive odor of urine, originating from the horses pulling the colorful carriages that made their way slowly through the narrow streets of central Vienna. The customers were romantic tourists that were willing to overpay for the illusion of being like the nobility in the good old days of the Austro-Hungarian Empire.

Ali couldn't understand why the municipality of Vienna, that was supposedly run by level-headed politicians, allowed this offense against the most sensitive olfactory sense. He felt that the odor could almost be compared to a chemical agent used for riot control. Surely, he thought, even in Isfahan where he came from, droppings and urine of horses, donkeys, and mules were a thing of the past in the center of the magnificent town. Even in the artificial light, he noted the big difference between the clean bright surfaces of the cathedral and the much darker parts that were still awaiting their turn, and the necessary funds, to be cleaned.

The evening was very chilly, but Ali felt that he needed some fresh air, preferably odorless, as he had just returned from a lengthy preparatory meeting with the Head of the Iranian delegation to the International Atomic Energy Agency, the IAEA.

Vienna that served as the IAEA headquarters was flooded by Iranian scientists, engineers, spies, and well-to-do tourists after the signing of the nuclear deal just a few months earlier between Iran the 5+1 countries (U.S., Russia, France, China, UK, and Germany).

Ali was concerned about the instructions he had been given by the senior Iranian diplomat to categorically deny that any research and development that were related to weapons were taking place in his laboratory. He was directed to lie through his teeth in the meeting with the team of IAEA inspectors that was scheduled for the next day.

The team of inspectors included professional scientists and engineers and was in charge of verifying that Iran was in full compliance with the agreement. Basically, Ali was an honest man who felt uncomfortable lying, but knew he had to do it for his country. Few people knew of the top-secret laboratory in which Ali worked as the lead physicist of the small, elite group that carried out complex calculations on solid state compression.

Ali came from a very poor family that lived in a small village near Isfahan. In the old days of the Shah he would have been doomed to life as a peasant, or at most, as a petty merchant in the local bazaar, even though he excelled in his elementary school studies. Fortunately for him, the Islamic revolution afforded him, and several other brilliant students like him, an opportunity to gain a proper education.

It turned out that Ali had an exceptional mind for mathematics and physics and was encouraged to study science at the local university. He was later sent to UMIST the famous university in Manchester, England, to obtain a doctorate in physics. After carrying out some ground-breaking research work, he was offered an academic position at the same university and a chance to live in the UK. But he felt that his country needed him, and he had an obligation to the Mullahs regime in Iran for giving him this opportunity.

Looking at the horse-drawn carriages, a fleeting smile crossed his lips when he remembered his father admonishing him. This occurred when he was ten years old and after he proudly told his father he had saved the bus fare by running after the bus and his father slapped him and said he could have saved more by running after a taxi.

It was a cold Sunday night at the end of November and there were very few people walking along the streets reserved for pedestrians and in the large St. Stephen square. Nothing like the swarms of happy and smiling people he saw when he attended a conference in Barcelona just a few weeks earlier. He strolled along Kartner Strasse toward the Donaukanal that was part of the Danube River that flows through Vienna. He wasn't quite sure about the right way to the bridge, so he looked for someone to ask for directions. He came across a bespectacled police-woman and in perfect English asked her if this was the way to the river.

She looked him over and in stilted English told him he only had to follow Rotenturm Strasse for a few hundred feet and he would reach the bridge that crossed the river.

Ali was so engrossed in his thoughts about the upcoming meeting that he did not notice the man who was following him. A young woman approached him and asked him something in German. He started to answer in English that he was not a local when he felt a drop of liquid in his left ear.

As it was not raining, he couldn't quite figure out where it came from. He scratched his ear to alleviate the annoying irritation the drop caused when suddenly everything went dark and he fell to the ground paralyzed. The last thing he saw was the beautifully illuminated St. Stephen cathedral in the distance. He didn't notice the man rapidly disappearing down the street that led to the river.

Security cameras recorded the whole scene, but no one thought any foul play was involved as it appeared that Dr. Ali Abdul Abadi suffered a stroke. After all, it was not unusual for a man in his sixties to have a seizure on a cold night, especially someone who was accustomed to a much warmer climate.

One Year earlier, Late November, Barcelona, Spain

Professor Ahmad Riza Kadoura attended a conference that was held at the main campus of the University of Barcelona right near the Barcelona Football Club, home of FCB the world-famous soccer team.

As a renowned analytical chemist Ahmad was invited to give a keynote speech at the opening session of the conference on, "New Methods in Analytical Chemistry." He gave a rather boring monotonous presentation, much to the disappointment of the organizers that had read his scientific papers but had never heard him address a live audience. He gave a very detailed description of the electrochemical device he and his students had developed to measure extremely low levels of uranium in drinking water.

As it turned out, the data he presented showed that the analytical performance of the device was inferior to instruments that could be purchased for less than one hundred dollars from manufacturers in China. The polite applause at the end of the presentation attested to the good manners of the audience rather than to the new insights they had gained from the presentation. Ahmad was unaware of the fact and was convinced that his performance was brilliant, and the applause was rightfully earned.

The last session of the day ended in the late afternoon, so it was already dark outside when Ahmad boarded the Green Line metro at Palau Reial station. As it was too early for dinner—no respectable restaurant in Barcelona fills up before nine pm—he decided to go and visit the Sagrada Familia church before looking for a restaurant. He had read about it in his tourist guidebook and knew that it was one of the most popular tourist sites in Europe, second only to the Eiffel Tower in Paris. He was impressed by the four main towers that loomed over the surroundings. The church was closed to visitors, so he first went to see the brightly-lit east side of the church from behind the metal fence. After reading his guidebook he understood that it represented the birth of Jesus and the promise of Christianity.

He then walked to the other side that was illuminated in a rather gloomy yellowish light and saw the scenes depicting Gaudi's design of the Last Supper and the crucifixion. After he had appreciated the genius of Gaudi's design, he took the stairs down to the metro station. He entered the station and waited on the platform for the train that was headed to Placa Catalunya Square, around which many restaurants were located. He didn't pay any attention to a heavily-built man who was standing right behind him on the crowded platform.

As the train approached the station the man gave Ahmad's back a small shove that sent him flying off the platform right under the wheels of the approaching train. The driver could not stop the train in time and Ahmad's head was severed by the train. In the panic that broke out, the hefty man disappeared.

The security cameras only showed a large man with a heavy overcoat and a scarf that covered most of his face and there was no way he could have been identified even with the most advanced facial recognition algorithms.

Ironically, this whole scene happened less than three hundred feet from the site where Gaudi, the legendary architect of Sagrada Familia, was run over by a tram some ninety years earlier.

One Year earlier, Late November, Taormina, Sicily

Dr. Mahmoud Al-Baida was a member of the elite science community of the Islamic Republic of Iran, and in recognition of his service to his homeland's nuclear program was appointed as a senior member of the Iranian delegation to the IAEA in Vienna.

He had grown up in a small town on the shores of the Persian Gulf, where the weather was warm most of the year and could not get used to the harsh climate of Vienna. In late November he felt that he was entitled to a vacation and found a nice package deal in Taormina, Sicily. The short low-cost flight from Vienna to Catania was not very comfortable and the in-flight service was nothing to write home about. Within one hour after landing he was driving out of the car rental's parking lot in a Skoda Octavia station wagon with automatic transmission.

He was smiling at his wife, Layla, and kept saying that they were very lucky to have received an upgrade from a small manual shift car to the larger Octavia. Layla was pleased that Mahmoud was so happy as she, too, was looking forward to the vacation in warm Sicily. The drive along the broad highway from Catania to Taormina was very pleasant but once they left the highway Mahmoud had to focus on the steep, narrow winding road that led to the center of the village.

Although they were using a modern GPS navigation system, they had trouble finding their hotel. They passed through the center of the village several times without finding the street that led to their hotel and because of the one-way streets had to go round and round in circles. After thirty minutes of wandering around they decided to use HUMINT rather than SIGINT—human intelligence rather than signal intelligence—and asked for directions, quite a degrading thing for a full-blooded Iranian macho man to do, especially one who considered himself as technologically savvy and brilliant. A polite shopkeeper told them they had to drive through the narrow stone arch they had passed by several times thinking it was closed to vehicular traffic, and then take a left fork up a steep dead-end street to the hotel.

They checked in to the hotel and while waiting for their room to be ready, chatted with the owner at the front desk and asked about the sites of Taormina. The owner was very helpful and in perfect English told them they should leave their car at the hotel's only parking spot and just take a ten-minute walk to the center. He added that driving around Taormina was not recommended, something that Mahmoud had already figured out and that all the main sites were within walking distance. He suggested they follow Corso Umberto, the main pedestrian street, and visit the Teatro Greco, the large ancient Greek theater that was built slightly after Alexander the Great defeated the Persian Empire.

They strolled down the street and reached the theater and were greatly impressed by it. They were amazed to see that it still served as the venue for concerts and performances more than two thousand years after it was used for the very same purpose. They sauntered to the Piazza IX Aprile and found a table in one of cafés on the large terrace that was built at the edge of the cliff. The view of the village of Giardini Naxos and the shoreline way down below was beautiful.

The sun was setting in the west and Layla said that she wanted to take a selfie photo of the two of them before it got too dark. They went to the edge of the terrace and leaned on the guardrail. Mahmoud extended his hand with the mobile phone and tried in vain to take a photo with the two of them in the foreground and the view of the shore in the background. Layla suggested they ask someone to take the picture and pointed to a young man who just happened to be standing nearby apparently also admiring the scenery.

Mahmoud asked the young man if he could take their photo and the man smiled politely and came closer to take the phone from Mahmoud's hand. Suddenly he stumbled and accidently fell, colliding into the couple. The guardrail was crushed under the combined weight of the three of them and the Iranian couple fell down the steep cliff while the young man managed to grab one of the poles of the guardrail and save himself.

The police investigation of the terrible accident found no one at fault. The Taormina public works department was accused of not taking proper care of the terrace's guardrail but as it was run by a local prominent member of the Cosa Nostra no action was taken. The young man who was requested to take the photo was questioned but released after it had been established that he was an innocent Canadian tourist who simply wanted to help the couple.

He did not mention the fact that Mahmoud's cell phone remained in his possession nor that his Canadian passport was a clever forgery. The bodies of Layla and Mahmoud were shipped to Tehran for burial. A post-mortem performed in Tehran found no foreign substances in their body and the story of the accident was accepted with some skepticism.

One Year earlier, Late November, London, UK

Dr. Mustafa Fahami sauntered down Gerrard Street in Chinatown. He was in no hurry and took his time to look at the display of cheap merchandize from China, imitations of famous Parisian designer clothes and accessories, typical London souvenirs, and strange looking things in jars that were considered by some as food delicacies.

Like many other people in London, he was enjoying the sunny day that was quite unusual for this time of year. He had been suffering from a persistent ache in his neck and shoulders, probably brought about by the tension he was feeling that he attributed to his clandestine mission. He was sent from the uranium enrichment facility at Natanz to interview a former-Iranian physicist, who was currently employed at the Atomic Weapons Establishment in Aldermaston.

The ex-patriot was an expert on the physics and metallurgy of highly enriched uranium and was ready to share his knowledge, or so Mustafa was told. There were two reasons for his willingness to cooperate—money and fear. He was promised a considerable sum for the information and was threatened that his aging parents and younger brother would be placed in the infamous Evin Prison in Tehran, where they would receive VIP treatment. In case he didn't understand the not-so-subtle threat, his contact explained that Evin Prison

VIP stood for Very Intense Pain.

Mustafa had another thirty minutes until the scheduled meeting with the scientist. He was gently rubbing his neck and trying to massage his left shoulder when a smiling Chinese man motioned for him to sit down on a wooden chair with wheels that was set on the sidewalk. A nearby store displayed a large sign that advertised a massage parlor and the sign promoted a special ten-minute massage for five pounds instead of the regular twenty pounds.

Mustafa asked him if he could do a neck and shoulders massage and the Chinaman nodded and in broken English said, "Inside or outside," indicating the chair and the store. Mustafa said, "Outside," and pointed to the chair hoping to continue to enjoy the sunny day while being treated. The Chinaman smiled and signaled for him to sit down.

An attractive young Chinese girl came out of the store and asked Mustafa if he wanted to remove his jacket and he answered that he would remain with it. She nodded to the Chinaman who started by gently massaging Mustafa's neck and twisting his ears, before moving down to his shoulders.

Mustafa wondered why the masseur had twisted his ears and was surprised by the pleasant sensation this caused. The Chinese man said something in Chinese to the girl, who told Mustafa in English to relax and not tense his muscles and stop resisting the soothing motions of the masseur.

Mustafa was not aware that all this time a tall man waited in the back room of the massage parlor and watched. The masseur held Mustafa's head in both her hands and tilted his head repetitively first to his right shoulder and then to the left shoulder until he felt that Mustafa let his neck muscles relax. He then motioned to the man who was still watching and the man stepped out of the store and silently exchanged places with the Chinese masseuse.

Mustafa was feeling the tension leaving his stiff neck and smiled. He tried to turn his head and look at the masseuse but a pair of strong hands twisted Mustafa's head to the right and back to the left a few times not enabling Mustafa to turn his head.

Meanwhile, the girl stepped into the middle of the sidewalk and started to do some acrobatics that were worthy of any "rubber girl" in a circus. That caught the attention of the people strolling down the street, who stopped to appreciate the flexibility of the attractive girl. The fake "masseur" looked around to make sure that nobody was paying attention to him.

In a sudden movement, he yanked Mustafa's head and twisted it almost one hundred and eighty degrees until he heard a sickening click when the neck vertebrae broke like twigs. Mustafa's head tilted forward but before anyone noticed the "masseur" wheeled the chair into the store and shut the door.

The ex-Iranian scientist from Aldermaston was surprised that Mustafa didn't show up for the appointment. He was terribly worried that he would be held accountable and his family in Iran would be persecuted, so he pulled out his cell phone and called the Iranian embassy. He explained the problem and was transferred to the head of security at the embassy who was a senior officer in the Iranian Revolutionary Guards (IRG).

He was told to come immediately to a new meeting point

near Piccadilly Circus and stay away from the embassy. The whole conversation was recorded by British intelligence and a team of agents were dispatched to the new meeting place. They managed to take a few photos of the meeting and the physicist was identified and arrested while the Iranian who had diplomatic immunity was declared persona non-grata and told to leave the UK within twenty-four hours. No one seemed to know what had happened to Mustafa and his disappearance was attributed to an operation of the British secret service. The Iranians didn't care if it was MI5 or MI6 and held the British responsible.

One Year earlier, Late November, Stockholm, Sweden

Dr. Jaafar Taghi was attending a conference that was organized by SIPRI—the Stockholm International Peace Research Institute. He tried to keep a low profile as the Islamic Republic of Iran was not famous for its peaceful operations but rather notorious for its support of terror organizations in the Middle East and elsewhere.

Jaafar was, nowadays, an intelligence officer who had rightfully earned his doctorate from Isfahan University but was enlisted to provide scientific support to the Iranian clandestine weapons program. His job was to attend scientific conferences that dealt with disarmament and nuclear non-proliferation matters and glean information that could help the program.

A tall, good looking dark woman whose nametag said that she was a member of a French anti-nuclear organization smiled at him and appeared to take a special interest in him. Jaafar was flattered by her attention and stealing a glance at her pert breasts then name tag, saw that her name was Genevieve. He had been trained to avoid "honey traps" but felt that he had acquired enough experience to recognize such a trap and was sure that the young woman had a genuine interest in him. She made certain he stood next to her during the coffee break and commented that as a French woman she detested the Swedish food and suggested they share dinner later. Jaafar asked her what kind of restaurant she had in mind and when she said that she loved seafood he was overjoyed as that was his favorite type of food.

After the boring scientific session ended, they headed toward a famous seafood restaurant in the center of Stockholm. Genevieve asked him if he drank alcohol and when he said that he occasionally enjoyed a glass of wine she ordered a bottle of good French white wine and said it would go well with the oysters they had both ordered. Jaafar thought about the properties that were attributed to oysters and wondered if there was any truth in the rumors and was looking forward to a chance to test this with Genevieve after dinner.

As if she read his mind she smiled and said that these were only rumors with no foundation in fact. He excused himself and went off to the restroom to relieve his full bladder. When he returned a few moments later a large plate of oysters was placed in front of him and another one was served to Genevieve. They ate the oysters while looking into each other's eyes and he saw great excitement and promise in Genevieve's eyes.

Suddenly Jaafar felt the room was spinning around him and his eyes became unfocused. Foam came out of his mouth as a series of strong convulsions twisted his body. The last thing he heard was Genevieve asking him what was wrong.

The medics that were summoned to the restaurant confirmed his death. Later laboratory tests showed that some strange, unidentified substance was found in the oysters that remained untouched on his plate. Genevieve was nowhere to be found. When other members of the French delegation were questioned, no one knew who the tall, good looking dark woman was.

One Year earlier, November, Chamonix, France

Hassan Sadeq had been looking forward to his long-awaited ski vacation in the beloved French Rhone-Alps. Two decades earlier, as a young agent of the IRG he had been posted in Grenoble and to oversee and keep an eye on the Iranian scientists who were attending graduate courses at **MaNuEn—Materials science for Nuclear Energy**—and at the Master **EMINE—European Master in Nuclear Energy.**

His job was to make sure that none of them chose to stay in Europe as that would be considered as defection, or even treason, by the Iranian Islamic Republic of Iran. Hassan was told to use any approach he found the most effective to achieve this goal. In some cases, he appealed to their patriotic sense, in others he reminded them that they had a moralistic debt to the country that paid for their education, others were promised good jobs and highly respectable positions on their return to Iran.

In some cases, where nothing else appeared to work, he threatened them that their families would be harmed. In the most extreme case, when a student who liked the French women, wine, and weather (the three W's), refused to return to Iran he simply cut his throat, trying to stage a foiled robbery. After that, he had to leave France in a hurry just one step ahead of the police that suspected the Iranian student's murder was not a simple robbery that was thwarted.

Hassan was in Chamonix, under an assumed name and a new identity. He was looking forward to taking the lift to the panoramic viewpoint at Aiguille de Midi, from which the majestic peak of the Mont Blanc could be seen on a clear day. He had been staying in a small three-star hotel near the center of the village waiting for the skies to clear and for the cable car to resume operations that had been suspended due to the weather conditions. Meanwhile, he enjoyed the food and wine and thought that he could now better understand the student who refused to return to Iran.

At long last the weather cleared, and he purchased a one-way ticket up to the panoramic view veranda. He planned to return down to the village on his skis. He was confident in his ability to negotiate the steep decline, although he knew that he was a bit out of practice as he didn't have many opportunities to go skiing in Iran. He was now a very senior member of the IRG given the responsibility of taking care of the physical security of Iran's nuclear facilities in Natanz, Isfahan, and Arak. He surmised that there were other secret facilities that were not under supervision by the IAEA, but these were not part of his mandate.

The cable car was very crowded, especially as several passengers had carried their skiing equipment, and everyone was wearing bulky warm clothes. Hassan didn't pay special attention to the young couple that appeared to be totally engrossed with each other. With their free hands they were holding on to their professional-looking ski equipment. All passengers exited at the viewpoint terrace and took a few minutes to get acclimatized to the depletion of oxygen at twelve thousand feet above sea level.

Nobody was in a rush to start the descent and the people simply stood on the veranda enjoying the magnificent view and taking photographs. After some thirty minutes, Hassan felt he was ready for the downhill skiing exercise and walked slowly to the exit that led to the slopes. He saw that the couple of lovebirds were just ahead of him and were already moving slowly on the downhill track. Within a few minutes he caught up with them. As he pulled up level with them and tried to pass, the young man extended his arm and slapped the back of Hassan's head with a short, lead pipe. Hassan lost his balance and veered off the path straight down a thousand-foot-deep abyss.

The young couple continued their way down the mountain and reached the village an hour later. Both were sure that no pathologist in the world would find evidence of the head injury in a post-mortem operation, even if any part of the head remained recognizable after the fall.

One Year earlier, November, Isfahan, Iran

The small Hyundai travelled along the broad Chahar Bagh E Bala Avenue that was one of the main thoroughfares of the beautiful city of Isfahan. The driver was the Senior Engineer at the nuclear facility, that converted uranium bearing ores in to feed material for the nearby enrichment plant, and his two passengers were his junior colleagues. Traffic was quite heavy as they approached Ayineh Khaneh Boulevard, which was quite normal during the morning rush-hour.

The queue of cars waiting to turn left at the T-junction was long and traffic was almost at a standstill. Small mopeds and large motorcycles passed the waiting cars on the left and on the right, ignoring all traffic rules and regulations that in any case were merely regarded as recommendations for good behavior. The noise from the exhaust pipe of the truck ahead and motorcycles overtaking the Hyundai were loud so none of the occupants were aware of the metallic sound made when a powerful pipe-bomb was attached with a strong magnet to the car's roof.

Seconds later the sound of a loud explosion reverberated and echoed from the surrounding building. Car parts and pieces of human organs flew up in the air and the ball of fire ignited the vehicles in front of and behind the Hyundai. Fatal wounds were received not only by the driver and passengers of the Hyundai but also by a young couple with their baby son that were crossing the avenue just behind the car. Over a dozen people were injured.

An alert policeman that was stationed at the road junction

noticed a motorcycle speeding away from the explosion but all he could see was that it was driven by a large, young man wearing a black leather jacket and a helmet with its visor down and a similarly attired smaller passenger, probably a woman, clinging to the driver's hips.

CHAPTER 2

Ten months earlier, Tehran, Iran

The small gathering was attended by the Senior Assistant of the Supreme Leader of the Islamic Republic of Iran, by General Aslawi, who was the commander of the Iranian Revolutionary Guards and by the head of the Atomic Energy Organization of Iran (AEOI).

Imam Mourtashef was also present in his special capacity as the liaison between the clandestine laboratory in Basement S of Evin Prison and the Supreme Leader. The general presented the findings of the committee that investigated the untimely deaths of the senior scientists and intelligence officers that were all intensely involved in Iran's nuclear weapons program. The investigation had taken a long time because the deaths in Vienna, Barcelona, Taormina, London, Stockholm, and Chamonix were apparently unrelated.

But the general who lived and breathed conspiracies knew better and searched for the guiding hand that directed these events. The mysterious explosion in the heart of Isfahan was especially challenging as similar incidents had occurred before, and in those cases the culprits were assumed to be Iranian opposition groups in cohorts with Mossad or some other foreign intelligence agency. The Imam was particularly concerned about the deaths of the scientists that were involved with the secret laboratory that he oversaw as part of his responsibilities to the Supreme Leader.

The immediate suspects were the three intelligence agencies that were the avowed enemies of the Islamic Republic of Iran, namely the American CIA, the British MI6, and the Israeli Mossad. After a careful examination of the modus operandi and the clean and successful execution of the operations the CIA was removed from the suspects list, as its track record was full of bungled operations and contrary to such a meticulous performance.

However, MI6 and Mossad remained on the list, until a Russian mole deep inside the administration of the British Secret Intelligence Service assured his handlers that MI6 was not involved. General Koliagin of the FSB, the Federal Security Service of the Russian Federation, passed this piece of information to Iran as a goodwill gesture. So, the four participants in the small meeting agreed that it was time to open a secret war against the Mossad in particular, and on the Israeli government and its citizens in general. Imam Mourtashef mentioned that two of the murdered scientists were also leading members of the elite group that operated in laboratory in Basement S and wondered aloud if this was a mere coincidence or deliberate targeting of prominent scientists in Iran's most secret nuclear project.

The Senior Assistant of the Supreme Leader said that after these acts all the scientists involved in the nuclear program ran scared and several had started seeking jobs elsewhere, in

Iran and even abroad. The high-profile murders had humiliated Iran, and in this part of the world losing face was anathema. Governments fell if the people, or even a small aggressive faction in the military, felt that their national pride and honor were derided.

The Senior Assistant declared that the Supreme Leader held the four of them responsible to restore national honor. He instructed General Aslawi to embark on a path that would involve kidnapping Israelis and holding them hostage until the Israeli government complied with Iran's demands.

The prime demand was that Israel would publicly admit that its Mossad agents were behind these murders and put them on trial at the International Court of Justice in Den Hague. In addition, Israel would be forced to dismantle its two nuclear research centers in Dimona and in Soreq and allow IAEA inspector free access to every site in Israel. They were well aware of the fact that this latter demand would never be accepted by Israel but wanted to use this to draw attention to Israel's nuclear activity and particularly that it had not joined the Non-Proliferation Treaty (NPT). Imam Mourtashef, who was by far the most sophisticated, cunning, and intelligent participant of this meeting was already plotting a devious scheme of using the hostages for a very special purpose but did not wish to share his thoughts with his companions at this stage.

Ten months earlier, Tel Aviv

The Chief of Mossad, Haim Shimony, called for an emergency meeting of his senior staff and representatives from the Israeli Security Agency (ISA) and the Israeli Atomic Energy Commission (IAEC). He asked David Avivi, who was now in charge of the Iranian desk in Mossad, to bring the participants up to date on the recent events that concerned the untimely deaths of senior Iranian scientists and intelligence operatives connected to the Iranian nuclear establishment.

David reviewed the cases and said that it looked as if someone was eliminating the scientists and trying to frame Mossad. He reminded the people at the meeting that two Mossad agents were captured in Amman, Jordan, when they squirted a poisonous liquid in the ear of a Palestinian Hamas leader. This ended badly as the agents were apprehended and as a result Israel was forced to deliver an antidote and release several Hamas prisoners. He also mentioned that Mossad had been suspected of pushing enemies of the state under approaching trains, down steep cliffs, and treacherous ski slopes, although such acts were more the stuff of movies than real intelligence agencies—where intelligence was not a suitable term. Even the use of poisoned food was blamed on Mossad agents in previous cases without any substantial evidence.

David added that he, too, had once had a massage in London's Chinatown and was a bit concerned that the masseuse would wring his neck like a chicken, but said that as far as he knew Mossad had never resorted to this trick previously.

Shimony said that he was worried that the Iranians would

believe that Mossad was behind these blatant murders and would retaliate against Israeli scientists and innocent citizens. He wondered who would be interested in making this look like Mossad's work and precipitate an all-out clandestine war between Iran and Israel.

He said that the CIA had tried to instigate such wars by provocation but doubted whether the CIA would dare to try this with Israel, its staunchest ally. "The Fish," who represented the ISA at the meeting commented that it couldn't be the CIA because of the clean professional operation, unknowingly repeating what his opposite number in Tehran had said.

The Russians were always held as suspects in such assassination cases but Shimony believed that they wouldn't bother to hide their involvement. He said that their approach to such accusations was the opposite. They were on record, tacitly if not publicly, when Alexander Litvinenko, a defector and former officer of the FSB, was poisoned in London by a lethal dose of polonium or when dissident journalists were found dead in Moscow. Shimony asked the participants if they had any idea who could be responsible, but nobody ventured an opinion. As the meeting was adjourned, Shimony appointed David to be personally in charge of investigating the matter.

Israeli nuclear scientists received a stern word of warning from the Prime Minister's office, supported by the Defense Ministry, that for their own security they should limit their participation in conferences in order to avoid being targeted by Iran. The Israeli scientists were still encouraged to actively attend conferences in the United States, China and Russia, but to avoid Europe. As most of them were aware of the risks they accepted the directive without questioning it. Israeli scientists who were already in Europe, on sabbatical or for other reasons, were urged to return to Israel without delay, and many did so for fear of what could happen to them or their families.

In a special press conference that was held at the Prime Minister's office, the PM and Mossad chief declared that Israel was not involved in the murder or disappearance of any Iranian nuclear scientist. This was in sharp contrast to the standard Israeli policy that had always refused to comment - deny or admit - on actions that were attributed to Mossad. The overall reaction to this statement in the world was skeptical, despite Israel's divergence from its regular behavior.

Ten months earlier, London, Washington, and Moscow

Meetings were held by national security advisers, intelligence officers, and nuclear scientists in London, Paris, Berlin, Moscow, and Washington to discuss the mysterious fate that befell the Iranian scientists. Mossad was the natural suspect and the culprit that first came to mind and the announcement of the Israeli PM was not considered credible. All the experts predicted that the Iranians would seek revenge and target Israelis, so a warning was issued by the administrations of these countries to stay away from Israelis in general and nuclear scientists in particular, especially at conferences that were held in Europe.

Eight months earlier, Tehran, Iran

The agents of the Iranian Revolutionary Guards in Europe were frustrated because after two months of intensive attempts to kidnap or assassinate Israeli scientists in Europe, they had not managed to snare even a single one. Once again, the Senior Assistant of the Supreme Leader, General Aslawi of the IRG and the head of the AEOI met to discuss the options for punishing Israel for its alleged actions against the Iranian scientists. Imam Mourtashef was not present this time because he was on a prescheduled visit to the laboratory in Basement S.

The meeting was quite short, and a consensus was reached within minutes: all Israelis were now fair game for kidnapping—they used the more politically correct term "taking hostages." However, Iran must retain plausible deniability for these actions so there should be no evidence linking Iran directly to the kidnappings. After all, the Senior Assistant said, Iran had signed the nuclear deal and was now a respectable member of the international community, so the idea was that everybody would "know" that Iran was responsible but there would be no substantiation to any such accusations.

The general said that he would use a worldwide network of Islamic supporters and sympathizers, but not official Iranian agents, to carry out these operations in places that were favored by Israeli tourists. Especially attractive were countries that were ruled by Muslims, even if they were not Shiites like Turkey or Azerbaijan, or countries that had a significant Muslim minority like India or Thailand, and even Cyprus that bordered on the Turkish controlled part of the island.

Another area where Israeli vacationers were particularly vulnerable was the Egyptian Sinai Peninsula with its sandy beaches, coral reefs, and free-for-all atmosphere. The general promised to issue a directive to his collaborators in those countries and use the same method that worked for "bounty hunters" in the Wild West—prize money and rewards for whoever would deliver live Israelis to the hands of the IRG.

Three months earlier, Tel Aviv

Captain Zohar Shemesh, addressed by everyone by his nickname Zorik, stepped into his Tel Aviv apartment and shouted to his girlfriend, "Honey, I am home. Come and see me," and walked to the bathroom. Inbal stuck her head through the bathroom door and watched him remove the flight suit overall from his sweaty body and unceremoniously toss it into the laundry basket. He announced, "This is the end of my career as a fighter-jet pilot, at least for now."

Inbal smiled broadly and applauded. At the age of thirty he had completed a twelve year stretch that included a bachelor's degree in computer science from Ben-Gurion University of the Negev, and pilot certification from the Israeli Air Force Academy. He had logged thousands of hours in a variety of the most advanced jet-fighter planes, starting with the aged F-4 Phantom that was removed from service in the Israeli Air Force in the early 2000s, through the latest models of the F-16 and F-15.

He had been on dozens of missions against terrorist

organizations, ranging from Gaza that was just a few miles from his base to targets that were thousands of miles away. He was summoned to an interview by the Commander of the Air Force (CAF) and invited to stay in the service with very tempting offers. These included promotion to the rank of a major, position as an executive officer in an elite fighter squadron, and a scholarship to advanced degree studies in science, engineering, or business at a school of his choice.

Zorik deliberated whether to accept the offer but told the CAF that he needed a time-out of six months to clear his mind and reach a decision. He explained that he would have to consult with his girlfriend, Inbal, as they had plans to get married and start a family. The Commander said that he fully understood and suggested that he take paid leave for six months. If he decided to leave the Air Force, he would have to return the payment but if he rejoined, it would a bonus for signing on.

Inbal watched him toss the flight suit and before he could step into the shower hugged him and said that for the next six months she didn't want to see him in anything except jeans and a tee-shirt, or a bathing suit. Zorik smiled and invited her to join him in the shower but she stepped back quickly and said they would have enough time for that later and she had to start packing for their trip to the beaches of Thailand and the mountains of India and Nepal.

The young couple went on a short round of farewell dinners with Zorik's parents and older brother, and then with Inbal's parents and younger sister. Zorik's father was a professor of physics at Tel Aviv University, and his mother was a research bio-chemist employed by a leading manufacturer of generic pharmaceuticals. His brother, Erez, was the founder of a high-tech company that had developed a cell phone application that was bought out by one of the major companies for an undisclosed sum that was estimated in the high eight-figure range.

Inbal was a talented mechanical engineer by training with the soul of an innovator and at the tender age of twenty-seven was already the co-owner of four registered patents and had declined several offers to sell them to large commercial bodies. Both her parents were senior partners in one of the largest law firms in Tel Aviv that specialized mainly in trading commodity futures and in real-estate deals.

Her mother, Anna, was in her late forties and the only daughter of the Israeli Prime Minister from his first marriage. She tried to keep in touch with her father, the PM, but at the insistence of his third wife was never invited to the official residence in Jerusalem. Despite the sour face his current wife made whenever he mentioned Anna, the PM met his eldest daughter about twice a year, always in unofficial settings, and closely followed the career of his two talented granddaughters.

He always attributed Inbal's successful career to his genetic heritage but never boasted in public about that. In fact, there was no public record that Inbal Sabatani was the PM's granddaughter although the security authorities were aware of it. Inbal's younger sister, Daphne was twenty-four years old, and an officer in Mossad but no one in the family knew what she did there, except that she spent a lot of her time outside Israel.

The farewell was very civilized and restrained as all involved refrained from public display of emotions, but the young couple had to promise to remain in touch by telephone, e-mail, or Skype. Inbal and Zorik said they would announce their intention to get officially married after their long vacation, much to the delight of both families.

***

The next day Inbal and Zorik boarded a flight to Bangkok, spent a night in the bustling city trying to ignore the noise, humidity, heat, and congestion. After a sleepless night, they continued to the resort of Phuket on one of the seven daily flights with Bangkok Air. They had decided beforehand that it would be their premarital honeymoon and they would spend one week in a luxurious hotel without caring about expenses—they called this the big splurge.

The hotel on the Shore of Katathani was very highly rated by the Trip advisor website, so they chose it for the first part of the vacation. They were favorably surprised by the cost that was much lower than they had estimated and by the facilities that exceeded their wildest dreams. For a few moments they considered extending their honeymoon but then the reality set in that their money wouldn't last anywhere near six months at that rate.

So, after that week they joined the crowds of young people from all over the world that tried to make their dollars go a long way and look for cheap places as they had planned on taking the full six months of vacation.

They moved to a beach resort that was a haven for

youngsters who were looking for cheap alcohol, plentiful drugs, and a ridiculously low cost of living. Most of the people on that beach were in their late teens or early twenties and Zorik and Inbal felt they were of an older generation. They were upset by the behavior of some of the young men, mostly their own compatriots, who were willing to bargain with the local shop owners for an hour in order to save a couple of dollars.

They quickly realized that for the local merchant these two dollars meant like twenty or even two hundred dollars for the tourists. Zorik felt he could put up with this behavior because bargaining was common in the Middle East, but he detested the manner in which these youngsters conducted themselves when they were drunk. They became abusive, aggressive, and violent under the influence of alcohol and reports of rape and vandalism were common occurrences.

When those youngsters were on a "chemical trip," some became zombies and didn't respond to any outside stimulation while others behaved as if they had been transformed from humans to animals. Zorik could ignore the zombies and tranquil animals but couldn't stand the young men who thought they were voracious felines and physically attacked anyone close to them.

The young girls were no better—some behaved like nymphomaniacs and tried to have sex with everything that breathed and even with inanimate objects, others just folded themselves in to a fetal position, hugged themselves tightly and cried quietly.

Inbal was totally disgusted by what she saw on the beach

and they decided to move to a small village further up on the coast. There, people their age and older, sought to enjoy the beautiful beaches, the peace and quiet afforded by the serene surroundings, and the plentiful tropical fruit juices and simple, yet delicious, cuisine. They stayed there for a couple of weeks soaking up the sun, surfing the waves, and talking about their future.

They knew this wasn't real Thailand—the guests were mainly European with a handful of Americans, Canadians, and many Australians, while the work force consisted of Thais. There was no opportunity for interaction with Thai people who were professionals like themselves.

They became restless and wanted to get a taste of real Asia, especially India, so decided to move on. It was getting hot in the south of India and they wanted a change of scenery from the beautiful beaches of Phuket, so they decided to go to directly Nepal and then to the north of India and the mountains and lakes of Kashmir.

Two months earlier, Nepal

The flight up north from Phuket back to Bangkok was a bit scary because the small plane was buffeted by strong winds just after take-off. Inbal clung to her seat with one hand and to Zorik with the other and he tried to calm her by saying that accidents rarely happened nowadays under these conditions. Zorik was impressed by the cool attitude and professionalism of the Thai pilot. He told Inbal that he was able to pass judgment of the pilot's performance because he had been in a similar situation several times during his career.

When the plane approached the Bangkok Suvarnabhu-mi International Airport (BKK), it was diverted to a small regional airport and the pilot announced that it was due to some emergency at the main airport but there was nothing to worry about as they would be transferred to Bangkok center.

Some of the passengers protested loudly saying they had to catch connecting flights from BKK. The pilot announced that all flights to BKK were delayed as well as the flights from the airport so they would not miss their connections. In any case, rapid transportation to BKK had been arranged and would get them to their flights in time.

Inbal and Zorik collected their luggage and took the airline bus to the center of Bangkok, where they found a hotel. After their experience on their way to Phuket they asked for a quiet room, and the smiling girl at the front desk assured them that all the rooms were soundproof and quiet and gave them a room on the thirteenth floor.

They slept soundly and the next morning, after having a lavish breakfast with fresh pineapple and papaya, they ventured to main street to find a cheap flight to Kathmandu Tribhuvan (KTM) Airport, Nepal. To their pleasant surprise there were many airlines that flew from BKK to KTM and they had no trouble booking a flight for the next day.

The three and a half hour non-stop flights were expensive, so they selected a cheap flight that first travelled south to Kuala Lumpur before heading north to Kathmandu. The travel time was nine and half hours, but the cost was much lower than the direct flight and the young couple had more time than money.

After landing in Kathmandu, they took a rickety bus in to town and looked for the hostels that were frequented by young travelers. The selection and variety were amazing with prices that ranged from a few dollars per person per night to a few dozen dollars. They selected one mid-range place and when they got there were happy to see that its residents were a far cry from the young people on the beach in Phuket.

There were many young people who were planning to take trails in the Himalaya mountain range. The most popular track for was a circular route around Annapurna. When Zorik looked at the description of the mountain in Wikipedia, he realized that there were many different tracks in the Annapurna Massif, some of which were accessible only to highly-skilled mountain climbers.

For example, Annapurna I main peak, soared to a height of twenty-six thousand feet, and was infamous for its death toll that statistically claimed the life of one climber for every three that managed to reach the summit and return safely to the base camp. The Annapurna Circuit, which circles the Annapurna Himal was the most popular track and was much less demanding. The starting point for this trek, and also several shorter treks was the town of Pokhara.

So, after talking to some young people that had returned from that track, Zorik and Inbal made their way to Pokhara on the western region of Nepal. The track was challenging but they were in good physical shape, and although they lost some weight, they didn't encounter any insurmountable difficulties.

A couple weeks later they returned to Kathmandu and started looking for a flight to Srinagar in India. They saw that there was a large selection of indirect flights but were a bit surprised to discover that for some reason the airfares on Tuesdays, Wednesdays, and Saturdays were lower than on other days. The distance between Kathmandu and Srinagar was slightly less than eight hundred miles and the flight time just under two hours for the direct flight. However, much cheaper flights were available with a stopover in New Delhi and they selected this route.

They did not wish to spend time in Delhi and didn't bother to leave the airport. After landing in Srinagar they went to a small booth at the airport that advertised itself as a travel agency and were put in touch with the owner of a houseboat who was more than willing to accommodate them for a reasonable fee. They felt that they had earned a peaceful vacation on the beautiful lake after the two weeks of hiking around Annapurna.

CHAPTER 3

September 11, Dal Lake, Srinagar, India

After dark, the two gunmen led Inbal and Zorik out to the deck of the houseboat. The hands of both young Israelis were cuffed with nylon cable ties behind their backs and smelly black sacks covered their heads.

One of the gunmen held a flashlight with a red lens and repeated a series of three long flashes pointing it away from the shore, towards the lake. Within minutes they all heard the stuttering sound of a small outboard motor. Zorik felt a slight bump when the small boat contacted the deck of the houseboat. He heard a short exchange in a language he recognized as Urdu but didn't understand between the gunmen and a person on the boat.

A moment later he was none too gently guided down the stairs and on to the boat. He heard Inbal protest as she, too, was led to the small boat. They were ordered to lie down on the bottom of the boat and a blanket was thrown over their prone bodies. Zorik managed to find Inbal's hand and squeeze it saying softly that everything would be fine. The gunman told him to shut up and bashed his shoulder with the butt of his gun to emphasize the point.

The small motorboat headed southwest toward a secluded point on the shore. The short trip ended when the boat gently docked at a wooden pier. The Israelis were ordered to stand up, with the help of the gunmen, and guided to the shore. They were transferred to a waiting van and instructed to sit on the floor and keep quiet. The van drove to a mosque on the outskirts of Batmaloo, and the Israelis were then taken out of the vehicle and led to the basement of a building that was right next to the mosque.

The basement smelled like carpet mold, an odor so strong that it permeated through the sack that covered their head. When the sack was removed, they could see the blue and green mold on the walls of the basement. The gunman took out his knife and cut the restraining cable ties and told them that if they didn't keep silent, he would use the knife to cut out their tongues. Zorik rubbed his sore wrists and said that they were thirsty and hungry.

The gunman growled and made a threatening move toward Zorik, but his mate barked something in Urdu and then said in English that they would get some food and drink shortly. He added that the basement had no windows, had a steel door, and that an armed guard would be posted outside the door. He warned them that although they were still in India, the area was completely Muslim and even if they got out of the building, they would probably be lynched by the mobs outside.

Zorik spoke up and said that their families would pay a handsome ransom for their release, but the gunman repeated they were not after money and both gunmen left the basement slamming the steel door behind them and locking it. Zorik went over to Inbal and held her tight while she sobbed quietly and asked him what was happening to them.

Zorik said they should avoid provoking their captors, especially the knife-wielding depraved creature and wait until an opportunity to escape presented itself. He suggested they call this gunman Creepy and the other gunman, who was obviously in charge, should be called Albert, as his curly hair reminded him of a friend with that name. Inbal smiled for the first time since they were kidnapped and agreed, she also thought he resembled their friend.

Twenty minutes later Creepy entered the basement carrying a tray with a bottle of water and a dish of chickpeas and rice. They had to use their hands to eat as no utensils were provided. Albert entered the basement a moment later with two blankets and a bucket that he said would be their toilet until the next move. He suggested they try and get some sleep as they would be facing a long journey.

September 12, Uri, Srinagar, India

Inbal and Zorik spent a restless night in the basement. Zorik admired the self-control of Inbal and her coolheaded acceptance of their plight. Both had gone over every square inch of the basement looking for weak spots through which they could possibly escape or for anything that could serve as a weapon in case an opportunity to overpower their captors would present itself. However, despite the filthy floor and walls, there was nothing useful to be found. They managed to get a little sleep cuddled together on the two thin blankets they were given.

At the crack of dawn Creepy came pounding down the stairs and banged on the steel door to wake them up. Another armed guard carried a small kettle and a couple of cups, which he filled with a murky fluid, that was supposed to be tea, and handed to them by Creepy, who held a gun in his other hand. He told them to use the bucket in the corner as they had a long journey and observed with a leer as Inbal relieved herself in the corner, while ignoring Zorik's spiteful glare.

They gulped down the tea trying to ignore its foul taste but as they were still thirsty, they even asked for more. Zorik told Inbal that it was safer than water as it was at least boiled, hopefully killing most of the bacteria or at least most of the pathogenic ones. Creepy told Zorik to turn his back and quickly slipped a nylon cable tie around his wrists and placed the smelly dark hood over his head and then did the same to Inbal.

Once again, he took advantage of the fact that Albert wasn't there and Zorik was blindfolded and allowed his dirty hands to fondle her. She tried to kick him with a strong backward swing, but he anticipated that and easily evaded her foot. He then opened the steel door and marched them up the stairs to the waiting van.

They were ordered to lie on the floor and a thin carpet was thrown over their bodies. The ancient engine came to life and they could feel that they were now travelling on a paved road with many potholes as they could feel every single one of the bumps. The van travelled from Batmaloo to Hussan Abad and then headed west through Kunzer towards Gulmarg, thus avoiding the busier highway to Pattan.

Before reaching Gulmarg, the van veered from the main road and took a dirt trail until it reached a clump of trees in Masjid Park. The door opened and the young couple was allowed out of the van. While Albert secured their feet with a new cable tie, Creepy drew out his knife and sliced the cable ties off their wrists. Albert removed the blindfolds and told them that they would take a short break. He offered them some more tea and a piece of the local bread and told them they could relieve themselves. They hobbled with their tied feet to a spot behind a tree and did so.

Zorik told Inbal that he thought they were heading west toward the Pakistani border and that they should try to escape before crossing the border because in India they could hope for assistance from the authorities but there would be no such hope in Pakistan. However, Albert ordered them to shut up and Creepy came over to make sure they stopped talking.

Their captors unceremoniously threw them on the van's floor without bothering to free their feet and bind their wrists again and covered them with the rug. As the van started moving, it headed back to the paved highway but after a few moments they felt that the road had changed from a relatively straight highway to winding sharp curves. They passed through the small village of Babareshi and headed almost straight north to Baramulla. The last part of the road was steep, narrow, and with hairpin bends that they could feel lying prone on the van's floor.

They turned west once more and Inbal could sense that the

road quality had once again improved, and they were picking up speed as they travelled through the valley in which a river ran. Had they been able to see the view they would have enjoyed it, but lying on the van's floor, not knowing what lay ahead was a different experience. They reached the relatively large village of Uri, whose claim to fame was that it contained a Government Degree College that was a large modern building with pink walls and a green tiled roof.

The dam on the river created a lake upriver while a hydro-electric plant generated electricity as the water fell with a roar and flowed downstream towards Pakistan. The van continued west and by nightfall reached Salambad, where they took another break, waiting until things grew quiet and resting a little before attempting to cross into Pakistan.

After midnight a small convoy of three cars that consisted of the van, in which the two young Israelis were held, a decrepit old Toyota pick-up truck and a small Tata, an inexpensive car made in India, left the sleepy village of Salambad. The van brought up in the rear and the Tata led the way. They all headed on the main road toward the border.

Before setting off, all the men took a couple of moments to pray to Allah asking for the success of their mission that was to transport the two captives into Pakistan. As they approached the border, they switched off their headlights. The drivers took an extra precaution and removed the light bulbs from the sockets in the back of the cars in order not to have them light up when the breaks pedal was depressed. This was an easy task as most of those bulbs did not function anyway.

They were expected on the Pakistani side of the border so

all they had to do was to evade a scrutiny by the soldiers on the Indian side. This was made even easier as a couple of bottles of cheap whiskey were "forgotten" at the Indian border post by a collaborator who crossed over an hour earlier. By the time the silent and dark convoy reached the border, the guards on the Indian side were in an extremely good mood, and when they were offered another bottle of whiskey by the driver of the Tata, they turned a blind eye.

The guards on the Indian side were not really concerned about people leaving India, as their main responsibility was to prevent an attack from the Pakistani side. The big sign on the side of the road, between both border posts read: *Welcome, Chakothi-Uri Xing Point.*

As the small convoy crossed into Pakistan with no hassle, the driver of the Tata held a small envelope in his hand and let it fall at the feet of the Pakistani sergeant major in charge. The driver was impressed by the sergeant major's huge mustache with its waxed ends in the best British army tradition but wisely refrained from commenting on it. The convoy continued to Chakothi, where they intended to spend the rest of the night.

Inbal and Zorik were ordered out of the van and led into a small building that served as the local police station. It was a multipurpose three room building: one room served as a detention cell, another as the office, and the third, as the bedroom for the two policemen that manned the station.

Zorik had hoped that he would be able to convince the policemen that they were forcibly kidnapped and ask for help, but when he saw the warm welcome his captors received from the policeman on duty, he realized that he too was involved in the plot. He didn't know if this was just some local enterprise or if it was condoned by the Pakistani government or intelligence services. Compared to their conditions the previous night, the holding cell in the police station was like a five-star hotel.

Albert came over to tell them that they had completed the most dangerous part of their journey and from now on they would be in the good hands of the Pakistani intelligence services. Inbal was relieved to see that Creepy would no longer harass her.

September 13, Tel Aviv, Israel

Anna Sabatani was worried. She had expected the weekly phone call from Inbal two days earlier and when it failed to materialize, she tried to contact Inbal on Skype to no avail. So far, in the three months since Zorik and Inbal had gone on their trip to the Far East this had never happened. Inbal knew that her parents were concerned and although they had great faith in Zorik, they insisted on hearing from her at least once a week.

Anna called her husband who was also troubled by the absence of any recent communication and he suggested speaking with Zorik's parents to find out if they knew what was going on. Anna called Zorik's mother and her response was that she, too, was anxious about not hearing from the young couple. Anna hesitated for a couple of hours but decided to call her father, the Prime Minister, and ask for his advice and assistance.

Anna called the PM's office and was answered by a secretary that the PM was at a meeting with a visiting head of state. Anna asked her to tell him that it was an urgent personal matter. An hour later the PM called and enquired about the urgent matter. Anna told her father that she was concerned that Inbal had not called and she wanted his advice. When she told him that Inbal was in Kashmir, the PM said he would ask his Aide de Camp, Dan Oren, who was a Special Forces lieutenant-colonel to look into the matter. He added that he was also concerned about Zorik who was a jet-fighter pilot and told Anna to expect a call from Dan. Anna thanked him and he hung up.

Later that night Dan Oren called and told Anna that the Indian police at Srinagar had received a report of a strange incident that occurred at one of the houseboats on Dal Lake. Apparently, the owner of the houseboat came over to collect the weekly rent and found that the place was a complete mess and the young couple was missing. He searched the bedroom and saw that their clothes and belongings were there, but their passports were not to be found anywhere. He then filed an official report with the police.

A policeman was sent to the houseboat but all he could do was confirm the report of the owner. Colonel Oren said that he would contact the Israeli embassy in New Delhi and ask them to send one of the diplomats from the embassy to Srinagar and would also try to obtain more information from the Indian security services with which Israel had a good rapport. Anna called Zorik's parents and updated them on these developments.

September 13, Chakothi, Pakistan

Zorik and Inbal were allowed to sleep until noon and were woken up by the local policeman they had seen earlier. He was accompanied by a gentleman dressed in an expensive looking suit who introduced himself as Colonel Hussain from the Pakistani intelligence services. He said that he was sorry they had to go through such an ordeal to get to Pakistan but promised that they would not be harmed if they behaved well.

Zorik was indignant and demanded their immediate release. Hussain smiled and said that it was beyond his power to do that but once they arrived in Islamabad they would be able to speak to the head of the intelligence service and discuss it. Inbal requested permission to make a phone call to her family because she was sure that they were worried sick about her, but the colonel said that this would be allowed in due course.

When Zorik tried to find out why they were kidnapped in the first place, the colonel said that high level politics were involved, and everything would be explained later. He added that a helicopter was waiting to fly them to Islamabad and that they should hurry. He showed them the passports that had been delivered to him by Albert and told them that they may be free to go after the "unfortunate event" came to its end.

September 20, Evin Prison, Tehran, Iran

Zorik felt a none-too-gentle hand shaking his shoulder. For a moment he thought that he was still having a nightmare, in which he and Inbal were taken hostage in Kashmir by two gunmen and transported to Pakistan. He opened his eyes and saw the bearded face of a very fat man looking down at him with a cruel smile, and saying in English, "Zionist dog, wake up. You have arrived at your final destination—Evin Prison in Tehran." This was followed by a backhand slap on Zorik's face and then a forehand spank.

Zorik tried to lift his hand to defend himself and realized that both his hands were chained to the metal frame of the bed on which he was lying. His face was still numb from the anesthetics that were given him before boarding the plane in Islamabad, which was fortunate because the slapping which would have been painful did not hurt as much as it was intended.

Although the face slapping woke him up, Zorik shook his head several times trying to clear it. He remembered that he had been with Inbal when he was kidnapped and stammered, "Where is my girlfriend?" but all he got was another cruel smile. He repeated his question and received another couple of slaps and his torturer said, "She is having fun with some real men."

Enraged and out of his mind, Zorik pulled at the chains that were restraining him and only managed to bruise himself badly, while his captor broke out laughing. "I only wanted to see if a Zionist pig had a sense of humor. She is in the next cell, all alone."

The heavy metal door of the cell opened with a loud bang, and a thin man with a neatly trimmed beard entered. He looked at Zorik and saw that his face bore the clear marks left by the fat man's fingers and said something terse in Farsi and pointed to the door. The fat man cringed and even Zorik, who understood no Farsi, figured out that he was asking for forgiveness and then slowly exited the cell making sure not to show his back to the boss.

The thin man said, "Mr. Shemesh, my name is Akbar, and I apologize for the barbaric behavior of this man. We are civilized people, with a proud three-thousand-year history and will treat you well as long as you cooperate with us." He added, "If you promise to behave nicely, I'll free your hands from the shackles. Let me remind you that you are in the most secure block in Evin Prison. If you have not heard of this place, let me assure you that no one has ever escaped from here—not in the days of the corrupt Shah and not since the people's Islamic revolution started running this place."

Zorik tried to enquire, "How did we get to Tehran? My last memory is that we were in Islamabad."

Akbar just mumbled, "Well, you were asleep for three days after being sedated. Once again, will you behave nicely?"

Zorik nodded and Akbar took a key out of his pocket and opened the lock on the chains. Zorik stretched his hands and as blood began to circulate the pain in his arms and face intensified. Zorik bit his lips and repeated the question he had asked the fat man, "Where is my girlfriend?"

Akbar's face did not show any emotion. "She is unharmed

and is being questioned right now."

Zorik said he had to go to the bathroom and Akbar released Zorik's feet that were still chained to the bed and he pointed to a bucket in the corner of the room.

Zorik relieved himself and then asked the question that had been on his mind from the moment they were kidnapped. "What do you want to do with us?"

Akbar's response was not informative. "We have yet to decide that. Meanwhile, you will be interrogated and if we are satisfied with your cooperation you will be allowed to join the other hostages."

Zorik did not know whether to be glad that he was not the only captive in Evin Prison or to be worried about that.

Akbar departed, saying, "You will get some food and water and we'll come back for you later." He left the cell. Within minutes, the fat man returned with a plastic tray on which lentil soup, pita bread, and a bottle of water were laid out.

***

Inbal regained consciousness and found herself on a bed with her feet chained to the bed posts. She looked around and discovered that she was all alone in a cell with bare walls and a massive metal door. A small panel in the door slid open and all Inbal could see was a pair of black eyes looking her over. Then the door opened and in came a tall woman wearing a hijab that covered most of her face and dressed in an abaya that failed to disguise the features of her supple body.

Before Inbal could say anything, the woman said, "I am

Farzaneh and in charge of your well-being here in Evin Prison. If you behave and cooperate, you will be allowed to join the other hostages, but if not then you will regret the day you were born."

Inbal was speechless when Farzaneh added, "You are probably wondering what happened to your boyfriend. I can tell you that he has been very cooperative and told us all about you and your relationship. We promised him that he will be allowed to see you."

Inbal was no fool and was well aware of the most basic strategy interrogators all over the world used to get their subjects to talk. She said that she needed to use the toilet and promised not to cause any trouble and to cooperate fully. Farzaneh unchained her and lead her to the corner of the cell where a small section was enclosed by a screen.

***

The interrogation of Zorik and Inbal was quite short and carried out in separate rooms. Their captors didn't really care who they were or what they did in Israel. They only wanted to know if they had relatives in Israel, who would be able to raise a public outcry for their release from captivity. Fortunately, Inbal and Zorik managed to hide the fact that Zorik was a fighter pilot in the Israeli air force, and more importantly that Inbal's grandfather was the Prime Minister of Israel. They assumed that the Iranians were treating them humanely because they had some strategic objective and could not be bothered with personal details.

Finally, they were allowed to meet in Zorik's cell after their separation that lasted just a few days but seemed to them like eternity. Although they knew that they were being watched by their captors and were sure that they were recorded on video, their relief at seeing each other alive was so great that they couldn't refrain from hugging each other.

Zorik whispered in her ear that they were probably on camera and Inbal quickly understood that she should not say anything that may raise the suspicion of their captors that they were anything but a young couple who were kidnapped at random while on vacation.

After ten minutes the door to the cell opened and the fat jailor prodded them to follow him. Inbal had a nickname for the sadistic fat jailor and whispered to Zorik that she called him, "Shamenchic," which could be translated as Fatso. Zorik barely managed not to chuckle as he knew that it would just enrage Fatso and lead to further abuse.

***

They were led through a long corridor and passed several metal doors that were locked with a heavy metal bar that was placed across the steel door and secured on both sides. Almost all the cells were occupied by people that were crying for God's mercy in Farsi and every now and then they could clearly hear the intimidating voice of an interrogator and occasionally the unmistaken whistle of a whip that was immediately followed by loud weeping.

Zorik tried to whisper in Inbal's ear that some of the sounds were just recordings but the fat jailor shoved him away before he could get the message across. Inbal was obviously affected by the sounds and a look of apprehension crossed her face. They continued down the corridor until they reached a large cell that did not have a solid door but was surrounded by thick metal bars. Two armed guards were seated at a small table outside the cell and were drinking tea and chatting.

Zorik noticed a leather whip studded with metal balls that lay beside the table. He could instantly tell that those inside the cell were obviously Israelis. None appeared to have open wounds or broken limbs and Zorik assumed that were also held as bargaining chips.

Inbal looked at them and at the bars and remembered the time as a child when her parents took her to the zoo and how she pitied the poor animals in their cages. Now, she realized, she would be one of those inside the cage and had to exhibit self-control to avoid weeping.

Fatso shouted something in Farsi and all the inmates cringed and turned to face the wall. When he was satisfied that no one was looking at him, he drew a large key from his pocket and unlocked the cell door while the two guards stood up and took positions on both sides of the door.

Fatso shoved Inbal and Zorik and they stumbled into the cell. Zorik held out his hand to stop Inbal from falling and said aloud, in Hebrew, that they were also Israelis. As soon as the cell door clicked closed the inmates that were facing the wall turned around and inspected the newcomers for a long moment. The oldest prisoner, who looked as if he was in his sixties said, "Welcome aboard to the gates of hell."

Zorik smiled and replied, "Thanks for the welcome, but we prefer not to enter through these gates. I am Zorik Shemesh and this is my fiancée Inbal Sabatani."

The old man said, "I am Morris Aladgem," and pointing at a woman his age added, "This is my wife, Vicki, and we are from Bat-Yam." He then motioned to a couple that appeared to be in their late forties and said, "These are Shulamit and Nate Levy and they are from Haifa. Those two young men are Ari and Avi, who thought they would have a great time in Thailand after their three-year army service and got this trip to Tehran as a bonus."

All the inmates nodded in acknowledgement. Zorik asked them how long they had been in prison and how they got there, and each couple told their story.

CHAPTER 4

One month earlier, Morris and Vicki Aladgem in Antalia

Morris and Vicki were enjoying their vacation in the touristic village of Kemer in Antalia, Turkey. They had purchased one of the luxury "all-inclusive" deals that offered a full week's vacation for the price of two nights with breakfast, if you were lucky, in a hotel in Paris, Rome, or London.

There were mostly German and Scandinavian tourists at the resort, but as almost everyone spoke a little English and this was the common language used by the staff and guests.

Some of the staff had lived in Germany as guest-workers and spoke fluent German, much to the delight of some of the German tourists, whose English was very rudimentary. There were few other Israelis at the resort so the Aladgem couple kept pretty much to themselves. At mealtime, which was almost at every hour of the day and night, "all-inclusive" meant that you could eat and eat until you couldn't eat anymore, the couple sat at a small table close to the large window that afforded a lovely view of the Mediterranean coast.

In the late afternoon they would take a leisurely stroll along the beach, watch the sun set in the sea and then head back to the hotel for another sumptuous dinner. Soft drinks were included in the price but for alcohol there was an extra charge. Nevertheless, Morris and Vicki were utterly enjoying the vacation and every evening ordered a bottle of wine that helped maintain their good mood. However, after three or four days of overeating, they became a little restless and went over to the front desk and asked if there were any special recreational activities offered by the hotel.

The woman in charge of guest relations opened a brochure that offered a myriad of activities from organized tours of the old town and the famous necropolis nearby, to yacht trips, jeep tours in the mountains, and bus tours along the shoreline. As Morris was looking at the brochure a colorful pamphlet displaying a hot air balloon caught his eye. He pointed to it and told Vicki that for years he had wanted to take a hot air balloon flight and frequently dreamt about it at night, and here they could do it for a very reasonable price.

Vicki saw how excited he was and once satisfied about the safety of the flight agreed to be a little adventurous. They asked the woman to book them on a balloon flight and after making a phone call and speaking in rapid Turkish she told them that a taxi would pick them up at six the next morning and that they should wear warm clothes. She explained that she was told the hot air balloon could not fly in strong winds and that just after dawn, or before the sun set, the air was usually very still, and conditions were ideal.

At six the next morning Morris and Vicki were excited and ready for the biggest adventure of their lifetime, although they didn't know how exciting it would actually be.

The taxi arrived on time, which was quite unusual for that part of the world, and without a word the driver took them to the open area where a large balloon was spread out on the smooth ground.

The balloon was much larger than they had imagined and very colorful—exactly as depicted in the pamphlet—and a young man was busy trying to inflate the balloon with a stream of air generated by a very large gasoline powered fan. As soon as the balloon started to inflate the young man directed the flame from powerful twin burners to heat the air in the balloon. While this was taking place, another young man approached the couple, consulted a note in his hand and asked them if they were the Aladgem couple.

When they confirmed that, he introduced himself as Azzuri and said he would be their pilot for today's flight. Morris introduced himself and his wife and asked Azzuri about the flight. The pilot explained that the flight usually lasted about ninety minutes, but the exact time depended upon finding a suitable landing spot. He then pointed at a wicker basket that stood upright near the balloon and said that it was suitable for five people, but that in today's flight only the three of them would occupy the basket so they would be free to move around the basket once they were airborne.

Vicki was a bit apprehensive when she saw the basket—until then she only used wicker baskets as ornaments or for storing fruit. Morris was fascinated by the way the hot air filled the balloon and watched it rise slowly and majestically. The pilot told them to get inside the basket and connected the ropes between the basket and the upright balloon. The young man, who turned out to be Azzuri's assistant, held the basket while the pilot slowly turned on the flame on the twin burners. The assistant let go and the balloon, with the two passengers and the pilot, detached from the ground and started rising above the tops of the trees that surrounded the open space.

The expression on Morris's face was of pure elation while Vicki was as still as a stone and she could only mumble a prayer. Azzuri told her that there was nothing to worry about, the balloon flights were safer than travelling by car and accidents rarely happened to experienced pilots.

Morris suddenly realized that they were flying over the hills where there were no roads and asked the pilot how that would get back. Azzuri said that they wouldn't have to return to the point where they took off as his assistant will follow them in the pick-up truck to their landing spot and they would always be in radio contact with him .

Morris looked down at the rough terrain and still worried but Azzuri assured him that they would land near a road that was accessible to the four-wheel drive truck. The pilot explained that the navigation of the balloon depended on the direction of the wind that varied at different heights. So, by altering the height of the balloon, they could find an air stream that would take them in the direction they wanted.

Vicki overcame her initial fear and enjoyed the view and the feeling of being free like a bird in the silent sky. After all they had been in the air for over thirty minutes and the only sound was from the flame whenever Azzuri turned on the burners.

Morris was enjoying the tranquil effortless feeling of floating through the air and looking down at the view of the hills, forests, streams, and mountains with the Mediterranean on the horizon. Azzuri was very quiet and let the couple soak in the silence and enjoy the apparent freedom from Earth's gravity.

After an hour Azzuri started to look at his GPS and kept searching for an air current that would take the balloon to the east. He saw a clearing and started venting the hot air out of the top flap of the balloon causing it to descend slowly. Once they could see the pick-up truck, Azzuri increased the descent rate but every once in a while turned on the twin burners to avoid going down too fast.

Finally, the balloon was low enough and Azzuri threw a rope down and it was caught by his assistant on the ground. Three other men stepped out of the pick-up truck and also pulled down on the rope gently bringing the balloon to touch the ground. As Morris and Vicki got out of the wicker basket, two of the men drew pistols and told the Israeli couple that they were their hostages.

They exchanged a few words with Azzuri, and Morris recognized that they were not speaking Turkish but some other language that he thought could be Farsi. One of the men handed Azzuri an envelope and Morris could see that it contained banknotes, probably U.S. dollars by the look of it.

The three men led their captives to a van with darkened windows that was parked under a bunch of trees. One of the men placed handcuffs on their hands and made them lie on the floor of the van. Vicki started sobbing in panic until the man, who was evidently the leader, told Morris in English to make her shut-up or else he would do it.

Morris spoke softly to her in Hebrew and said that probably

all they wanted was ransom money and that he would promise them to pay whatever they wanted for their release. The
van headed north-east on a dirt road and soon after started
climbing into the mountains on dirt roads until they got close
to Konya.

The leader introduced himself as Suleiman and said that
they had a very long drive ahead of them. When Morris asked
how far they had to go, the answer was an impatient, "very
far." Morris said money was not a problem, that he was a very
rich man and they would pay anything to be free and promised
they would not mention the whole episode to anyone. Suleiman
just smiled and said they were not after money but had bigger
things in mind.

The driver of the van said something in rapid Farsi—by now
Morris was sure that was the language they were speaking—
and pointed ahead. Morris could not see anything as he was
lying prone on the floor of the van, but a gag was placed on his
mouth and on Vicki's mouth and an old rug was thrown over
them.

Morris could feel that the van hit a paved road and then
came to a stop. He could hear an exchange of words in Turkish
and guessed they had reached a roadblock. A moment later the
van was on the way once again and Suleiman sighed and said
something in Farsi to his two buddies. Morris recognized the
word "dollar" and surmised they had to pay some dollars to the
Turks manning the roadblock.

Once they were a few miles from the roadblock, Suleiman
bent down, removed the old rug and the gags. He said that if
they behaved, they would be allowed out of the van to relieve

themselves. As they approached the village of Aksaray, the van stopped in a cluster of trees and one of the captors got out and surveyed the area and then signaled that all was clear.

After the door opened and their handcuffs were removed Morris and Vicki slowly managed to get out of the van. Suleiman indicated that Vicki could step to the side of the van while all the men looked the other way. Morris appreciated the gesture of respect that they paid to the woman and said so. Suleiman was more relaxed now and promised again that no harm would come their way if they cooperated. Morris asked for some water and Suleiman pulled a bottle out of a cardboard box and offered it to the captives.

Once again, he said that they had a long drive ahead of them and this time he said that it would take them two or three days to reach their destination. Morris did a quick mental calculation and figured out that the distance from Antalia in western Turkey to Iran was just over twelve hundred miles and considering the state of the roads and the busy traffic, would take three days. At a suitable moment he whispered to Vicki that they were probably being taken to Iran. The bad news, he said, was they probably would be held as hostages for negotiations and the good news was their value depended on their being alive so they need not worry the kidnappers would kill them.

In the evening, when it got dark, they took a side road that led to a small village and stopped again to stretch their feet, eat some dry bread and cheese and drink water. Morris had chatted a little with Suleiman, who appeared to be quite a nice guy whose country had sent him on a mission to kidnap Israeli citizens. Suleiman did not know why the Islamic Republic of

Iran wanted Israelis, and like Morris, he assumed they were to be held as hostages for bargaining of one sort or another. He said they were close to Gaziantep, but Morris said that the only two places in Turkey he recognized were Antalia and Istanbul. Suleiman said that would take a short nap and then continue to Iran as travelling at night was faster on the narrow roads.

They continued driving through most of the night, stopped for breakfast that pretty much depleted their meager food reserves and continued their way east. They reached the outskirts of Saliurfa, a town that had a large Kurdish population they wanted to avoid so they headed north-east towards Diyarbakir making sure to evade the large military base and airfield. By now Suleiman felt that Morris and Vicki wouldn't cause any trouble and allowed them to sit on the back seat rather than lie on the floor of the van. Morris asked where they were heading, saying he knew that Iran was their final destination.

Suleiman looked at him and nodded and then said they wanted to avoid getting close to the Syrian and Iraqi borders and were, therefore, going on a slightly longer route that would take them a safe distance away from the conflict areas. He added he was a bit concerned that Russian aircraft would mistakenly cross into Turkish airspace, as had already happened, and fighting could break out unexpectedly. He then mumbled something about the Kurds, whose loyalty could change overnight from side to side and, therefore, they should get away from population centers.

Vicki said she needed her medication that kept her blood-pressure under control because she was feeling a little lethargic and Suleiman said he would try to get something suitable at a pharmacy in the next town. Morris said there was no need to handcuff and gag them and promised not to do anything that may risk their captors. Suleiman looked at the two of them and said something in Farsi to his two colleagues. The driver took the van through the main street of the small town and when they spotted a pharmacy stopped for a moment to let Suleiman out and then continued to the outskirts of the town.

A few minutes later the driver's cell phone rang, and he immediately turned the van back and picked up Suleiman near the place that he had dropped him off. Suleiman was holding a couple of plastic bags with groceries, bread, and bottled water. As he entered the van, he took a small box of tablets out of his pocket and handed it to Vicki, who acknowledged it with a smile of gratitude.

From Diyarbakir they continued north-east to Tatvan and stopped for the night on the shore of lake Van. The next morning, they continued along the shore of the lake and turned to the south-east before the town of Van and travelled on secondary roads to Baskale and Yuksekova and to the border crossing at Esendere. Suleiman told Vicki and Morris to lie down on the floor of the van and once again threw the rug over them.

The van passed over a couple of bumps and came to a stop. Morris heard a rapid exchange in Turkish and the unmistaken sound of money changing hands. Had Morris been able to look out of the window he would have seen the sign that said: "Turkiye cumhuriyeti, Esendese Sinir Kapisi, Gule Gule—Goodbye."

The van continued for a very short distance, stopped again and now Morris heard an exchange of some words in Farsi. The sign in English announced: "Welcome to the Islamic Republic of

MISSION PATRIOT | 69

Iran," and probably said the same in Farsi and Turkish.

Suleiman and his people relaxed noticeably, and they all started singing and clapping. He said they had just entered Iran, near the town of Urmia and from there they would pass through Tabriz. He estimated it would take about seven hours on the highway through Zanjan and Karaj to Tehran.

Morris asked him what would happen once they reached Tehran and Suleiman said they would be held in captivity, but no harm would come to them.

Evin Prison, Tehran

Morris finished his story and Zorik understood they were all hostages and would be released only if Iran's demands were met by Israel. Zorik asked, "Morris, do you think that someone knows that you were kidnapped?"

Morris looked at Vicki and replied, "We thought a lot about this. Obviously, the hotel in Kemer would notice that we did not check out and one look at our room would alert them that something happened to us as our luggage and even our passports are there. They may have notified the Israeli embassy or consulate, or at the very least the travel agent that booked our package deal."

Zorik asked if they had any family is Israel. Vicki burst out in tears. "Yes, we have a son and a daughter. Both are very close to us and they would alert the police and probably the Israeli Foreign Office if we didn't return on schedule. We are sure that the circumstances of our disappearance would be investigated. We hope they will speak to Azzuri the pilot of the hot air balloon, but I doubt he will tell the truth about our abduction."

Zorik nodded and said, "Our government is very sensitive to sudden disappearance of citizens and I am sure they will investigate the matter until they find out what happened. I am not sure they will get to the bottom of this and figure out you are held here in Tehran, but the case will not close until they find out."

Shulamit Levy said, "Now, I remember that before we went on our trip to Georgia there was something on the news about an Israeli couple had gone missing in Turkey and the anti-terror branch of the government issued a warning about going to Turkey, which is why we decided to go on an organized tour to Georgia. A lot good that did—"

Morris interjected, "Why didn't you tell us about this earlier?"

Shulamit answered, "We didn't know that you and Vicki were that couple. You never mentioned the circumstances of your kidnapping."

Zorik saw this was leading to an argument and cut it short. "Please, relax. We are in this together and must stay unified and support each other. Inbal and I left Israel months before this happened and Ari and Avi have also not been in touch with news from Israel."

Zorik then looked at the other couple, Shulamit and Nate Levy, and asked them how they were captured. There was little doubt that Shulamit was the talkative one in the Levy family and indeed she started to describe how they were captured.

Two weeks earlier, Shulamit and Nate Levy in Tbilisi, Georgia

The Levy couple wanted to celebrate their silver wedding anniversary and the fact that their youngest daughter had moved out of their small apartment in Haifa to study at the university in Beer-Sheva. They had intended to go on one of those "all inclusive" deals in Antalya but when they heard that an Israeli couple disappeared under mysterious circumstances, they changed their plans and joined a guided tour to Georgia.

They had heard a lot about that country with its magnificent mountains, good food and wine as well as nice, hospitable people. They were also attracted by the low prices for the "last minute" deal. The flight from Tel Aviv to Tbilisi was a bit scary as the old airplane seemed to be on the verge of breaking apart, as cheap charter flights sometimes seem to be but almost never really crash. It was a no-frills flight, so they were really hungry and thirsty when they landed in Tbilisi in the evening.

They were driven with the rest of the group by coach to the Marriott Hotel on Shota Rustaveli Avenue. As soon as they got the key to their room and put their luggage in the room, Nate said he was starving and wanted to go look for something to eat. Shulamit said he should not go alone and offered to join him as she, too, was famished. They didn't bother to unpack and took the elevator down to the lobby and enquired at the front desk about a place to eat.

The woman at the desk said they could order room-service and when they asked for the menu, they saw that at that time of night only served cold sandwiches. So Shulamit said to Nate it would be better to look for a restaurant near the hotel and get some hot food, so out they went.

The streets near the hotel were lit up nicely but they didn't see a restaurant that looked inviting, so they wandered a little further. As they crossed a small alley, they saw a neon sign that looked like a restaurant. They started down the dark alley when suddenly they were surrounded by four men wearing black leather jackets. The leader asked them something in Russian and when they didn't respond said in heavily accented English, "Tourists?"

Nate just nodded as he was at a loss for words for a moment.

The man didn't see this silent response and immediately got angry and demanded in an aggressive tone, "Where from?"

Nate was still unable to respond but Shulamit proudly said, "Israel."

The man looked at his three buddies and muttered something and then smiled nastily and Shulamit could see a couple of gold teeth reflecting the neon sign, and said in English, "Come with." He drew something out of his jacket's pocket.

Nate heard the sound of a knife flick open and saw the blade glinting. He lifted his hands and said, "Dollars? Do you want dollars?"

The man turned serious and grabbed Nate by the collar and pulled him deeper in to the alley. Two of the younger guys grasped Shulamit's hands and twisted them behind her back. Her scream was muffled by coarse hand that was placed over her mouth.

The Israeli couple was forced to walk down the alley while one of the young men pulled out his cell phone and spoke to someone in rapid Georgian. A few minutes later a pick-up truck with a double-cabin appeared and the Israelis were forced into it and thrown on the floor under the back seat. Once again Nate tried to offer dollars, but the response was a slap on the back of his head. The older man and the driver of the truck started arguing and shouting about something. Nate couldn't follow the conversation that was taking place above his head but understood that the word Iran was mentioned several times.

The older man warned Shulamit and Nate that if they as much as muttered a syllable he would cut their throats. Of course, they didn't understand his exact words but there was no doubt what his intentions were. They cowered on the floor of the truck and tried to hold each other for comfort.

The pick-up truck drove along the right bank of the Kura River and then along the Rustavi Highway and finally straight across the border into Azerbaijan. There didn't seem to be any formalities while crossing the border, probably because it was close to dawn and the guards on both sides preferred to stay in their sheltered shacks rather than worry about the light traffic. The leader of the group was busy talking to someone in Russian on his cell phone and probably making some kind of arrangement to hand them over.

They reached Gazakh and stopped near the Olympic Complex and were met by three men in a van. The Israeli couple was ordered out of the pick-up truck and as soon as they saw the three men, Nate was sure that they were devout Muslims. Some money changed hands and the pick-up truck headed back north while the van with the hostages continued south-east. Crossing from Azerbaijan into Iran was even easier, and within *a few hours Nate and Shulamit found themselves incarcerated in Evin Prison.*

Evin Prison, Tehran

The irony of the situation was not lost on all the Israelis in the cell—here the Levy couple tried to evade the risk of going to Turkey only to suffer the very same fate they had tried to get away from. Even Zorik, who prided himself on being a pragmatist and realist, had to accept this was an act of fate rather than an act of faith, while the others regarded the whole affair with fatalism.

Shulamit said they had not suffered any ill-treatment by the kidnappers in Georgia or by the Muslims that took them from Azerbaijan to Tehran. The only abuse they endured was from the fat jailor in the Evin Prison and even that was more because he was a sadist than because their captors wanted to extract sensitive information from them.

Zorik asked all the people in the prison cell whether they knew if the Israeli authorities had been aware of the missing couple. Nate said he was sure their tour guide would have noticed their absence in the morning following their abduction and would certainly report it, but he didn't have any direct knowledge if that had happened.

Zorik then turned to Avi and Ari, the two Israeli guys in their twenties and asked them how they landed in Evin Prison. Avi was a muscular, tall man with a large, fresh scar on his right cheek. He pointed to the scar and said the fat jailor had violently pushed him in the cell and when he fell his face was scratched by the latch on the door. Ari was thin and short, but his blue eyes were burning with an internal rage. Apparently, he was the talkative one and described briefly how they ended up in Evin Prison.

A week earlier, Ari and Avi, Phuket, Thailand

They were dancing with a large bunch of young men and women at a "full moon" party on the west coast beach at Kata. The loud music reverberated in the air, echoed back from the trees and pinged like a sonar directly on the brain. The young beachaholics, a term for people addicted to beach parties and alcohol, were moving about mechanically like zombies in time with the music.

They were fueled by copious amounts of cheap alcohol and by low quality marijuana, amphetamines, and an assortment of other drugs. Most of these were homemade by enterprising locals and tourists, who didn't care about any after-effects that users may experience once they sobered, if they bothered to do so. Two blonde girls, who said they were from Sweden, encircled Avi and rhythmically imitated his every move, while Ari looked on a bit enviously at the laughing threesome. Avi quietly said something to the girls and one of them turned to Ari and invited him to join their dance.

The four of them continued dancing for another couple of hours and then the girls said they had to go to the toilet and indicated that the guys should follow them in ten minutes to the nearby guesthouse where they were staying. Avi and Ari nodded and said they would pick-up a little more "fuel" and join them shortly. Ari said something to Avi in Hebrew, and both laughed, patted the girls on their backside, and sent them on their way. Then they headed for the cluster of trees where they knew every variety of drugs or alcohol could be purchased.

A dark-skinned boy of about fifteen approached them and asked if they were Israelis because he had a special deal for them. When they nodded, he motioned for them to follow him and headed along a trail that led further into the trees. The two Israelis were already a bit high and were looking forward to a night of a thousand pleasures.

They didn't pay attention to the four large men who surrounded them until a dirty rag with something that smelled like ether was placed over their mouths and their hands were pinned to their bodies. They passed out almost immediately and were carried to a truck waiting on the dirt road that ran close to the beach.

They came to a little later with a splitting headache and discovered that their feet and hands were tied with coarse ropes. It took them a while to orientate themselves and realize they were captured. Avi tried to speak but his mouth was so dry from the alcohol, drugs, and ether that his tongue felt like sandpaper and no sound came out.

Ari was in no better shape but managed to make some noise by stumping his feet until one of the captors hit him across the back of his head and told him to shut up. Finally, when he noticed their condition, he held a bottle of water close to Ari's mouth and gave him a couple of sips and then did likewise to Avi. He said that they would soon reach their destination.

The two Israelis had no idea why they were captured or

where they were taken to. Ari knew that the island of Phuket was thirty miles long, so reckoned they must still be on the island and not too far away from Kata beach. The truck left the paved road and moved on to a gravel road and then came to a stop. They heard someone get out the truck's cabin and open a gate. The truck moved a few feet and stopped, while the man closed the gate and got back in the truck. The truck moved a little further and stopped and the driver switched off the engine.

Ari and Avi were brusquely unloaded from the truck and unceremoniously led by two men to a small wooden shed, where they were chained to a metal pole. Dawn was rapidly approaching, and they could clearly smell the ocean and see it. But then every place is near the beach in Phuket, so that didn't add any information until they heard a plane taking off and understood they were near the airport.

At long last, a man dressed in a safari suit addressed them in accented lilting Hebrew and told them they were hostages of the Iranian Revolutionary Guards and would soon be sent to Tehran. He introduced himself as Colonel Shirazi, a senior officer in the IRG and head of the Counter-Intelligence Department that dealt with the Zionist entity that some called Israel.

He said if they behaved and cooperated, they would not be harmed and added that in the evening a private jet would take them to Iran. Ari asked if he could go to the bathroom and the Colonel said Iranians were civilized and an ancient people with a proud history and treated their prisoners well. He said something in rapid Farsi and one of the captors untied Ari's feet and took him outside to the toilet. The guard drew his pistol and led Ari outside. Avi looked up at the Colonel and said they would cause no trouble.

Suddenly a shot was heard and Avi cringed with fright and moments later the door opened, and the laughing guard led the shocked Ari into the room and tied his feet again. The Colonel smiled when he saw that Avi had wet himself and said this was just a demonstration that they were serious.

After dark, the Israelis were escorted by the Colonel and two guards and driven to a hangar in a jeep with dark windows. A small private jet was waiting with its engines already turned on. The Israelis were forced to board the plane and seated on both sides of the aisle at the back of the plane. The plane taxied to the runway and took off toward the west and then headed north. The small jet covered the distance of almost thirty-five hundred miles in a nonstop eight-hour flight and landed in Tehran.

There was a small welcoming committee consisting of IRG members, who greeted Colonel Shirazi and without further ado led the two Israelis to Evin Prison.

Evin Prison, Tehran

The eight Israeli prisoners now understood they were being held as hostages, as none were interrogated for military or secret information. Apparent to all was the fact that the Iranians were not selective—any Israeli would be fit to serve their purpose—regardless of age, gender, position in society, or personal history. The fact that they were grabbed from Turkey, India, Thailand, and Georgia indicated that this was a global operation by Iranian intelligence, or more likely by the Iranian Revolutionary Guards.

They also realized that there could be more hostages brought in to Evin Prison soon or even hostages being held in other locations. For the time being they were treated quite well, despite the sadistic behavior of Fatso the fat jailor.

CHAPTER 5

September 25th, Tel Aviv, Israel

The Head of Mossad received yet another phone call from the Prime Minister inquiring if any progress had been made regarding his granddaughter. The PM told Shimony that the young diplomat sent to Srinagar from the Israeli embassy in New Delhi submitted his report to Colonel Dan Oren and didn't discover any new information about the whereabouts of the young Israeli couple.

Haim Shimony replied he already knew that, and Mossad was investigating the matter of the disappearance of several other Israelis under similarly mysterious circumstances and there was a theory that the incidents were related. The PM asked who was behind this and Shimony answered there was no definite evidence, but he believed the Iranians were responsible.

The PM then wondered aloud if these incidents could be connected to the fate suffered by the Iranian nuclear scientists. Shimony answered this was also part of the theory. The PM said he wanted a full report by the end of the month and hung up without giving Shimony a chance to respond.

Shimony looked at the silent phone in his hand and

shouted to his secretary to summon all Mossad divisions heads, as well the head of military intelligence, the representative of the Israeli Security Agency, and David Avivi for an urgent meeting in the evening.

With a stern expression, which contrasted with his usually relaxed features, Shimony addressed the meeting.

"I am sorry to have summoned this meeting at such a short notice, but the PM is putting a lot of pressure on me. He is worried not only about his granddaughter and her fiancé but that the recent series of disappearances of Israeli citizens could somehow be connected to some global operation by the Iranians. He has instructed me to give this matter top priority and pool our resources. Does anyone wish to comment?"

The head of the Mossad section that dealt with international relations said, "Our colleagues in the Indian Intelligence Bureau, India's internal intelligence agency, had raised the possibility that the couple was kidnapped and transported over the border to Pakistan. They found that during the week of September 13th, close to the time the Israeli couple had disappeared, there were incidents of heavy drinking among the border police at the Chakothi-Uri Xing Point. The sergeant in charge of the post was dishonorably discharged from the service for negligent behavior and it also turned out he had received monetary bribes and alcohol. Putting two and two together I guess that it is where and when they were moved to Pakistan."

The ISA participant said, "We have found no connections between the missing people. Morris and Vicki Aladgem are in their sixties and from Bat-Yam, Nate and Shulamit Levy are in their forties and from Haifa, two young men Avi and Ari had just completed their military service and are in their early twenties, and Inbal and Zorik are in their late twenties and from Tel Aviv."

David Avivi raised his hand quietly and said, "Looking at the timing of the disappearances—this has to be connected to the Iranian nuclear scientists. Also, the fact that the missing Israelis were kidnapped, or so we assume, at different locations indicates there is a powerful organization involved. This is not a series of random acts or incidents and certainly not a simple ransom demand situation."

Shimony looked around and saw that all the participants seemed to agree with David's comment, so he asked, "What do we do now?" When no one volunteered to speak, he added, "I think we have to approach the Iranians through back channels and convince them that we were not involved in the incidents with their nuclear scientists. We can do this through our European friends that were so eager to do business with Iran after the nuclear deal was signed and implemented and the sanctions were removed."

He then looked at David and said, "I appoint David Avivi as my personal envoy to head our efforts in resolving this matter. It is his prerogative to also enlist the help of the Americans and Russians or even the Chinese, if he sees this as helpful. You are all required to fully cooperate with him."

After leaving the meeting, David used a secure line to call his friend from the American National Nuclear Security Agency (NNSA), Dr. Eugene Powers. He gave him a short update on the missing Israelis and asked him to enquire if the

American intelligence community had picked up anything relevant. Eugene promised to get back to him.

David then called one of his colleagues, Dr. Fritz Mayer, in the German Federal Intelligence Service, known by its German acronym as the BND. Dr. Mayer was glad to cooperate and said that the BND had heard about the Iranian scientists and missing Israelis and suspected there was a direct connection. He added that several German firms were doing a thriving business with Iran, and mainly with firms controlled by the Iranian Revolutionary Guards. He promised that he would enlist the help of their contacts in Iran to try to discover the whereabouts of the missing Israelis.

Finally, David called General Dmitri (Dima) Koliagin, who was in charge of the Iranian desk of the FSB, the Russian state security organization, and asked for his help. Dima asked what he had to offer in return and David, who had expected this question, said that he would reveal something that would truly surprise the general. The general agreed to see what he could find out and arranged to speak to David the next day.

David considered calling the Chinese but then decided they were too enigmatic. In any case the Russians were more deeply involved with the Iranian nuclear program, especially after the agreement to remove sanctions was signed. The Russians had received the Iranian stocks of low-enriched uranium and in return supplied Iran with natural "yellow cake" uranium. They were also negotiating a deal to build a couple of new nuclear power plants in Iran in addition to the one operating in Bushehr.

September 25, Tehran, Iran

The Senior Assistant of the Supreme Leader of the Islamic Republic of Iran summoned General Aslawi, commander of the Iranian Revolutionary Guards, for a private meeting to discuss the progress of the plan to retaliate against Israel.

The general asked, "Is the head of the Atomic Energy Organization of Iran (AEOI) late?"

The Senior Assistant replied, "His presence is not required, because what we are going to discuss may upset him."

The general shrugged and brought the Senior Assistant up to date. He said, "So far, eight Israelis are held in Evin Prison. All of them had been captured without any evidence of our involvement. The Israelis are probably suspicious that Iran is behind the kidnappings, but our agents made sure there would be no proof of that."

He then asked the Supreme Leader's representative, "When should we present our demands to Israel. Do we need more hostages?"

The Senior Assistant looked at him and answered, "We'll wait until there is a public outcry against the Jewish government, until Israelis fear to travel abroad, until everyone who dares to leave the safety of Israel will look over his shoulder every moment. Yes, we should continue to capture a few more hostages to strengthen our bargaining position."

The general, who knew that Israelis were not easily intimidated, sighed and said, "This could lead to an extended confrontation without any winners. The people of Iran want revenge and want it to be seen and want it now."

The Senior Assistant's face turned red. "This is the decree of the Supreme Leader. Perhaps you want to join the hostages at Evin Prison? I am sure the Israelis will gladly pay a nice price for getting you alive."

The general could barely restrain himself from getting up and walking out of the room or perhaps even slap the guy who tried to threaten him.

The Senior Assistant realized that he had gone too far and in a conciliatory tone said, "General Aslawi, I know you are doing your best. Perhaps we should look for hostages with a high profile in Israel—journalists, celebrities, people closely related to the ruling elite, important scientists, high ranking officers, or intelligence operatives."

The general nodded his approval, and the Senior Assistant added, "Make a list of prime targets that may be accessible by our agents or collaborators and give me operational scenarios that could be implemented."

The next day the general returned to the Senior Assistant and brought a list of two dozen names of senior Israelis that were currently in Europe. Some were regarded by Israeli security authorities, and of course by themselves, as worthy of having bodyguards when they travelled abroad. These were initially ruled out because an armed confrontation on foreign soil would not serve Iran's objective of appearing not to be involved. Some others were currently in countries where the local police was very effective like Switzerland, and others were on a family vacation with small kids that could complicate their quiet extraction across international borders.

The general recommended that they focus on an elderly

member of Knesset—the Israeli parliament—from the coalition, who was on a very private, and semi-secret, vacation in Cyprus with his young boyfriend. The Senior Assistant approved and said the potential for a scandal that would be noticed by the international media was very promising. He cautioned the general, quite unnecessarily, to avoid leaving any evidence of an Iranian operation.

September 26, Tel Aviv, Israel

David didn't receive any useful information from his American and German colleagues. Eugene said that the U.S. had not managed to develop a network of informants inside the IRG and that official ties between the two countries were progressing slowly.

He added that the U.S. was still regarded widely by the Iranian government and masses as the Great Satan, while the students and intellectuals wanted to copy everything from the West but had to do so surreptitiously. Dr. Fritz Mayer of the BND said that he needed more time because the commercial firms were unwilling to cooperate with the BND as they didn't want to risk their lucrative business arrangements in Iran.

General Koliagin was more forthcoming and willing to discuss the situation. He said, "David, I have information. First, let me tell you that the Iranians are simmering with anger about the assassinations, they called them 'nefarious murders', of their nuclear scientists. They regard this as a plot to make them lose face in the world and to throw a wrench in their peaceful nuclear program. They hold Mossad responsible for this, as they are sure that the CIA and MI6 are incapable of executing such an operation without getting caught. Second, they are set on exacting revenge. They know how sensitive public opinion in your country is when it comes to freeing captive Israelis. Third, this time they do not want you to release what you call terrorists in an exchange but want to force Israel to change its non-transparent nuclear policy. Finally, the FSB knows that one of the hostages is related to your Prime Minister but will not inform the Iranians."

David was speechless for a couple of minutes, only when Dima said, "Hello, are you still there?" David managed to speak. "General Koliagin, if this fact gets out, Israel may have to strike out with great force."

Koliagin suppressed a sigh. "Yes, you primitive tribes of the Middle East always react emotionally and not rationally. Do I need to remind you that Stalin did nothing to release his own son from Nazi captivity?"

David knew that Stalin's eldest son, Yakov, was held as a prisoner of war by the Nazis and that Stalin refused the offer to exchange him, leaving him to his death. The general continued, "So, David, what can you tell me that the FSB doesn't know?"

David answered, "You have my assurance that Mossad is not involved with any of the deaths of the Iranian scientists. You have our solemn word we were not responsible for any of those deaths."

The general was quiet for a moment. "So, I can tell you that all your missing citizens are held in a basement of the terrible Evin Prison in Tehran." He stopped talking when he heard

David gasp, but then continued, "They are treated well as the Iranians are looking forward to exchanging them in return for your government's policy change, as I said."

David said, "Thank you, General Koliagin. Israel would be grateful if you could convey the information I gave you to the Iranians. It would be best if it were not officially passed to them but made to look as if leaked out."

The general laughed. "I never thought Mossad was naïve, but do you really think that the Iranians would believe that this operation of eliminating nuclear scientists could be professionally executed by anyone else? Even in the good old days, when the KGB carried out "wet" operations, I doubt if they could get away with "terminating" seven senior scientists without leaving any traces. No, my friend, it would take more than your assurance and solemn oath to convince the Iranians. There is only one thing you can do—find the offenders and turn them over to the Iranians."

David stuttered. "Dima, I understand your point. Mossad will do everything in its power to apprehend the culprits. Thanks again."

David called Shimony and gave him a summary of his fruitless efforts. The only positive piece of information was that all the prisoners were held in Evin Prison and were unharmed.

September 29, Dahab, Sinai Peninsula

Eyal was napping under a palm tree on the sandy beach of Dahab. The sound of a soft voice singing a popular song woke him up and he lazily opened his eyes looking for the source of the harmonious melody.

He made a double-take when he saw that his girlfriend, Yanna, emerged from the water wearing nothing but sandals and holding a mask and snorkel. For a moment he felt just like James Bond—Sean Connery if you really care for details—in the movie "Dr. No" when Honey Ryder—he liked the choice of the name for Ursula Andress—came out of the ocean carrying a large shell and wearing an unforgettable white bikini. Eyal liked what he saw, and his attention was so fully focused on the rhythmic movement of Yanna's breasts that he didn't notice the two Bedouins that approached him from behind.

One of them was holding a curved sword while the other had an automatic rifle that he identified as an outdated M-1 carbine. In broken Hebrew, the man with the rifle told Eyal to put his hands behind his back, and the other guy stuck his sword in the sand and quickly bound Eyal's hands with a plastic cable tie. Yanna tried to run back in the water but the Bedouin with the sword was much faster and tackled her before she could reach the water line. He was in no hurry to get up from her, but his buddy shouted something in Arabic and tossed Yanna's Abaya and told her in broken Hebrew to cover herself and then cuffed her.

A battered pick-up truck stopped just a few meters from the group and the two Israelis were hastily thrown into the back of the truck and were covered with a dirty tarpaulin. The truck sped toward the small port where a fisherman's boat was waiting. The Israelis were transferred to the boat that reeked of stale fish—even worse than the tarpaulin's smell—and were dumped in the small hold below deck.

The fishing boat headed north-east towards the Jordanian Red Sea port of Aqaba. Yanna and Eyal were taken off the boat and placed in a closed van that left the port area and headed north to Amman. A private jet with Iranian markings, the very same plane that had flown Avi and Ari from Thailand a few days earlier, waited at the airport and they were flown directly to Tehran and transported to Evin Prison. There they were taken to the cell in which the other Israelis were held.

They received the same welcome that other newcomers got and after overcoming the shock of being transported from the lovely, sandy and warm beaches of Sinai to the dreary prison in Tehran told their story. The veteran prisoners told them that they had been treated nicely and had nothing to fear, except perhaps some abuse by Fatso.

September 30, Ayia Napa, Cyprus

Yonathan Shmaryahu, honorable MK (Member of Knesset) known by one and all as Johnny, was lying on a straw mat under the shade of a colorful parasol and sipping a cold beer. Despite his fashionable sunglasses, the late-September Mediterranean sun was reflected from the white sand of the beautiful beach, and he had to narrow his eyes and squint in order to see his much younger boyfriend, Oded, cooling himself in the water.

He was not glad to see that a tanned muscular blond guy was taking an active interest in Oded and the two young men seemed to be talking and laughing. Johnny had hoped that

Oded would be so grateful for the opportunity to spend a week in the resort town of Ayia Napa and would not indulge in flirting, as he tended to do whenever attractive young men were around.

Johnny and Oded had travelled from their five-star hotel in Ayia Napa to the small beach of Kermia, that was practically exclusively for gay people. Heterosexuals were not chased away from the beach but were made to feel uncomfortable and usually left after realizing that most of the bathers, surfers, and sun lovers had a different preference.

Oded and his new friend came out of the water and approached Johnny, who sat up. Oded introduced his friend as Gustav and said that he was from Denmark and appeared to be lonely and looking for company. Johnny looked closely at Gustav and liked what he saw, so he invited them to sit down and passed a couple of cold beers from the icebox they had brought to the beach. He invited Gustav to join them for dinner at one of the fanciest restaurants in Ayia Napa that was in an old building that used to serve as a fortress.

Johnny had made a fortune as the founder of a start-up company that had created a website that served gay people who were looking for partners—for life, or for spending a vacation, or for a short fling—that managed to maintain the anonymity of its users. The main advantage of this website was that it maintained a firewall that thwarted all attempts by criminals, extortionists, and curious media reporters to acquire the identity of the site's members.

Johnny had used the money he got from selling his website to launch a political career as a successful businessman with an astute sense for identifying technological and social trends. Whenever he appeared in public he was always accompanied by his bodyguard, who doubled as his very close and very personal boyfriend, a position that was now taken by Oded.

The three men had a delicious dinner that lasted for several hours and included copious amounts of alcohol in cocktails before dinner, three bottles of wine during dinner, excellent cognac after dinner, and finally coffee with Kahlua. After the meal the three men stumbled back to the hotel in which Johnny had reserved the most expensive and largest suite for the whole week. At Johnny's suggestion they all took off their clothes and pulled on bathrobes supplied by the hotel.

Johnny called room service and had a couple of bottles of chilled champagne delivered to the suite. The three of them got into the Jacuzzi, not bothering with bathing suits and continued sipping champagne. They stayed in the Jacuzzi until the skin on their fingers became all wrinkled. As the three of them got out of the Jacuzzi and entered the bedroom, Gustav said that they had to drink a nightcap as a token of gratitude to fate that had brought them together.

He drew a silver flask from his backpack and poured its ivory colored content into three shot glasses. He raised his glass and said that this drink will take them to astonishing places and to new heights they had never even dreamt of. Oded and Johnny looked each other in the eye and drank, while Gustav just tilted his shot glass and only pretended to drink.

***

When Johnny woke up it was close to noon. He had to keep his eyes closed because he had a brain-splitting headache, much worse than any hangover he had ever experienced. He figured out that he was in a moving vehicle but had no idea how that was possible because the last thing he remembered was a nice warm Jacuzzi in his hotel suite. He tried to put his right hand on his forehead to see if he had a fever but found that his movements were restricted by something. The same happened when he tried to move his left hand.

Finally, he opened his eyes and after adjusting to the pain from what seemed to be a blinding light, realized that he was lying naked on a narrow stretcher with both hands and both feet tied with plastic cable ties to the stretcher. A beach towel covered the lower part of his body and he was embarrassed when he noticed that it was wet near his midsection. He turned his head slightly to the left and saw that Oded was struggling to free his hands that were bound to another stretcher. He looked to the right expecting to see Gustav trussed in a similar fashion but instead he saw Gustav seated on a deckchair smiling.

Johnny's mouth was dry, but he managed to mumble, "Gustav, please untie us."

Gustav just looked at him, uttered an expletive about gullible homosexuals, and said, "Well, I did promise you that this drink would take you to astonishing places that you had never even dreamt of. I only forgot to add 'dreamt of in your worst nightmares. ' So, now here you are already in the Karpas Peninsula that is in the Turkish controlled northern part of Cyprus."

Johnny thought that he could get out of this problem, as he had many times before, and offered, "Gustav, I'll pay you one million dollars if you let us go." When Gustav didn't react, he added, "I mean one million for each of us. It can be in your bank account tomorrow. Just release us."

Gustav only laughed at this and said, "If you knew where you were going you would offer me ten times as much but even that would not help you. You may be surprised to know that my mother was a Danish woman that had fallen in love with my father, who was from Iran. Both my parents died in a car crash when my father hit a guardrail and wrecked the car while under the influence of alcohol. I was raised by my uncle, who is a senior officer in the Iranian Revolutionary Guards. He told me that I could atone for my father's sin of marrying outside the faith and drinking alcohol by proving that I would do anything for the IRG and my country. I agreed to do so and was put in charge of the operation to kidnap a senior Israeli politician. I have been following you and your bodyguard and must say that you both were an easy push-over. So, don't tempt me with money."

Gustav leaned over, withdrew a couple of syringes from a small metal box and injected each of the Israelis with a powerful anesthetic and within seconds they were both in a deep sleep. Blankets were thrown over their bodies to cover them and keep them warm, but they were not even aware of the fact.

A few minutes later the van entered the Gecitkale air base where a private jet with no markings was waiting. Four men approached the van and removed the two stretchers with the prone Israelis and carried them to the waiting plane. A customs officer came over, was handed an envelope stuffed with bills and a couple of official looking papers stating that this was a medical evacuation of two tourists that had fainted and needed to be transported to a hospital in Ankara. The customs officer countersigned the documents and within minutes the plane took off on runway zero nine heading east.

October 1, Imam Khomeini International Airport, Tehran

Johnny and Oded were fully conscious by the time the transport plane landed at Imam Khomeini International Airport in Tehran and taxied to a hangar at the edge of the large airfield. The plastic cable ties were cut with a sharp knife and two men were released from the stretchers. Oded instantly understood where they were and quietly said to Johnny that they were in Iran.

Johnny needed a few minutes to recover from the shock of this revelation. He told Oded that they would probably be held as hostages for some kind of deal and that he was sure his political party would pressure the government to expedite their release. Oded was not so sure about that but remained silent.

They were taken to a washroom where they were given fresh underwear and clean khaki overalls, which they were glad to put on. They were also given cheap plastic sandals that were a couple of sizes too big.

After they were dressed, they were taken to a small office at the airport hangar. A respectable looking man met them and introduced himself as Imam Mourtashef and said that he was sent by the Supreme Leader. He was sitting in a comfortable chair and wearing the standard clothes of a high-ranking religious leader. In excellent British accented English, he invited them to sit down on a sofa facing his chair. He then called a guard in a military uniform and ordered some hot tea and pastries for his guests.

Johnny seemed to relax a little after sipping tea and having some sweet pastries. His headache had abated with the help of a couple of aspirins, which he had asked for and got after they had landed in Tehran. He looked up and said, "Why are we in Iran?"

The Imam answered, "Mr. Shmaryahu, Honorable Member of the Knesset, you are our guest. You'll be free to leave as soon as your government agrees to the legitimate and miniscule demands of the Islamic Republic of Iran."

Johnny wondered why the Imam bothered with such niceties like tea and pastries if Iran wanted to present demands to the Israeli government. "Imam Mourtashef, surely there are better ways to open discussions with the Israeli government than by kidnapping a Member of the Knesset. You could use one of your allies like Turkey or China or even Russia to open covert negotiations. You know that Iran and Israel used to be great friends. This friendship was based on the common interests of the two most scientifically and technologically advanced countries in the Middle East. In addition, there is the fact the Sunni Muslim world surrounding us, regards both our countries as foreign entities that should be eliminated.

Furthermore, there is a mutual respect between our two ancient and proud cultures. We Jews are especially indebted to King Cyrus the Great who decreed twenty-five hundred years ago the return of the Jews from the Babylonian exile to the land of Israel after the destruction of the First Temple in Jerusalem."

The Imam listened patiently and said, "You have a very selective memory. You forgot to mention the military and political support that Israel gave the corrupt and illegitimate regime of the Shah. You neglected to mention that the CIA and Israelis trained the hated Savak—the domestic security service that was feared by every decent Iranian for decades."

Johnny was taken aback but this statement and replied, "The Shah was the legal ruler of Iran and as far as I know made great efforts to develop Iran and implement democratic institutions—"

He was cut short by the Imam whose outburst surprised the two Israelis. "Nonsense, the Shah was a tyrant who usurped power with the help of the CIA and British Secret Service."

Johnny tried to intervene, but the Imam continued, "The people had voted democratically to elect Mohammad Mossadegh as Prime Minister in 1951, based on his promise to nationalize the oil fields. He intended to give Iran and its people their just share of the proceeds from our natural resource and to put an end to control of the Iranian oil industry by Anglo-Persian Oil Company. They exploited not only our God given treasure but also our people that were employed at less than minimal wages in the oil fields and refineries while their British bosses were handsomely paid. He also started to introduce social and political reforms for the benefit of the common people. The British regarded this as an affront to their international interests and managed to persuade the Americans that Mussadegh was a communist—a word that to the CIA was like a red rag waved in front of a raging bull. A coup was organized by the CIA and MI6 and executed by an Iranian renegade general. When the coup started the coward Shah tried to escape from the country but the senior CIA agent, Kermit Roosevelt, who was a nephew of President Roosevelt, forced him to return to his palace. Since that coup the Shah had ruled Iran with an iron fist with the help of the American bayonets and the terror instigated by the Savak secret police."

Johnny asked, "I have never heard of this. What happened to Mussadegh?"

After his outburst, the Imam cooled down a little and said, "He was placed under house arrest until his death three years later. The Shah made sure he was buried quietly in his home-town. Maybe now you understand why Iranians have such a strong hatred for anyone who supported the Shah. We regard the United States as the Great Satan because of that and Is-rael as the Little Satan. You may not know that we used to call the Soviet Union the Lesser Satan because of its atheism, but now we don't regard Russia as such because it has come to our assistance several times and denounced the atheistic communism."

Johnny looked at Oded for silent approval and asked, "What do you want?"

The Imam smiled and said, "You'll be taken to Evin Prison

and join your compatriots who are there. You will receive humane treatment as we want you as human bargaining chips. However, if your government rejects our demands and threatens to take military action against our people or our country you will be transferred to other places and used as human shields." He then called the guard and told him to escort the hostages to Evin Prison.

After they left, the Imam smiled to himself and was content to know that his grand plan had taken another small step to being implemented. He knew that the Israeli government, media, and people could not ignore the disappearance of a Member of the Knesset and that public pressure would surely intensify driving the government to open negotiations with Iran. He was also pleased that the abduction of Johnny and Oded was so neatly carried out by a person who looked Scandinavian and not at all like his Iranian father.

The Imam's English was perfected when he was sent to his post at the Iranian embassy in London. He was responsible for the religious teachings and political indoctrination of the embassy's staff. There were a great many temptations in London and not all Iranians could withstand the lure of alcohol, food that may have contained pork, and overtly friendly women.

For some of the staff, including the young Ahmaddi Mourtashef, it was not attraction to alcohol, food, or women, but the open way in which gay couples behaved in public. Furthermore, young men were drawn to the striking charismatic Mourtashef. His mysterious figure and the exotic garb he wore at ceremonious occasions, and the vibe he unconsciously and unknowingly sent, magnetized some of the younger and older men who had crossed paths with him.

In particular, a mutual attraction developed between him and a British officer, Major Ian Leopard who was in charge of liaison with the Iranian embassy. Ian was a major in the Queen's Royal Guards and seconded to the Foreign Office to expand his international acumen, as a step toward being promoted. Ian, like Mourtashef, was a repressed homosexual, and like him had completely abstained from sex. Their work brought them together on many official occasions, but they unconsciously kept finding excuses for spending more and more time with each other.

One evening, after they had finalized the details of an upcoming meeting between a visiting Mullah from Iran and a minor functionary at the Foreign Office, they found themselves alone in the major's office. It is unclear who made the first move but within minutes they were engaged in a strong embrace that caught them both short of breath. The expression on both their faces was a mixture of excitement, fear, and horror but neither of them wanted to break the magical moment. This may have been a small step for improving the Anglo-Iranian relations but a huge leap for the two repressed gay men. They got carried away and couldn't stop until fully satiated. Ian and Ahmaddi, as they now called each other, lay cuddled on the Afghan rug in the major's office. Half asleep Ian said that he didn't know what came over him, but he didn't regret it although as a Jewish man he shouldn't have gotten close to a Shiite clergyman.

Upon hearing this, Mourtashef who had also been a bit drowsy, jumped up and almost banged his head on the major's desk. He quickly dressed and said that this had never happened, and it was all just a bad dream. Ian looked up at him with embarrassment and agreed never to mention this and never to do it again.

The honorable Imam Mourtashef shook his head in disgust as he remembered the incident in London. He had never done that again and had kept his vow to abstain from sex. However, seeing the two gay Israelis brought back a flood of memories over which he had no control. Oded looked as if he could have been Ian's son or younger brother—the similarity was striking, or it could just have been a trick of memory. One part of him wanted to tear the young Israeli to shreds while another part wanted to cuddle with him. Perhaps, he thought, this was the reason for his avowed hatred to Israel, not the long explanation that he had given Johnny and Oded earlier.

CHAPTER 6

October 1, Evin Prison, Tehran

Fatso approached the cell in which the Israeli hostages were held and with his baton beat on the bars of the cell. When he had the attention of the inmates, he ordered them to face the wall. Two armed guards stood by his side when he unlocked the cell door. Fatso pushed the two new hostages, Johnny and Oded, into the cell and slammed the door shut.

The inmates looked at the newcomers and instantly recognized the Member of the Knesset, who was more famous because of his scandalous sexual escapades than for his prowess as legislator.

Zorik was the first to speak. "Welcome to hell, Mr. Shmaryahu." He introduced all the inmates, explaining briefly where and when each was captured. Johnny looked at the varied collection of Israelis and said something about them being a representative sample of the Israeli society.

Johnny introduced Oded as his bodyguard and explained that they had been captured in Cyprus. He also gave a shorthand account of their conversation with Imam Mourtashef and his threats. He added that there was no public outcry in Israel about the missing Israelis but as a member of one of the

Knesset's select committees on foreign affairs, he was briefed by a senior intelligence officer from Mossad that Iran was involved.

Zorik motioned to Johnny to keep his voice down and whispered that there were probably recording devices in their prison cell. He added that he suspected that this was the reason why they were all allowed to stay together. He also said that they had so far avoided speaking about anything except how they were captured—information that their captors obviously possessed.

Johnny looked at Inbal and a look of recognition crossed his face but before he could utter a word Zorik approached him and murmured something that only Johnny could hear. Johnny nodded and promised to keep this very sensitive piece of information to himself. Zorik didn't really trust him to do so, especially under pressure, but couldn't do anything about it.

Johnny said aloud that he was pleased to hear that the hostages were indeed treated well. He added that his sudden disappearance from Ayia Napa was sure to raise an alarm in Israel—after all, an elected Member of the Knesset had never disappeared into thin air before—and he was sure a thorough investigation was already under way.

October 2, Ayia Napa, Cyprus

David Avivi was sent to Cyprus to investigate the sudden disappearance of Johnny Shmaryahu the Member of Knesset. Johnny had been expected to contact the "whip" of his parliamentary party the previous day and tell him how he intended to vote on a certain issue. When all attempts to contact Johnny had failed, the "whip" called the security service and as Johnny was abroad when he disappeared the matter had been passed on to Mossad. The Head of Mossad suspected that Johnny's disappearance may have been connected to that of the other Israelis and briefed David about the incident.

It took no great effort for David to find the hotel in which they had been staying. A couple of crisp American dollars changed hands and the hotel manager showed David the suite that Johnny and Oded occupied. A few more American dollars were transferred, and the manager called the person in charge of room service and was told that a bellboy was sent to deliver two bottles of champagne to the suite.

David asked the manager to summon the bellboy and when he arrived, David asked the frightened young man if he saw who was in the suite. The bellboy said that he saw three men and described them. David instantly recognized Johnny and Oded from the description. He pulled a few more bills out of his pocket and said that these should refresh the bellboy's memory and asked him to describe the third man in detail.

The bellboy's eyes lit up as he looked at the bills and said that the man was in his late twenties, well-built, and had short blond hair. He added that the three men were already very inebriated and kept laughing. He noted that they were all wearing bathrobes.

David, like many members of the public, was aware of Johnny's sexual preferences and knew that Oded doubled as a bodyguard and boyfriend. He understood that the blond man was invited to join the party but had no idea who this man was. He suspected that he must have been involved in the disappearance of Johnny and Oded that he now suspected was another kidnapping.

He looked around the room and noted that it was tidy with no evidence that a fight had taken place in the suite. He reckoned that some kind of drug must have been used because there was no other way the blond man could have taken the two Israelis by force without a fight. David was aware that Oded was well-trained in unarmed combat and would surely protect his employer and lover.

David asked the hotel manager if surveillance cameras were installed in the hotel and the manager just laughed and said that there was nothing to fear in Cyprus, so these were not necessary. David thought that there was nothing else he would find at the hotel, so he thanked the manager, asked him to pack the guests' belongings that were left in the suite and send them to Israel.

He called Haim Shimony and reported his meager findings and asked if he should try to locate the blond man. Shimony told him that the two men were probably already in Iran or on their way there and there was no point hanging around in Cyprus. He added that Mossad knew that Iranian agents were very active in Cyprus, as well as agents from many other intelligence services.

The small island had become an entry point for people trying to covertly get into the Arab countries of the Middle East as well as the exit point for people travelling in the opposite direction. Finally, Shimony told David to catch the next flight from Larnaca, the major international airport of Cyprus, back Tel Aviv, and to meet him at his office in Mossad headquarters as soon as possible.

October 2, Tel Aviv, Israel

Haim Shimony asked for an urgent personal meeting with the Prime Minister. The PM demanded to know what progress had been made regarding his granddaughter and the other missing Israelis. Shimony told him about the circumstances of the disappearance in Cyprus of a Member of the Knesset and his bodyguard and reiterated the main points of David's report.

The PM wanted to know if there was any hard evidence that the Iranians were responsible and became truly agitated when Shimony said that there were only indications but no definitive proof, except for information delivered by General Koliagin that the hostages were held in Evin Prison in Tehran. Shimony added the Russians could not be fully trusted because they had their own interests and their dirty fingers were stuck in many pies.

The PM concluded the meeting by saying he wouldn't tolerate this situation for much longer and if Shimony could not provide substantial irrefutable evidence within three days then the PM would find someone who could do the job. Shimony was stunned as no PM had ever so blatantly threatened a Mossad head.

***

By the time David Avivi entered Shimony's office it was past ten in the evening. David immediately noticed that Shimony looked very tired and under great stress. He took the bottle of Ouzo that he had purchased at the duty-free store at Larnaca airport, poured some into a glass and added cold water. The clear liquid turned in to a cloudy white drink and David invited his boss to sip some "milk," as the drink was nicknamed by its aficionados throughout the Middle East and the Balkans.

A tiny smile crossed Shimony's lips as he took a sip and relaxed a little. He then told David about the phone call from the PM and its implications on his own career, and on the careers of several senior Mossad operatives that he had promoted. He didn't need to add that if he was fired the next Mossad head would be one of the PM's cronies, who knew nothing about intelligence operations and would always act to please the PM, even if it was not in the best interests of the country.

CHAPTER 7

Three years earlier, Boston, Massachusetts, USA, and Tel Aviv, Israel

Mr. and Mrs. John and Angelica Smith got out of the taxi that they had picked up at Boston Logan airport and checked in to the small family hotel on Massachusetts Avenue that was located on the same block as the St. John Evangelist Church. The Chinese clerk at the desk did not believe that their real name was Smith nor that they were Americans as John's driver's license claimed, but as they paid cash up-front for one week he didn't really care who they were or where they came from.

He tried to pry what they were doing in the area, but John answered curtly that they were visiting their family and also had some business meetings at MIT. The clerk gave them a key ring with two keys and explained that their room was in the building next door and one key was for the front door and the other for their room. They got a small room on the second floor from where they could see the traffic moving along the busy avenue.

After settling in the small room, John removed the SIM card from his telephone and inserted a prepaid local SIM card and Angelica did the same with her phone. They detested airline food and were hungry after the long flight from Paris. So, in search of food, they strolled up Day Street to Davis Square, where they found an Italian restaurant that looked appealing. They ordered two of the dishes recommended by the owner, who was also the cashier, and had a cold beer while waiting for their food.

Two steaming plates that smelled delicious were placed on their table. After the first bite both rolled their eyes and felt as if they had just reached heaven and were served ambrosia, the food of the gods and goddesses. The beer wasn't exactly the gods' nectar, so they ordered a bottle of lush, deep red Chianti. John beamed at Angelina, who smiled back, and after consuming the large plate they each ordered a double Espresso and relaxed on the comfortable seats. They strolled back to the hotel and wearily climbed up the stairs to their room. Jet-lag was setting in and within minutes they fell into a deep sleep.

John and Angelina Smith were Mossad agents whose real names were Shmuel (Sam) Jacobs and Rina (Ruby) Rabinov and they were sent on a special mission by the ambitious chief of Mossad's operations division, who was also Shimony's senior deputy. His nickname was Segan (Hebrew for deputy), and he earned it because he was not trusted to be the chief and was doomed to retire as a deputy. People who saw him for the first time and knew about his career almost automatically thought "always a bridesmaid never a bride," because of the vibes they got from him. Segan was sure that he would not be the PM's selection for the next Mossad head unless he did something truly exceptional, some grand achievement that would be attributed to him alone, a patriotic act that could not be ignored. That is why he trusted his two close cronies, Sam and Ruby, with a delicate and sensitive mission. He promised them promotions if they succeeded and warned them that he would absolutely deny his involvement if they were caught.

***

Segan had explained that their mission was vital to the defense of Israel and would in no way affect the national security of the United States. He didn't need to tell them that the relations between Israel and the U.S. were in a very delicate state, mainly because each country quietly, but not very subtly, tried to meddle in the internal politics of the other. The Israeli right-wing government supported the Republican Party while the left-wing openly sided with the Democrats. These relations were reciprocal—the Republicans favored the Israeli right-wing and the Democrats wanted to see a change of power in Israel. There were also some personal scores to settle between the U.S. President and the Israeli PM—everything is personal as the Godfather said in the famous movie.

In addition, since the Pollard affair in the mid-1980's when some members of the Israeli intelligence community accepted the offer made by a young officer in US Naval Intelligence and recruited him, Israel had vowed never to spy on the US. Pollard happened to be Jewish, and the fact that he passed classified information to his Israeli handlers brought forth accusations of dual loyalty of the whole US Jewish community. After all, Pollard and his handlers committed the worst sin of all—they got caught red handed. Israel officially claimed that this was a rogue operation by individuals who disobeyed their orders and stated that the classified information was used in the fight against terrorism for the benefit of the US and its allies. The US did not accept these excuses and made sure that Pollard was severely punished and that the careers of the Israelis involved were callously terminated in the intelligence community.

Segan had briefed the two agents he sent covertly to the U.S. He said that he had clandestinely formed a closely-knit group of adherent backers of Israel in the U.S., but they were instructed to refrain from showing their support openly. They were mainly people who were respected members in their society and above suspicion. He promised that he would never ask them to do anything against the interests of the U.S.

As yet, he had not asked them to provide classified information but had recently learned that one of them was a key player in a major technological development that was funded by the Defense Advanced Research Projects Agency (DARPA). Possession of this unique technology could enhance Israel's operational capabilities and, in effect, allow it to attack its enemies with impunity.

Sam asked what this technology was and Segan said that it was a material that greatly improved the stealth properties of aircraft, missiles, and unmanned drones. Segan said that as a senior Mossad officer it was his patriotic duty to obtain this technology, regardless of the risks involved. He repeated his warning that they were to evade getting caught at all costs. When Ruby enquired what he meant by "all costs," Segan smiled cynically and said even at the cost of your life or the lives of others.

Before departing Segan gave them the details of their

preliminary contact and told them that a devout Catholic woman would be expecting them. After confirming that they were not followed by agents of the FBI or Homeland Security, she would provide them with contact information to the next member in the group of supporters. This man would also make sure they were not under surveillance and then hand over the sensitive technology.

***

The next day Ruby and Sam crossed Mass Avenue and entered Pemberton Farms and Garden Center. They ordered bagels with cream cheese, strong coffee, and sat at one of the handful of small tables in the garden center, surrounded by orchids and other exotic plants.

They had arranged to meet their contact at the annual sale held in the basement of St. John Evangelist Church that was Roman Catholic despite its name. They followed the old adage that meeting in public did not raise nearly as much suspicion as trying to conduct a secret meeting. They were to carry out a "bump"—an engineered encounter to penetrate an organization—and meet the contact that Segan described only as a devout Catholic woman, who was an avid supporter of Israel. He told the two agents that she believed in the role Israel had to play in the battle of Armageddon and the return to earth of Jesus Christ to defeat the Antichrist and was willing to help expedite the cataclysmic event.

There were several cars parked in the church's ample parking lot, many of them with infant car seats as a testament to the pro-life sign in the yard. They entered the building through a side door that had a notice directing the people to the annual sale in the basement. They descended the stairway and could hear the sounds of young children and infants even before they entered the large room where the sale was held.

At a glance the goods displayed looked like those found in a poor neighborhood yard-sale—an assortment of knick-knacks, old toys, plates and cups, old pots and pans. Sam and Ruby were not there to buy anything but kept up a pretense of being interested in the merchandise. According to Segan's instruction, they reached a small table at the far end of the room where some reasonably-priced nice quilts were spread out. The matronly looking woman saw the young couple, who were obviously strangers to the tightly knit community of the church regulars, guessed who they were and held up a beautiful quilt.

She pointed to a square piece of fabric in the corner and said, "Can you see the image of the Jordan River here?"

Ruby answered, "The Jordan River is now just a small stream with great public relations, not a mighty river as it was in Biblical times."

The woman smiled. "Perhaps the river will flow again."

This time it was Sam who responded, "With the help of the Almighty and his devout servants."

Ruby intervened, trying to move the conversation to more practical grounds. "I love this quilt. Is it for sale?"

The woman, who did not introduce herself nor did she ask the names of the young couple, said, "The quilt is for sale, but you will have to return to collect it in the evening. Make sure to check it carefully when you pick it up. Please go to cashier and *pay there and I'll put a "Sold" label on it."*

***

Sam and Ruby left the basement and returned to their room to catch up with some more sleep. After they had rested for a couple of hours, they discussed the encounter with the woman, whose name they didn't know so decided to call her Quilty. Ruby wondered what possible information she had that was so important that Segan had sent them to gather—she didn't really believe Segan's story about stealth technology. Sam had no idea but said that Quilty must have received some training in clandestine operations as she neither mentioned her name nor what her daytime job was.

Ruby was not so impressed by this. She wondered aloud if the fact that they had to return to the church's basement to collect the quilt could not be a trap or even some kind of "sting operation" by the FBI. She emphasized that since the arrest of Jonathan Pollard some thirty years earlier, Israel had avowed to refrain from spying on the U.S. She added that if they were caught it could create a real rift between Israel and the U.S., as the tension between the allies was very high anyway.

Sam tried to dissuade her but had to admit that her suspicion was not unjustified. He emphasized that there was no incriminating evidence against them, and they hadn't done anything illegal. Ruby said that they may be accused of entering the U.S. under false identities and that alone could send them to prison or at the very least have them deported.

Eventually they agreed that she would go to a café at Davis

Square, while he returned to collect the quilt. If all went well, he would call her and say something that included the code word "Metro." If he failed to call or to use the code word, she was to leave the U.S. as quickly and secretly as possible or go in to hiding somewhere safe until she could be sure that all was clear. They were aware of another possibility that he wouldn't be picked-up by the FBI immediately but would be followed until they met and then both would be gathered like Easter eggs. However, both were experienced field agents and knew how to spot and evade people who followed them.

***

Ruby left the hotel with her laptop computer and walked to the café and settled down with a latte on a high stool at the counter overlooking Elm Street. Sam waited fifteen minutes and then walked the short distance to the same side entrance of the church and descended the staircase. He didn't look over his shoulder, but his keen senses assured him that he was not being followed. He held the receipt he was given earlier and approached the table where Quilty was seated. She looked quite tired after a long day but when she saw Sam she smiled and held out a transparent plastic bag and he could see that the quilt was inside it.

He thanked the woman and she wished him farewell and added that she hoped he would enjoy the quilt. He assured her that he would and bid goodbye. With great apprehension he strode up the stairs and exited the door that led to the now almost deserted parking lot of the church. He had half expected to see police cars and black vans with dark windows but saw no-body around. It took him less than three minutes to get back to his room and remove the quilt from the plastic bag. He spread the quilt on the bed and saw that a label had been sewn on the same square with the scene of the Jordan River. At first, he saw nothing written on the white label but when he looked closely against the light, he noticed that there was a ten-digit number that had been created by a series of small holes, probably made with a pin.

He phoned Ruby and told her to meet him at the Davis Square Metro station in twenty minutes. According to their arrangement this meant that he expected to see her at the next Metro station, Porter Square, in one hour and twenty minutes.

***

Sam and Ruby met as planned after making sure that nei-ther of them was followed. Sam told her about the ten-digit number that was produced by a series of pin-pricks on the label and both guessed that it was probably a phone number. Sam recognized the first three digits were six one seven as the local area code. He called the number from his prepaid phone and re-ceived a voice message box. "You have reached the office of Dr. Josh Levin at the MIT advanced materials laboratory. I cannot answer the phone so please leave a message after the beep." To Sam the "beep" sounded like something from the first Star Wars movie so he guessed that Dr. Levin must be an aficionado of the film and probably not a very young man.

Sam hesitantly said, "Dr. Levin, this is the man who

purchased the beautiful quilt. Could you please call me back between eight and nine tonight or between eight and nine tomorrow morning"? He gave the number of his cell phone and ended the call.

He then looked at Dr. Josh Levin's webpage on the MIT website. He saw that Dr. Levin was in his late fifties, as he had guessed, and that he was not a professor, which was surprising in view of the impressive list of publications on the webpage. He showed this to Ruby and she said that something must have impeded Levin's career because academic researchers that were much younger were already professors. When they looked more closely at Levin's CV, they saw that he had worked for quite a few years at a private high-tech company under contract to one of the U.S. National Laboratories before joining MIT just last year and this probably explained his academic position. Sam switched off his cell phone, planning to turn it back on only at the time when he expected Levin's call.

***

Sam's phone rang just minutes after eight that evening and he heard a man's voice saying, "This is Josh returning your call."

Sam asked, "Can we meet tonight?"

Levin said, "Could you please come to my office at MIT. I'll be here at least another hour."

Sam looked at his watch and agreed to meet Josh and asked for directions. Thirty minutes later Ruby and Sam found the office on the third floor. They knocked on the door and it was answered by a gaunt man who looked emaciated as if suffering from a terminal disease. He looked very fragile, like he could fall apart any minute.

He welcomed the Israeli couple. "I was told to expect you and was instructed to hand over this little parcel." He took a small plastic box out of the top drawer of his desk and gave it to Sam.

Ruby asked, "Are you feeling okay?" Not waiting for an answer, she went over to the cooler and fetched him a glass of water.

Josh Levin said, "Thanks, but a glass of water will hardly solve my health problems. I have been diagnosed with a very aggressive bladder cancer and my physicians have given me just one more month. What I am going to give you now is highly confidential and the only reason I want the Israelis to have this information is that my days on this earth are nearly over."

Sam and Ruby looked very concerned, as Levin continued, "That is why I am working late tonight. I need to complete a crucial part of the work before I weaken much further."

Sam saw that the long speech took its toll and Levin leaned back in his chair. Sam asked what was in the parcel. Levin gestured and said, "There is a thumb drive with blueprints of a new stealth material that was developed by the private company I worked for before moving to this position at MIT. This project for developing advanced stealth materials was funded by DARPA for the sole use of the U.S. Air Force and Navy. I know that Israel will put it to good use, and I am also sure that the U.S. interests coincide with those of Israel."

He added a highly technical explanation about a breakthrough in material science and something about a completely innovative system called Active Frequency Selecting Surface

(AFSS). The idea was that a very thin absorber could change the properties of the surface with the use of broadband receivers that would reduce the reflected wave from radar systems and thus provide stealth features to the object it coated.

Ruby approached Levin's cluttered desk to place another glass of water in front of him. As she straightened up, she noticed a framed photograph in which a much younger Josh Levin was standing next to a slim blonde woman. She looked at it closely for another moment and suddenly realized that the woman in the photo was the very same woman that had sold Josh the quilt. She motioned for Sam to get up and they both thanked Levin for his help and wished him well as they left the office.

On the way back to the Metro station, she told Sam what she had seen in the photo. Sam said that the story about the exotic stealth material was unbelievable and he thought that Dr. Josh Levin was a bit too far gone. Ruby said she thought he was rational and lucid and although what he said was on the verge of science-fiction she had seen stranger things come true. Sam said there was no point in arguing and they should check the thumb drive and if the information was valid, they should leave the U.S. promptly.

They hurried back to their hotel, inserted the thumb drive into Ruby's laptop and saw that there were several directories and files with names like: "Principles of defeating radar systems," "Microwave reflection," "Ultra-thin broadband devices," "Schematics of the fuselage of advanced jet-fighters," "Testing radar silhouette of ship hulls with AFSS," etc.

They looked at each other and Ruby told Sam to start packing. Within five minutes they were ready to leave their hotel room and head to the airport. It was already late at night and there were no pedestrians and very few cars on Mass Avenue. They tried to flag a passing taxi, but none stopped, so they decided to walk to up Mass Avenue to Porter Square hoping to find a taxi there or take the Metro to a busier part of town where taxis would be available.

Fortunately, just before reaching Porter Square they saw a taxi going in the opposite direction. Sam jumped in the road and managed to get the driver to turn around. The trip to the airport was very quick as the roads were wide open with very little traffic.

The driver dropped them off at the international terminal and they checked the departures electronic notice board for the first flight to Europe or Canada—anywhere that would get them out of the United States in a hurry. They found an Air France flight to Paris that was scheduled to depart within an hour and rushed to purchase tickets. The economy class was fully booked but they managed to get two seats in business class. Sam used his John Smith credit card to pay for the tickets.

The Air France representative raised his eyebrow at the name and carefully checked the passports, made sure the credit card was valid, then sold them two tickets at a cut-throat rate.

They rushed through airport security and passport control, reached the gate in time, and boarded the flight. Once the aircraft doors closed and the plane left the gate and taxied to the take-off position, Sam and Ruby relaxed. Soon after they were airborne, they were offered drinks by the male cabin attendant that served the business class, and both asked for neat whiskey.

The snotty French attendant said, "Wheeskee is coming up."

They had to restrain themselves from laughing. They had their drinks and told the cabin attendant not to disturb them for food and wake them up before landing. He seemed offended as if he had cooked them a gourmet meal himself but left them alone after muttering something about uncivilized American passengers under his nose.

***

Ruby and Sam had to wait for a few hours before getting a flight from Paris back to Israel, but the time passed quickly on a couple of very comfortable recliner chairs. They landed in Tel Aviv less than twenty-four hours after getting the thumbdrive from Josh Levin and took a taxi straight to Mossad headquarters.

On the way they heard something on the radio about a new crisis between the U.S. and Israel, but they couldn't figure out what exactly was happening. Sam switched on his Israeli cell phone and saw what the headline news about—Israel was caught spying on the U.S. and stealing classified technology.

The taxi driver started swearing quietly at the stupid Mossad heads that never seemed to learn anything. Sam looked at Ruby and told the taxi driver that he had changed his mind and asked him to take them to his apartment that was in the center of Tel Aviv.

After they left the taxi and entered Sam's third floor apartment, he called Segan's office. Segan's secretary, Yardena, answered the phone and when she heard Sam's voice, she said that Segan was at a meeting and couldn't take any calls. Sam tried to inquire when he would be available and Yardena, who really liked Sam, whispered that he was summoned to an urgent meeting by internal security affairs.

Sam thanked her and said that he would be coming in with Ruby but Yardena cut him short and said he should wait for Segan's call before coming in. Sam replied he would be available at his apartment and Yardena promised to pass the information to Segan.

Two hours later there was a knock on the apartment door. Sam looked through the peephole and saw a very nervous Segan waiting impatiently for the door to open. Sam unlocked the door and Segan rushed in, closed the door behind him and locked it.

He spoke in a hushed tone, "The shit has hit the fan. The Americans have arrested Josh Levin and within a few hours he confessed that he had passed classified information to Israeli agents. You were lucky to get out of the United States or else you would have also been arrested. Apparently, Dr. Levin's office had been bugged by the FBI and everything that took place there was recorded. When the eavesdroppers heard about your meeting with Dr. Levin, they alerted the police, but as there were no visual images, only audio, they didn't know your identities. Josh held out long enough for you two to be on your way from Paris to Tel Aviv so you were not caught red-handed."

Sam and Ruby just looked at him, not believing their luck in getting away. "So, what do we do now?"

Segan thought for a moment and said, "Destroy the thumb drive, format your laptop, and never admit to any wrongdoing. If you are interrogated by internal security affairs, as you surely *will be, deny everything. Just say that you were on vacation in Boston. I warned you that if caught you would be on your own, so this little meeting has never taken place." As he headed toward the door he added, "Well, this is the end of the career of three good patriots—yours and mine. We would be lucky to avoid a prison sentence. Fortunately, we know too much about Mossad operations, so they would never hand us over to the Americans. Also, I hope that the Americans would like to downplay this whole affair and have it disappear quietly. Let's pray that this affair is treated as if it had never happened."*

As soon as he left, Sam said, "Perhaps we should go to Shimony and confess everything. After all, we acted on direct orders from the Deputy Director and what we did was certainly for the good of Israel."

Ruby was skeptical if that would change their predicament but agreed.

***

The meeting with Shimony was not a simple matter. First, he refused outright to see them but after some reconsideration felt that after their long and loyal service to Mossad, they deserved to be heard. He summoned the legal advisor of Mossad to hear their account and brief him on the legal implications. After hearing their story, he asked them to leave the office and wait outside while he discussed the matter with the councilor.

The legal advisor said Ruby and Sam would have to be protected from the wrath of the Americans but there was no way they could continue to work for any government office in

Israel. Shimony called them back and told them to turn in their employee IDs and never set foot again in Mossad headquarters. They would receive severance payments but would never again work for the Israeli government.

Just as they were about to leave the office, the councilor asked them about the thumb drive with the information. Reluctantly Sam pulled it out of his pocket and handed it over, saying it was the original and no copies existed.

***

After Ruby and Sam were dismissed, Shimony told the legal advisor to stay in his office for another moment. The councilor knew what Mossad head wanted and said that Segan would have to go with a laconic public announcement that he retired from his job for personal reasons. He said that Segan would probably start his own security firm but Shimony said that whatever he did he would not be able to remain in Israel.

The councilor said the government would have to assure the Americans this was a rogue operation that was not sanctioned or authorized by Mossad and that the PM was unaware of this. Shimony doubted this would placate the Americans but the councilor assured him they did not want to have the breach of their security publicized. He added that if the thumb drive was returned quietly, and the technology safely retained, the Americans would probably be satisfied with a secret reprimand. Naturally, Segan, Sam, or Ruby should never enter the U.S. if they wanted to avoid prosecution and imprisonment.

CHAPTER 8

Two Years earlier, Berlin, Germany

A few months after the great fiasco in the U.S., Segan estab-lished a security firm. Its main office was located in Berlin, with branches in Madrid, and London. He mainly employed former soldiers that had served in Special Forces units in the UK, U.S., Germany, France, and Russia, as well as Israel.

Most of them had been dishonorably discharged and forced to leave the service of their country and often even their coun-try. Segan didn't care about the exact circumstances of their compulsory retirement and was satisfied with their willingness, in some cases almost desperation, to do anything for the right price.

The main service he provided was personal security, namely bodyguards, but his employees were often used as enforcers and debt collectors. A few of his select customers contracted his firm for "special functions," that was a euphemism for removal of competitors and elimination of competition. These tasks were usually handled by Russian ex-KGB (or FSB) commandos or "soldiers of fortune," and sadly, their victims were "unfortu-nates," no witticism intended.

He preferred to employ ex-Mossad or Israel Security Agency (ex-ISA) personnel for the more delicate contracts that involved finesse and subtlety, rather than brute force. As a true Israeli patriot, he had only one rule—never accept a contract that was against the interests of Israel.

***

One day, Segan received a phone call from a man with an upper-class British tone of voice, who identified himself as Alan Ross and asked for a private meeting. Segan recognized the accent and after looking at his schedule said that he would be in London at the end of the week. However, Ross said he was already in Berlin and would be glad to discuss a large contract over dinner that evening. Segan said he already had a dinner appointment but could make himself available after dinner and suggested that they meet at 'Allan's breakfast and wine bar'.

Alan Ross laughed when he heard the name of the place but then saw that it was highly recommended by TripAdvisor and agreed to meet there at nine thirty that evening. Ross said he would recognize Segan, which already rang an alarm bell for the experienced ex-Mossad man, but he made no comment on that.

Before the meeting, Segan asked his secretary to look up if there was any information on the web about Alan Ross. A few minutes later she said it was a common name and she couldn't be sure which one was the contact. Segan shrugged and said that in any case this was probably not the man's real name.

As was his habit whenever he was about to meet a stranger, he was escorted by his two most trusted employees, Ruby and

Sam who were now working for his firm. According to their standard modus operandi, they entered the wine bar thirty minutes before Segan and took a corner table that overlooked the crowded room. They ordered coffee and cake and settled down to watch the patrons. They also checked both the Damen and Herren restrooms and when they were sure that no ambush had been set up, they sent a short text message to Segan in Hebrew that all was clear.

Segan walked in and took a table across the room from his two agents. Shortly afterwards, a middle-aged man wearing an expensive looking suit with a striped silk tie, and even more expensive hand-made leather shoes, approached Segan's table and introduced himself as Alan Ross.

After going through the usual niceties, they got down to business.

Ross said, "You realize, of course, that Alan Ross is just the name I have adopted for this meeting. I used to work for British Intelligence, MI6 actually, and am now a consultant at large."

Segan replied, "I figured that out, but who are you serving as a consultant?"

Ross shrugged. "I am merely a messenger sent on a mission that would be lucrative for all involved, as well as in line with your main interests."

Segan asked, "How lucrative?" When he heard the eight-figure sum he nodded but enquired again, "Who exactly is your employer?"

Once more Ross avoided a direct answer, saying, "Please, first listen to the description of the mission and then decide if you really want to know about the employer."

Segan's curiosity was reflected in his eyes, so Ross continued, "The target is the Iranian nuclear program. My employer believes that if this program is obliterated, the world would be a better place, safer for the Middle East, and everywhere else. The public annihilation of this reprehensible effort of the Islamic regime to obtain an atomic bomb would bring about its downfall. This will enable the peace-loving, liberal forces in Iran to gain power, install a true democracy, and exterminate the Mullahs' regime and their supporters."

Segan swallowed twice and took a deep breath before responding, "The progressive countries in the free-world have been trying to do this for years. How do you expect me, with my small firm, to succeed where the CIA, Mossad, and British Intelligence have failed? They had practically unlimited funds, support of the international community, and backing from the most powerful countries on Earth."

Ross just smiled and said, "It is all a matter of timing. This is like Judo—you use the strength of your opponent to throw him to ground. When he comes charging at you, all you must do is use his own momentum to bring him down. After the nuclear deal, the opposition in Iran is ready to make its move. All that is needed is the trigger, the match to ignite the fuse, the sign that the regime is vulnerable and ready to be toppled down."

Segan was unconvinced. "How do we light the fuse when we don't even know that there is a fuse?"

Alan Ross bent over and whispered in Segan's ear for a few minutes. Then he rose from the table and said he would let Segan sleep on it for a few nights and would call him the following week when he was in Berlin again.

***

After Alan Ross left, Segan signaled to Sam and Ruby to join him at his table and gave them a brief summary of the intriguing conversation.

Sam's immediate reaction was that something didn't seem right with the questionable mission that Ross had proposed. Ruby was even more skeptical and suggested they should not even consider the project. She said she thought it was a test and not a genuine proposal, perhaps even some "sting operation."

However, Segan was blinded by the eight-figure sum that had been discussed and said he would not reject the idea outright and was determined to meet with Ross again to hear his specific plan of action.

***

A week later Ross and Segan met again at the same place. Ross asked, "What did you think about my proposal? Have you reached a decision?"

Segan said, "I need to know more about your plan."

Alan Ross leaned back in his chair and his eyes seemed to stare in to space for a moment. Then he sat straight up. "The contract calls for the elimination of a number of Iranian key scientists and security personnel who play an important role in Iran's nuclear program. This will be done by your most experienced and trustworthy people, preferably former Mossad agents with field experience. They must not be caught alive, meaning that if there is a risk of them being captured, they must be willing to sacrifice their lives. As you correctly reckon, this will do your home country a great service. I was led to believe that your ex-Mossad agents, like yourself, are Israeli patriots and willing to give their life to fight Israel's most bitter enemy. The people of Iran are not the enemy, the hateful Islamic regime and the Mullahs are.

"Once the regime is stripped of its nuclear weapon capability and is forced to give up the dream of becoming a nuclear power and dominate the region through intimidation, then the people will rise and overthrow the confining tyranny imposed by the Iranian Revolutionary Guards. The IRG has manipulated the Mullahs and now controls the economy and strangles it. They have become so greedy that the leaders have fat bank accounts in Switzerland and the Cayman Islands. The common people know this but are afraid to say anything. Once the IRG is toppled, this information will become common knowledge with bank statements as proof and the voice of the people will resonate throughout Iran and the world."

Segan was shocked by the emotional outburst and began to doubt if Ross was indeed an Englishman and not an Iranian. He asked, "You mentioned a large sum of money. I know the Iranian opposition is pitiable and without outside financial support would have crumbled long ago. Where does the money come from?" Segan knew well the old axiom that was taught to all intelligence operators and police forces across the globe: "follow the money trail."

Ross looked a bit uncomfortable. "I cannot say where the money for this operation comes from, but I can give you a brief review of the recent developments in the region and their roots.

You can then draw conclusions at your own risk. You know, as all experts on the Middle East discern, that Iran regards itself as the leader of the true Islam while Saudi Arabia sees all the Shiites, and the Iranians in particular, as infidels and traitors. No love is lost between these two rivals.

"Periodically the tension between them erupts overtly. For example, when hundreds of Muslims, including several Iranian Shiites, were trampled to death in Mecca, Iran blamed the Saudi royal family. When a Shiite leader was executed by the Saudis, together with dozens of Sunni Al-Qaida terrorists, the Saudi embassy in Tehran was sacked, supposedly by crowds that gathered spontaneously. When Iran threatened to develop an atomic bomb, the Saudis ran to Pakistan begging to purchase one of their nuclear bombs to counter Iran's threats.

"So, you can guess who is funding the opposition groups in Iran. Unfortunately, there are several such groups that operate separately, and each faction wants to lead the opposition resulting in an uncoordinated effort against the Mullahs. Only if the regime is perceived as ready to fall will they unite. That's why the operation is so important."

Once again, Segan was surprised at the flare-up of temper by the apparently cool man. He said, "Do you sincerely believe that eliminating a number of nuclear scientists would be the proverbial straw that breaks the camel's back?"

Alan Ross just nodded, before Segan said, "Well, in view of the potential rewards for the financiers of this operation, and the risks involved to my people, I would have to add to the contract a clause that ensures a bonus for success. And I would need a list of targets and detailed information about them, particularly where and when they can be hit outside of Iran because my resources inside Iran are practically non-existent."

Ross responded, "The bonus is agreed in principle, but we need to agree on its size. I could add twenty-five percent to the original offer as a reward for toppling the regime and another twenty-five percent, if my sponsor's group gains control of Iran. I'll prepare a list of vulnerable and worthy targets. I have to stipulate, just in case it wasn't obvious, that all the operations must not be traced to me or my group and certainly not to the source of our funding. No official announcement will be made—"

Segan interrupted, "The Iranians will suspect their natural enemies—what they call the Great Satan and the Little Satan—and who knows what their response would be."

Ross continued, "I was just about to say that your bonus would be doubled if the Lesser Satan could be blamed."

Segan thought about this and said, "Realistically, this would be impossible. The Russians would not jeopardize the large market that has opened up after the nuclear deal. There are already advanced negotiations for the construction of two more nuclear power plants at the Bushehr site to be built by the Russians. These are multi-billion projects that will be signed by the Mullahs regime, while a democratic government would probably prefer French technology or even American power plants that have a better safety record."

Ross shrugged and said, "As long as we are not caught red-handed, you can let the Iranians speculate and guess but leave no footprints or fingerprints."

Segan said, "Before we sign, well not literally of course, a contract for the job, I'll need to know how many people are to be eliminated and the schedule. I would prefer to carry out the job within less than one month because once we start, the level of watchfulness would rise, and the next targets will be harder to strike."

Ross replied, "This is a good point. I'll gather the background information and we'll set the schedule for the beginning of the operation and the timeframe for its completion. I suggest we meet in six months to conclude our deal. Meanwhile, make sure that you use your most reliable and capable people for this operation."

Segan said that he needed an advance payment of ten million American dollars in addition to the fees for the contract and when Ross agreed, he gave him the number of one of his accounts in a Swiss bank.

***

Segan checked that the money was transferred to his account and called on his two most trusted operatives—Ruby and Sam—and briefed them on the upcoming contract. Once again, Sam was skeptical and Ruby cynically said that this operation should have been carried out a decade earlier as that would have stopped the Iranian nuclear weapons program in its infancy.

Segan agreed with her on this point but said that in this case, "better late than never" applied. He proudly said that this operation could possibly reinstate the three of them as true patriots and that their dishonorable discharge from Mossad would be forgotten. In his own mind, he hoped that this spectacular *operation and outcome would renew his chances of becoming Mossad head after Shimony. None of them stopped to reconsider the whole operation and the dangers involved.*

***

Six months later, after Segan and his people had almost forgotten about the affair, Alan Ross called Segan's office and set an appointment. The two men met again at the wine bar and this time Segan didn't even bring his bodyguards.

Ross said he had compiled a list of targets that comprised some key Iranian nuclear scientists and engineers as well as intelligence officers that played a role in the nuclear weapons program. The list included a dozen names and Ross promised a payment of three million American dollars for each successful job—the words murder, targeted killing, elimination, or even termination were never used in public by the professionals, just in case someone was recording them or lip-reading.

He repeated his instructions that the jobs should be carried out within a short timeframe, forgetting that it was Segan's suggestion. Segan proposed a different payment method—he said the first job would be free, the second would cost one million American dollars, the third two million, and each consecutive job would cost one million American dollars more than the previous one. Ross thought about it and agreed.

Then Segan said that in cases like this, collateral damage was inevitable, and Ross said he understood that in some cases innocent bystanders may suffer and that didn't bother him as long as the objective received the proper treatment.

The two men shook hands on the deal and Ross left a London telephone number that would accept messages twenty-four-seven. The messages should be very short and include two or three words that corresponded to the initials of the eliminated target. Segan thought that this was a stupid arrangement but agreed to comply with this childish code.

One Year earlier, November

Vienna was the site of the first job that Segan's people carried out. Segan called the telephone number he was given and said, "Another apple appeared." Then he hung up, thinking he must have had a mental blackout when he composed this triple A sentence.

The meaning was that Dr. Ali Abdul Abadi had been eliminated in a quiet manner by Ruby, who had distracted the scientist and Sam who squirted the poison in to Abadi's ear.

A couple of days later Segan called again and left another short message. "Another Romantic Knight." Referring to Professor Ahmad Riza Kadoura's early demise in a tragic train accident in Barcelona, implemented by Sam.

Segan hoped that Ross would know the difference between Knight and night and not bust his brains looking for an Iranian scientist with the initials ARN. He knew the message was quite stupid, to say the least, but was glad to verify that one million American dollars was received in his bank account.

Three more days passed before Segan called the same number with the news about Dr. Mahmoud Al-Baida's unfortunate mishap when he and his wife fell to their death from a cliff in

Taormina, Sicily, when Sam "accidentally" stumbled into them. Segan just said, "Miniature boats." He figured the prefix Al was not really a part of the name.

Once again, he wasn't sure that the message would be correctly understood. So, he was relieved when two million American dollars appeared in the bank account the next day.

The job in London was more complicated as it involved recruiting the Chinese masseur and his daughter, but the payment was also higher—three million American dollars, so the elimination of Dr. Mustafa Fahami took place almost at the same time as the one in Sicily.

Segan himself carried out the neck-wringing after he persuaded the Chinese father and daughter to collaborate with a "carrot and stick" tactic: he promised them a quarter million American dollars if they successfully cooperated and allowed the fake "masseur" to take over during the massage and combined that with a threat that he would report their illegal status to authorities if they did not oblige.

After Fahami's neck was broken he made a local call to the London number saying, "Many foxes." Which again he thought was a brainless way of passing the good news.

A day later, Segan made another call saying, "Jolly toffee." After Dr. Jaafar Taghi consumed some bad oysters in Stockholm that were spiced by Ruby in her guise as a French scientist. The four million American dollars arrived promptly in the Swiss account. These last three jobs were carried out more or less simultaneously by Sam in Sicily, Segan in London, and Ruby in Stockholm.

Four days later, Hassan Sadeq suffered a bizarre ski accident *in Chamonix as he was nudged down a precipice by Ruby and Sam who posed as a couple of skiers. This was the sixth job carried out by Segan's team and the five million American dollars that were deposited in the account helped ease the conscience of the Israelis. After all, they were convinced they were carrying out a patriotic mission.*

There were a few other names on the list that Ross handed over, but the intended targets didn't leave Iran. No sane Iranian scientist, and they were all wise people, wanted to risk foreign travel as rumors spread that so many of their number had suffered mysterious accidents.

When Segan calculated his revenues from the project he realized that he should have accepted Ross's original offer of three million dollars per capita. He laughed to himself as he reckoned that Iranians were reputably known for their business acumen and negotiation skills.

When he heard about the bombing in Isfahan, in which three more scientists were killed, he figured out the Iranian opposition had gained confidence from his own work and carried out this job on their own, but he could not take credit for it.

CHAPTER 9

Present time, October 2, Tel Aviv, Israel

By the time Shimony and David had finished the bottle of Ouzo that David had brought from Cyprus, both lowered their guard and relaxed in each other's company, as good friends who trust each other do.

David felt free to bring forth a wild idea that had been in the back of his mind for some time. "I am sure that the Iranians are holding our people as hostages for some reason. There must be an element of revenge for the series of mishaps that their nuclear scientists suffered but I feel there is something else involved here. After the nuclear deal and removal of the international sanctions against Iran, in return for curtailing their attempts to obtain fissile materials and cessation of their military nuclear program, the stranglehold of the Iranian Revolutionary Guards and the Mullahs on the Iranian people has weakened.

"This has encouraged the opposition groups and secular population to raise their heads and increase their instigation against the religious leadership. What if the elimination of the scientists was orchestrated by the opposition and the regime is now retaliating against Israel because they think that we worked in cohorts with the opposition? You and I know that Mossad had nothing to do with the Iranian scientists but what if some wise guy in the PM's office launched an independent project without our knowledge but with the PM's tacit approval or even without it? After all, such things had happened in the past."

He was referring to an operation that was carried out by amateurs that were recruited by the IDF military intelligence in Egypt in 1954. This operation literally blew up in the face of one of the perpetrators and resulted in a scandal that almost toppled the government of Israel a few years later when details of the affair were revealed.

Shimony was momentarily at a loss for words and pondered the idea for a long time before saying, "David, are you implying that there is a renegade within Mossad. Someone who has interpreted suggestions that came up in our meetings and took a personal initiative right here under our nose."

David immediately rejected this idea. "Haim, there is no way that this could happen here without your knowledge. But what if former Mossad agents were behind this? What if your ex-deputy, Segan, who was driven away with disgrace, decided to do something like this? He could be doing this to redeem his reputation, to undermine the interests of Israel as a means of seeking revenge for his dishonorable discharge, or even because he is just out of his mind."

Shimony countered, "There is no way Segan is a traitor, but he could well be a misguided person, who thinks that he is doing a patriotic thing. He was always a good tactician and operations officer but never really understood anything about strategy. Yes, David, he could be involved in this. What's more, when he was kicked out of Mossad for his private enterprise in America, we had to expel two of our best operatives who were sent there by him. Indeed, Ruby and Sam are certainly capable of carrying out the operations against the Iranian scientists without leaving a trace or a shred of evidence."

David took some minutes before replying, "So, I think that I should find Segan and ask him about the operation."

Shimony warned him that Segan and his people were extremely dangerous, especially if they felt cornered, but endorsed David's suggestion.

October 3, Berlin

David arrived at Berlin's international airport in the afternoon. His plan was to meet Ruby and confront her with his suspicions. He knew that if he called in advance, she would avoid him and disappear, so he intended to "accidently" bump into her.

He hoped that as an old colleague, or rather ex-colleague, who showed sympathy for her plight she would accept his invitation for a cup of coffee. He knew she was perceptive and sharp, and he would have a hard time convincing her that their meeting was not premeditated but as one of Mossad's best operatives he hoped she wouldn't reject him outright. He really worried she would alert Segan and that would complicate things considerably.

Berlin was one of the main hubs for intelligence gathering and mutual spying. The Cold War was almost forgotten by the younger population of Berlin, but old habits die hard and intelligence agents still favored the vibrant city. It was said that you could buy anything and everything in Berlin if you have enough money and the right contacts.

In Berlin money could buy you love, drugs, weapons, and contracts to dispose of your enemies. The local Mossad station head, Julia Carmon, was one of the rising stars with high hopes of being promoted to a Division Head soon. Provided, of course, that she did a good job quietly without attracting any media coverage, and more importantly, managed to avoid scandals.

Julia was a vivacious woman in her late thirties who looked a decade younger. She had recently divorced her husband, who was so busy making money and running one of the largest law firms in Tel Aviv that he refused to join her in Berlin.

According to him, her career was anecdotal and important only because of the connections and the clients she brought to his law firm, while she regarded it as a service to her country. In her younger days, before they were married, she was a field agent and had participated in several clean clandestine operations that were attributed to Mossad although there was never any hard evidence.

After her posting to Germany, Julia and her husband used to get together every week-end either in Tel Aviv or Berlin. However, as happens in many arrangements of this type, the frequency of their meetings slowly dwindled and eventually they decided that they would be better off separated and finally got divorced.

Now each of them was free to pursue their happiness,

whatever that meant. In Julia's case, happiness was to immerse herself in her work and forego personal life. Sex to her was like exercise—something you did to feel better with your body and soul without any emotional involvement.

Some senior Israeli politicians who visited Berlin regularly expected the Mossad station head to respond to their beck and call and satisfy their every whim, including things they wouldn't dare do in Israel. Julia did her best to comply but had her own red lines that she refused to cross. When the demands of those VIPs bordered on illegal fantasies, she referred them to the embassy.

The "cultural attaché" at the embassy was an administrative worker in the Israeli Foreign Office who received the posting in Berlin from the new general manager in order to get him away from the headquarters where he caused more trouble than he was worth. He was not a career diplomat and quickly became more familiar with the Berlin "sub-culture," that consisted of a rich mixture of sex, drugs, and the pursuit of fulfilling the most eccentric desires and perversions.

***

Julia knew that Segan had set up his own security firm and that its main office was in Berlin. Like all senior Mossad employees, she was aware of the fact that he was disowned by Haim Shimony and left Mossad under a cloud of disgrace, but the details were vague and known only to a select few. The official version was that he sought new challenges in the private sector—a common euphemism for someone whose

Mossad career was over and now wanted to make money by marketing the skills he acquired in government service to the highest bidder.

As long as Segan's operations did not collide with her own work, Julia couldn't care less about his firm. She had received information that he had no scruples taking on jobs that were not perfectly within the law and that some of his employees were of disreputable character, not to say fugitives from the law in their own countries.

Julia and David had worked together previously, so she was pleased when David called her and said that he was in Berlin and immediately invited him for dinner. However, he said that he needed to meet with her on urgent official business and had time only for a quick cup of coffee, but that perhaps they would be able to get together later that night. He said he preferred to meet at a café rather than in the embassy building that was probably under surveillance by all kinds of organizations from the local polizei to various terrorist groups.

Julia gave him the name of a quiet little place not far from the embassy that was located on Augustae Victoria Strasse. David took a taxi from the airport directly to the café and when he arrived there, Julia was already nursing her second cup of coffee and a large slice of chocolate cake waited on a plate in front of her.

Julia stood up and gave David a hug and pecked both his cheeks. David responded in kind and smiled warmly at her. He gave her a brief explanation of the reason for his sudden visit, without going into details about the suspicions that

Segan's outfit was involved in the mysterious deaths of the Iranian nuclear scientists. He just said that Shimony asked him to make sure that Segan was not acting against the interests of Israel.

Julia replied that she had not been instructed to keep an eye on Segan, and on the contrary was discouraged to have any official contact with him. She added that he, and all his Israeli employees, were considered as *persona non grata* at the embassy and, therefore, kept pretty much to themselves. David asked her if she had come across Ruby, and Julia said that she had heard that Ruby and Sam were now a real couple, not just colleagues, but other than that she knew little about their private lives and even less about their professional activities.

However, she said that they now lived in an apartment building on Gruntaler Strasse near the corner of Badstrasse. David took out his cell phone and checked the address on Google Maps. Julia said that like many young German couples, they probably shop for fresh food products at a nearby supermarket or mini-market and pointed to a Lidl supermarket near the corner but added there were two other similar stores, Kaiser's and Euro Gida on Badstrasse, also within a short distance from the apartment building.

They drank the excellent coffee and enjoyed sharing the delicious rich chocolate cake. David said he had to leave now because he had to engineer a meeting with Ruby without Sam's presence. Julia said she believed that there was a good chance Ruby would be at the Lidl supermarket as it was the closest and had good products at reasonable prices.

David then decided he could use Julia's help and asked her if she would join him in staking out the three stores. Julia gladly agreed to go back to the field and relive her days as a young field operative.

***

David positioned himself on the sidewalk of Badstrasse between Lidl and Kaiser's supermarkets, while Julia waited on the other side of the broad street near the other mini-market. They were only about fifty feet apart but could not maintain eye-contact because of the traffic on Badstrasse that was heavy at this time of the evening. They agreed that there was no point in hanging there after eight in the evening, so they had a window of opportunity of about one hour in which they hoped Ruby would appear, or else they would have to devise a different approach for the planned "accidental" encounter.

Minutes before eight o'clock, Julia saw a familiar female figure approaching the Euro Gida supermarket and as the woman got closer she recognized Ruby. She turned away and started walking south on Badstrasse to avoid getting too close to Ruby.

She texted David that she saw Ruby entering the super-market and picking up a shopping cart so assumed that she intended to take her time shopping. David immediately hurried from his post between the two other stores and crossed the road toward the supermarket.

He picked up a small shopping basket at the entrance and looked around until he saw Ruby carefully viewing the tomatoes and trying to select those that looked fresh and juicy. David approached the stall on which the tomatoes were displayed and selected one of the finest he could see and then quietly spoke to Ruby saying, "This would really taste good in your salad tomorrow morning." Knowing that Israelis liked a fresh vegetable salad for breakfast.

Ruby was startled to hear someone speaking to her in Hebrew and looked up with a confused expression. Then she recognized David, who was something of a legend in Mossad and smiled innocently. "Wow, imagine running across you by accident here."

She was too experienced to believe that the meeting was really a coincidence, but she knew that creating a scene would draw unwanted attention and not serve her well.

David saw that she was not going to buy any of the cover stories he had prepared so he cut to the chase. "Ruby, I need to speak to you in private."

Ruby looked around and said, "I have nothing to say to you or to the people that sent you." She continued her shopping as if nothing had happened without another glance at David.

David said the magic words that he had planned as a last resort, appealing to her patriotic feelings. "Your country needs you. I know that you and Sam have been mistreated by Shimony and have been punished for following direct orders from your boss. He has sent me to make amends—"

Before he could complete the sentence Ruby interrupted, "A bit late for that, don't you think? I have started a new life and am quite pleased with it. I owe you nothing but contempt."

She abandoned her cart and walked past the cashier before

storming out of the supermarket with David close on her heel. She walked rapidly up Badstrasse, pulling out her cell phone as she turned the corner heading up Gruntaler Strasse. She was gesturing excitedly with her free hand as she passed the Willy-Brandt Oberschule and reached her apartment building.

David had no choice but to follow her into the building and expect the confrontation with Sam, who had already opened the apartment's door and was waiting for Ruby with one hand hidden behind his back. It didn't take a genius to guess what was concealed in his hand, so David held both open hands far from his body and put a smile on his face. "Sam, indeed, it is a nice surprise to meet you, too."

Sam was not smiling. "David, I wish I could say the same. Walk slowly through the door, turn left into the living room and sit on the sofa. Don't make any sudden movement and keep your hands where I can see them."

David obliged grudgingly and said, "Sam, I told Ruby that I have come to make amends." Seeing the expression on Sam's face, he quickly added, "Shimony feels bad about the way you were treated and sent me on a special conciliatory mission. Please let me speak freely."

Sam looked at Ruby, who nodded, saying, "Okay. Let's hear him out."

David repeated the message he had earlier said to Ruby, "Your country needs you. I know, and Shimony does too, that both of you are true patriots. Segan got you in trouble with his unauthorized initiative. You two just followed his instructions, that, to you, seemed to be a perfectly legitimate task, coming from your superior officer. It was not your place to question his motives and certainly above your pay-grade to worry about the consequences of being found out."

Sam instinctively responded, "So, why were we thrown out of Mossad?!"

David honestly said, "Because the PM needed a scapegoat and just sacrificing Segan was not enough to satisfy the Americans. They wanted more blood and you were not exactly innocent bystanders."

This last sentence enraged Ruby. "So, here's the truth coming out at last. The Americans had to be placated and we paid the price. Effectively, we were banished from Israel in to exile. We cannot safely return to visit our families for fear that a journalist, or worse a CIA informer, would discover us entering the country. Without Mossad's blessing we cannot even do this under assumed names and fake passports. If you want any degree of cooperation from us, you first have to remedy this."

David hastened to say, "You have my word that you can freely enter the country. We'll provide you with valid, legitimate new passports under any name you wish to choose."

Seeing the skeptical look on Sam's face David continued, "You don't have to say anything to me until you get the new identities. In fact, I would prefer you to visit Israel and meet Shimony at Mossad headquarters. Then and there, we can continue this conversation."

Ruby and Sam exchanged another look and Sam spoke, "Okay. Contact us again with the new passports and then we'll see. We demand that you alone do this. Here's my private unlisted and untraceable cell phone number. Call me when you are ready."

Before parting, David said, "It is best that this little meeting and agreement is not shared with Segan. He is very unpredictable, and his reaction may be violent."

While all this was taking place, Julia was nervously pacing up and down the apartment building on Gruntaler Strasse. She was getting worried that David had not come out or called and even considered breaking into the apartment.

However, she had second thoughts about trying to take the two veteran Mossad field operators by force. She was relieved to see David walking unharmed out of the building and approached him discreetly. She took David's hand and whispered that she was glad he was unscathed, and he answered that he needed a stiff drink urgently.

***

David and Julia walked up Gruntaler Strasse, turned right on Klever Strasse and found a nice pub with the improbable name of 'Offside Pub and Whiskey Bar'. They sat at a corner table under a few paintings that depicted realistic scenes and admired the old radio sets in the display cabinet near their table.

After each had downed a double whiskey, they had some greasy snacks, then a cold beer to wash them down. David reiterated the main points of the conversation he had with Sam and Ruby. Julia asked him if she could help. David emphasized that they demanded his personal handling of the matter and said that it was best if the Mossad Berlin station was not involved.

Julia wondered why they really insisted on new Israeli passports. "After all," she said, "Ruby and Sam had used Israeli fake passports and probably a myriad of other passports that were illegally obtained for their operations in the service of Mossad and certainly when working for Segan. I would be surprised if they didn't keep some of them or if Segan had not supplied them with all kinds of new passports."

David said, "They are considered as pariahs in Israel. Even if they enter the country with a false identity the face recognition algorithm at the border control posts in Tel Aviv airport are sure to identify them and trigger an alarm. That is not to say that they will be arrested on the spot—after all they were allowed to leave the country after the U.S. fiasco—but Mossad, the police, and the ISA will know about them. They may be followed or harassed, depending mainly on Shimony's decision, and whoever they meet would be under surveillance. This they want to avoid, so they have required a kind of official pardon that will remove them from the list of "most wanted persons." This will enable them to meet freely with their families and friends."

Julia said, "I had only heard rumors about this face recognition algorithm and had no idea that it was used against Israeli citizens who were not on a 'most wanted' list."

David smiled. "Julia, you are so young, so naïve, and so beautiful that it makes me ache." In fact, David was a bit younger than Julia, but he felt like the older of the two.

She smiled at the compliment and said, "Well, I agree with

the last part of your sentence, and we'll have to see if your ache can be somehow relieved."

After they had satisfied their hunger pang and unwound a little with a glass of cognac, the conversation became more personal. David told her, without being prompted, "You have probably heard on our grapevine that my relationship with Orna is over."

Julia laughed quietly and said, "This is common knowledge in Mossad gossip. I am now officially divorced after quite a long period of not having an effective marriage."

This was hardly earth-shattering news to David, who was aware of the extremely high divorce rate among Mossad employees. The circumstances of their work often made them find themselves in strange countries and unusual situations, where normal family life was impossible to maintain. Julia didn't beat around the bush and asked him, "What are your plans for the night? Have you booked a hotel?"

David just smiled. "I am completely free and at your service until the morning flight back to Tel Aviv."

They exited the pub together and took a taxi to Julia's apartment, where they spent the night satisfying each other's needs and releasing the tension that their jobs induced.

October 4, Tel Aviv

Before boarding his flight to Tel Aviv David called Shimony's office and set an appointment. An official car was waiting for him at the airport and rushed him directly to Mossad head's office.

David reported the deal he had made with Sam and Ruby

and although Shimony was not pleased with the *de facto* pardon given to the two former field agents, he complied and called in his secretary to attend to the issuance of two new passports. He asked David if they had chosen their new names and David smiled and said that they wanted to be known as Anna and Kristoff Berliner. He laughed and said that the first names were probably influenced by the main characters in Disney's animated film *Frozen* and the last name by their city of residence.

Shimony failed to see anything funny in the selected names and said that Elsa and Hans would be more appropriate for that couple.

Shimony instructed David to hand over the passports only after getting the information he sought about the operations of Segan's firm. The passports were ready the next day—Mossad had good connections with the passport office in the Ministry of the Interior—after all they were one of its best customers and were always in a rush to get the passports they needed. David made sure that the Mossad experts doctored the passports, so it appeared that they were issued in Tel Aviv twenty-four months earlier and they contained a few stamped pages of leaving and entering Israel as well as several other countries outside the European Community.

On second thought he reckoned it would have been simpler to take two passports that were seized by Mossad and switch the photos and personal details to those of the personas requested by Sam and Ruby. Of course, this could also be done with passports from other countries, not only with Israeli passports.

CHAPTER 10

October 6, Berlin

David's flight to Berlin was uneventful and he managed to take a short nap between the incessant interruptions for meals, duty free items, announcements by the captain that they were over this country or that mountain range, and the preparation for landing.

David particularly disliked the film clip explaining how to buckle the seat belt and what to do in case the plane had to land on water—bend forward with your head between your legs and kiss your ass goodbye, was what he thought more appropriate. He even had a stronger dislike, not to say revulsion, from the older planes in which the cabin attendants—stewards and stewardesses to the older generation of passengers—actually stood in the aisle and clicked the seat belt closed and released it as if it was some kind of ancient ritual—it was.

To him, it was like the stories his grandfather had told about crossing the equator on board a cruise ship and the passengers who dipped in the swimming pool and were adorned in symbolic feathers and received a certificate for being fearless travelers. He had also heard that a similar ritual, this time in freezing water, was customary for those sailing to Antarctica and crossing the Southern Polar Circle. At least in that case, they had to brave the freezing water to earn their free glass of cheap cognac.

Anyway, the reception he received from Julia was as far from freezing as paradise was from hell, that is if you believed those who had been in both places and returned to tell about their experience. He told her briefly that he had to meet privately with Sam and Ruby and that this had to be done without Segan hearing about it, so he asked Julia if she could distract Segan somehow.

She said he would immediately get suspicious if she tried to contact him or have him invited to a social event organized by the Embassy, but she could use one of German colleagues from the BND to summon him under some excuse like checking his resident status or that his office complied with the fire regulations.

David liked the idea and said that he would inform her when his meeting with Sam and Ruby was to take place so she could set things in motion.

***

The call to Sam's private cell phone was answered by the voice mail box. David left a short message with his prepaid phone number and waited for the return call. A couple of hours later he received a call with a cryptic message that the owner of the phone will be out of town for the next two days. He told Julia about that and suggested they both pay a visit to the couple's apartment just in case Ruby was there.

When they reached the apartment building, they saw a light in one of the windows but when they knocked on the door there was no reply although they could hear sounds that must have come from a radio or television set.

Julia pulled a small leather wallet out of her purse and within fifteen seconds the Yale lock on the apartment door opened with a soft click. David called, "Hello, is anyone home?"

When there was no response, he stepped through the living room and checked the bedroom and bathroom before calling Julia to join him. There were no signs of Ruby being in the apartment. Julia shrugged and said that the couple must have left the light and radio on with a timer in order to deter burglars or simply confuse whoever tried to follow them.

David responded that they were much too sophisticated for this naïve ploy. They surveyed the apartment meticulously and David spotted a small camera lens inside the smoke detector. He pointed at it and said to Julia, "Smile, you are on candid camera." He then waved his hand at the camera in a silent salute and took off his imaginary hat in a theatrical gesture of respect.

Julia was a bit disgusted with this whole affair and led the way out of the apartment making sure that the Yale lock on the door automatically locked the door behind them.

When they were back on the street, she asked David how he intended to spend the next two days as the week-end had just started. David grinned at her and said that he needed to spend as much time in bed as possible to catch up on his sleep, and that in any case the weather was getting chilly and an unseasonal cold front was approaching.

As soon as they got back to Julia's apartment she went to her laptop and put on Tchaikovsky's Waltz of the Snowflakes and suggested they drink a cup of hot tea spiced with some brandy as an antidote to the snowflakes. David said he preferred the more popular Waltz of the Flowers, but Julia responded that she would consider his request in the spring, and meanwhile they had to get away from the snowflakes and what better place than under the warm blankets.

On Monday morning Julia and David crept out of bed and were glad to see that the storm front had passed, and the sun was shining. David said that was a good omen and called Sam's cell phone number. This time Sam answered in person and they agreed to meet in the apartment on Gruntaler Strasse in the evening.

***

David asked Julia to stay behind and keep an eye on the apartment building in case some uninvited visitors, especially Segan, showed up. Reluctantly, she agreed to play a secondary role in this affair.

When the door opened, Sam smirked. "David, that was a very nice gesture you and Julia performed in front, or rather underneath, our camera."

David smiled. "I must say that I didn't expect something so simple and crude. What burglars believe nowadays that when lights and the radio are turned on it means the apartment is indeed occupied? The camera in the smoke detector is also not very high-tech, but I give you full marks for being deceptively simple."

Ruby, practical as ever, said, "Did you get Shimony's approval for the deal we proposed?"

In response, David put his hand in his pocket and produced two passports with a blue cover and lettering in Hebrew and English saying these were passports of the State of Israel. He told them they were in the names they had requested of Anna and Kristoff Berliner. He didn't repeat Shimony's comment that Elsa and Hans were more appropriate names.

Sam held out his hand to take the passports, but David put them back in his pocket. "Just a minute. First you two need to fulfill your part of our deal and answer some questions."

Ruby broke the silence. "We'll answer all your questions and tell you as much as we can. However, there are certain things which we cannot say, and you must understand that we have some obligations to Segan."

David considered the situation and disregarding Shimony's directive, handed over the passports and said, "I fully understand your position. Although we need very detailed information from you as soon as you are willing to give it, a comprehensive interrogation session can be delayed until you visit us in Israel. Meanwhile, there is only one urgent matter that needs a short answer now: is Segan's organization involved in the fatal mishaps that befell the Iranian nuclear scientists in Europe?"

Ruby looked at Sam and said, "The short answer is affirmative. The long answer will be given after our visit to Israel. Surely you know that we are not gullible enough to believe that we'll be allowed to leave Israel after we disclose everything we know about this affair. If you want our full cooperation, let us visit our families and friends in Israel and when we are safely back in Berlin come and see us again for an interview, in which we'll tell you everything, including some things you would never be able to find out without our help."

David said that he fully understood their reservations and distrust and gave them his direct Mossad phone number and asked them to call him when they arrived to make sure that the agreement was honored by Israeli authorities.

October 7, Tel Aviv

David had returned to Tel Aviv on the night flight without spending another night in Berlin, much to Julia's disappointment. This time he managed to get almost three hours of uninterrupted sleep on the flight, so he was quite fresh and ready for work after they landed at the crack of dawn at Ben-Gurion airport.

He wasn't surprised to see that, despite the early hour, the parking lots at Mossad headquarters were almost full. He saw that Shimony's car was already parked in his allocated parking spot and when he entered the outer office of the Mossad head, he was welcomed by Shimony's personal assistant who ushered him in to the chief's inner sanctum.

Shimony rose from his chair and said, "Well, what did our friends tell you?" He motioned for David to help himself at the coffee machine.

David took his time and made himself a cup of espresso

using the strongest capsule marked fourteen. He knew that the chief was impatient and didn't like to be kept waiting but decided in this case he wanted another minute to gather his thoughts and correctly phrase what he had learned from Sam and Ruby. He took a sip of the dark liquid from the miniature cup and said, "Yes, Segan's firm is deeply involved in the Iranian affair, but I cannot elaborate."

Shimony was unappeased. "What do you mean?"

David proceeded to tell him about the deal he'd made and that he had no details.

Shimony was livid with rage but had his complete trust in David so refrained from saying anything for a full minute. Finally, he said, "Okay. So, when will we get the whole story?"

David shrugged, saying, "We don't have to wait for the details. We can begin to counteract the allegations of Mossad's involvement in the elimination of the Iranian scientists and defuse the hostage situation with Iran by offering them a fair trade for some of the Hezbollah prisoners we are holding. After all, the Iranian regard Hezbollah as their allies, not to say servants, in Lebanon and Syria, so should be glad to liberate some prisoners as a gesture of appreciation."

Their discussion was cut short by Shimony's assistant, who knocked on the door and barged in without waiting for an answer. He looked very pale as he approached the chief with a slip of paper in his hand. Shimony took the paper, read the short sentence that said the bodies of Ruby and Sam were found in their apartment in positions that looked like a murder and suicide. He showed it to David and ordered him to return immediately to Berlin and investigate what had really happened there.

October 7, Berlin

David was a bit disoriented—as far as his current trip was concerned, he wasn't sure if he was coming or going from Berlin or to it. It was an afternoon flight, so he didn't nap and was so deep in thought that he even welcomed the commotion of the flight crew. He figured there were at least two organizations that would welcome the murder of Sam and Ruby.

First and foremost in his mind were the Iranians that might have discovered that these two ex-Mossad agents were responsible for the deaths of their nuclear scientists and decided to take revenge. David thought that Segan might be behind the murders, if he had suspected the deal between the two agents and Mossad that was in the making.

Such a deal would place him and his firm in a direct collision course with both the Iranians and Mossad. He would have been concerned in case Sam and Ruby had retained some hard evidence about his pact with Alan Ross or could just testify in a secret hearing set up by Shimony and get the PM's blessing to eliminate him.

David wondered how the Iranians and Segan could have discovered these developments and then a terrible thought occurred to him. What if Julia was involved? After all, she knew about their role in Segan's firm and about the deal with Mossad. What if she had been forced to eliminate the couple by a foreign security service that was interested in keeping up the tension between Iran and Israel, or even worse if she acted on her own initiative due to a false sense of patriotism? David decided he'd contact Julia as if this latter suspicion had not existed and see how she reacted as the investigation progressed.

***

Julia was waiting at the airport when his flight landed and as soon as he emerged from customs, she walked up to him and gave him a warm embrace. She said, "It looks as if the gods wanted you to spend some more time with me. The circumstances for your speedy return are less than joyful but the result certainly is. I have started to look into the bizarre deaths of Sam and Ruby and have enlisted my informants in the BND and the Berlin police force. I have managed to get permission for the two of us to visit the crime scene so that's where we are heading straight from here."

David turned on his charm, allaying his suspicions of her involvement in the crime, and said, "I am very glad to see you personally and admire your efficiency organizing the visit to the scene. I understand that you reported the murder to Mossad, even before the German official announcement to the Israeli embassy about the slaying of the two citizens."

Julia led the way to her car that was double parked at the terminal among the taxis. A heavyset policeman with a pockmarked face was standing by the car and looking up the registration when they approached. Julia flashed her brightest smile and in perfect German said that she had diplomatic immunity and was there on urgent official business.

The German policeman knew that tangling with Israeli

diplomats could be very messy and sensitive due to the history of Germany's treatment of the Jews some seventy to eighty years previously. So, he said she shouldn't do this again and this time, he would let it go.

As soon as they were inside the car and on their way to crime scene, Julia looked at David and said, "It never fails. I am yet to get a ticket for a traffic violation."

David queried, "What about automatic speed traps or cameras that take a photo of your car crossing a red light?"

Julia smiled and replied, "You know the quote attributed to Stalin, *no man, no problem*, with me a traffic police it's the opposite, *no (police) man, big problem.*"

David laughed. "I hate to correct you, the whole sentence is, *Death solves all problems–no man, no problem.*" I wonder if this is the reason for the double murder of Ruby and Sam?"

Julia turned serious, saying, "We really need to find out who did the crime. I think the standard forensic approach of finding the means, motive, and opportunity is a good starting point for our investigation."

David nodded and didn't reply as they had reached the apartment building on Gruntaler Strasse and were trying to find a parking spot. Eventually one of the police cars pulled out, and Julia quickly parked her car there. A policeman motioned for her to move her car, but she flashed her diplomatic ID accompanied with a smile and he let her remain parked in that spot.

***

The Berlin police forensic investigation technicians had carried out their work methodically and professionally and had already left the scene. A lone police sergeant stood at the door to the apartment and allowed them to enter after Julia once again flashed her ID and captivating smile.

The forensic team had taken many photos of the victims and of the crime scene, collected fingerprints, and placed yellow plastic signs where the empty cartridges were found. The two bodies were still left where they lay—Ruby on the carpet with a couple of 9-mm bullet holes in her chest and Sam in a reclining chair with a bullet hole straight through his heart.

The gun itself, a semi-automatic 9-mm Jericho 941 pistol, was still in his hand. David looked at the scene and his immediate thought was that it looked like a textbook murder and suicide—too good to be true.

Ignoring the sergeant and speaking in Hebrew, David told Julia that everything looked too neat and tidy.

Julia shrugged and said, "I am surprised that Sam needed to shoot Ruby twice. With his experience and expertise one shot should have been enough. I agree, this looks more like a double execution staged to appear as a murder and suicide. But who could surprise these two experienced field operatives and kill them both?"

David said, "Let's get back to the three classic fundamentals of criminology: means—quite obviously this Jericho pistol is not commonly used by criminals but has been deployed by police forces and intelligence services as well as by the military in several countries. I would like to verify that both victims were shot with the same gun before speculating further on the means. Motive—that's the big question. The proximity of the time of their murder to the planned visit to Israel, where they were expected to disclose all details about their involvement with the elimination of the Iranian scientists could point either at Segan trying to silence them or at the Iranians who were taking their revenge. As far as the opportunity is concerned—they were alone in their apartment and they would not hesitate to let in someone they knew well, like Segan. On the other hand, a trained Iranian assassin or a contract killer could get them to open the door under false pretenses and then shoot them and arrange the bodies to look like a murder and suicide."

Julia thought about this for a moment and said, "Well, David, this doesn't really get us any closer to solving this problem. We know that Segan and the Iranians were the obvious suspects. How should we proceed?"

David asked the police sergeant if the apartment had been searched by the forensics team and the sergeant called the headquarters before saying that nothing had been touched, awaiting the Israeli embassy representatives, pointing at Julia.

David nodded and said that they were ready to start searching for clues. Julia took two pairs of powder free disposable nitrile gloves out of her bag and handed one pair to David.

They started by taking a close look at the bodies. David bent down to closely examine the two bullet holes in Ruby's chest. It was evident that both pierced her heart. There was only one way to know if they were fired at the same time—and that is by a meticulous autopsy and certainly not by their cursory inspection.

They scrutinized Sam's body and David focused on the pistol in his right hand. It was held at an awkward angle but that could have occurred after he shot himself, if indeed he had.

Julia stood behind David as he bent over Sam's body. David said, "I never thought that Sam was the type who would commit suicide, and certainly could find no reason for killing Ruby. They became close together after the mission in Boston and their expulsion from Mossad. There were rumors they were a couple even before that, but I doubt if that was true although they did pose as Mrs. and Mr. Smith for that mission."

Julia nodded. "I didn't see much of them in Berlin, as I had told you they were considered as *persona non grata* at the embassy. But sharing the same fate after their ejection from Mossad, carrying out jobs together for Segan's firm, and being kind of outcasts among the official Israeli community would certainly bring them together."

David had an epiphany. "What if someone entered the apartment, shot Sam through the heart and then shot Ruby the first time. He then placed the pistol in Sam's hand and shot Ruby again so that traces of gunshot residue would remain on Sam's hand as if he did the shooting. He then staged the two bodies in the textbook murder and suicide posture."

David was thinking about a famous incident that happened in Jerusalem some years earlier when a high-society hairdresser shot his super-model girlfriend and committed suicide. His brother, who was the first on the scene, removed the pistol from his dead hand and placed it in the girl's hand as if she was the one that committed the murder and then shot herself.

Julia thought about this for a moment before saying, "This is an interesting theory. How can we obtain proof to confirm or contradict it?"

David said, "I read about a new forensic test that can help. It is based on taking an imprint of the palm to determine if there are traces of iron that fit the metallic parts of the gun grip. The special point is that the imprints are left when the perspiration present on the palm interacts with the iron, containing parts of the gun grip. If it is placed in the palm of a dead person then there will be no iron traces, or only very weak traces, on the palm imprint, although the classic forensics would show that the gun was fired from the same hand."

David observed Julia very closely as he made this last statement to see how she reacted. He had expected to see an expression of confusion if she was involved or curiosity and relief if she was truly only trying to solve the mysterious double death.

Julia maintained a "poker-face"—and David saw no change in her expression. He didn't like this, although he knew that she was a trained Mossad field operative that excelled in her job. Finally, Julia said, "This is very interesting. Do you think that the Berlin police can perform this test?"

David said that his colleagues in the Israeli police would be glad to instruct their Berlin counterparts on performance of the test. However, he thought the proper chemicals should be flown from Israel, perhaps with an experienced technician as the murder of the two Israelis could be directly connected to the country's national security.

Once again, he scrutinized Julia trying to see how she responded, but she maintained her "poker-face," and he didn't know how to interpret her lack of reaction.

October 8, Berlin

The technician from the Israeli police forensics laboratory arrived with the kit for taking palm imprints. He was met by a representative of the Berlin police, who drove him straight to the crime scene where David and Julia were already waiting.

The technician got to work immediately and within minutes it was clear that Sam had not fired the pistol when he was alive and that the gunshot residue was the result of someone else firing the gun in his palm after he was murdered in order to stage the murder-suicide scene.

David thanked the Israeli police technician and told him to enjoy the evening in Berlin before catching the morning flight back to Tel Aviv.

David called Shimony and gave him an update on the findings and his suspicions. Shimony said that he should continue his investigation on the obvious suspects—Segan and the Iranians—and do that with Julia's help. When David pressed and asked whether he should also consider Julia's possible involvement Shimony instructed him to focus on the other suspects and leave Julia alone.

***

David asked Julia if she thought that it was time to summon

Segan for an interrogation, but she pointed out they had no jurisdiction in Germany and could only invite him to give his testimony voluntarily.

David wondered aloud if Segan would cooperate after the treatment he had received from the head of Mossad and the PM's office. Julia said there was nothing to lose if they called him in for questioning. She added that he was probably upset about the murder of two of his most senior agents unless, of course, he was the one who did it.

So, David called the main office of Segan's firm, identified himself to the secretary who answered the call as an old friend and asked to speak to Segan. He was told that Segan was out of town and would be back the following day. When he tried to enquire when Segan had left Berlin the secretary said she had a call on the other line and hung up without responding.

David turned to look at Julia and said he didn't like the reply and asked Julia to try and trace Segan's movements just before, and during, the time of the murder. Julia said that it wouldn't really help because he could always have one of his other agents do the job while arranging a waterproof alibi for himself.

David said that they should wait for Segan's return to Berlin and try to interview him, and perhaps they could learn something from his responses and body language, if he agreed to meet them.

CHAPTER 11

October 8, Office of the Senior Assistant of the Supreme Leader, Tehran

The Senior Assistant of the Supreme Leader of the Islamic Republic of Iran summoned the General Aslawi, and demanded to know what progress has been made with regard to Israel.

Imam Mourtashef was also present at the small meeting and looked at the general like a bird of prey observes a squirrel trying to avoid its fate by freezing on the spot. The general was not intimidated by the Senior Assistant but was evidently made anxious by the Imam's stare.

He said, "So far our agents and collaborators have captured a dozen Israelis, including a Member of the Knesset. The Israelis are running around themselves in circles trying to figure out what was happening. Naturally they suspect us, but we have been careful to avoid leaving any evidence that would lead to Iran. I have some more news—"

The Imam spoke up, interrupting the general, "I believe that they are not too concerned about these hostages."

General Aslawi met the Imam's glaring eyes. "Please let me continue."

When the Imam nodded, the general added, "We have

managed to trace the two Israeli agents who murdered our scientists. Alas, before we could lay our hands on them, we got information from our contact in the Berlin that they had been sent straight to hell—"

This time the Senior Assistant intervened. "General, do you mean to say that two Mossad agents did all this damage. Do you realize that our nuclear scientists are afraid to go out of Iran, our secret nuclear program has gone to an almost complete standstill, and our whole regime is receiving a serious threat to its stability from the opposition factions? Two people—it is unbelievable."

The general said, "Obviously these two were not operating alone. The Mossad, CIA, and MI6 must all be behind this."

The Senior Assistant said, "I have received a secret visit from General Koliagin of the Russian FSB, and he had a very interesting message. He said he was contacted by a trustworthy senior Mossad operative—if there is such an entity—who wished to convey that the Israeli Mossad had nothing to do with the murder of our scientists. Furthermore, he suggested an informal meeting, hosted by the Russians, between our representatives and Israeli officials. The Israelis will try to convince us they were not responsible for the heinous acts of terror committed against our people."

The Imam and the general were silent as they pondered this improbable suggestion. The general responded, "This must be a trap. The Israelis are masters of disinformation and fabrication. I suggest telling General Koliagin that we don't need his services."

The Imam said, "On the contrary. We must get to the

bottom of this. If the Israelis are not responsible, then someone else is. We have to find out who is killing our people and trying to undermine our regime or else these acts might continue."

The Senior Assistant concluded the meeting by saying, "Thank you both. I'll inform the Supreme Leader of these developments and wait for his decision."

October 8, Tel Aviv

As soon as Shimony received the update from David, he didn't wait for the PM to call him but initiated the call himself despite the late hour. After being transferred to the PM he said, "Prime Minister, there are some important developments in the hostage situation and in the elimination of the Iranian scientists. First, the man I put in charge of the case, David Avivi, has contacted General Koliagin of the FSB. The general assured him that the hostages were being treated well and indicated that although the FSB know of the family ties you have with one of the captives the Iranians are not aware of that. Second, the general also agreed to try to arrange an informal, off the record, meeting between David and the Iranians to give him a chance to convince them that Mossad and the Israeli government have not sanctioned the elimination of the scientists. Third, most recently two of our former Mossad agents, Sam and Ruby, who were dishonorably discharged after the U.S. fiasco were found dead in their Berlin apartment. The bodies were staged to look like a murder and suicide but with the help of our forensics experts it was shown to be a double murder. At this point we are not sure whether they were killed by their boss, my former Deputy Director that we all call Segan, or by the Iranians."

Shimony didn't mention that David suspected that Julia may be involved as he thought this would make the PM raving mad.

The PM answered, "Haim, I have given you a lot of credit and ample leeway to solve the problem. I have also allowed you more time than I had initially allotted but I realize that the matter is very complex. If we handle this incorrectly, we may find ourselves in an unwanted conflict with Iran. We must discover who is behind this, what their motives are, and provide irrefutable proof. I understand that you shouldn't rush to conclusions. You have put my mind at ease with regard to my granddaughter's fate—as long as the Iranians remain ignorant of the fact. If they do find out that I am her grandfather and use this to blackmail Israel, I'll resign my office in order to avoid a conflict of interest between my official position as PM and my family."

Shimony was surprised by this bold statement, but as a true cynic he doubted if the PM would really step down from his high office because of something so sentimental. He knew that deep down in his heart the PM was not as hardened as the Steel Man, Stalin, but was no less determined to maintain his stronghold on the coveted job.

So, he tried to comfort his boss by saying, "Sir, I hope that it never comes to this and that we bring all the captives safely back to Israel. I have great faith in David and his abilities to succeed in convincing the Iranians, and actually the whole world, that Israel was not involved in the sordid affair of murdering innocent, or not so innocent, Iranian scientists."

The PM was silent for a moment and then said, "Well, Haim, at least this time we are not guilty, but will the world believe us?"

The PM hung up and called his most trusted consultant, the only person he trusted absolutely, his wife. "Honey, I need you here. Could you please come down to my study?"

She answered, "As soon as I finish my glass of wine, or should I bring the bottle with me? After all, it is already quite late in the evening."

The PM's impatient reply was, "Honey, come down now with the glass and bottle."

The PM's wife had already consumed a few glasses of wine, so it took her some time to collect herself, find a couple of empty glasses and an open another bottle of expensive red wine, usually only served at official dinners with visitors on the PM's A-list.

The PM looked at her as she entered his study and said, "I hope you are in full control of your faculties because I need your advice on a very crucial matter."

When she nodded, he continued, "I am not pleased with the performance of Shimony on several matters. He failed me miserably with the U.S. fiasco when he didn't manage to keep his own house, the Mossad, in order. Fortunately in that affair, the Americans were as embarrassed as we were and didn't want to make a public issue of their own shortcomings in safeguarding their national security. Haim got away by firing his Deputy Director, Segan, and a couple of top operatives and now these two operatives were murdered in Berlin while working for Segan.

"This is related to the current situation with Iran and the fact that they are holding a dozen Israeli citizens, including Inbal, my own flesh and blood, in captivity and trying to hold the state of Israeli for ransom. Shimony doesn't know how to get them back safely. I am considering replacing him by someone I can rely on to carry out my wishes. What do you think about this?"

The PM's wife was now completely sober—there is nothing like shocking news and high-level backstabbing to get out of the stupor induced by alcohol. She said, "I never liked Shimony, he was always too independent. He never acknowledged that he owed his promotion to Mossad head to you. We need someone who would be grateful and indebted to you personally. Let's wait until this crisis is resolved one way or the other. If he fails, then we can easily hold him accountable and replace him without any public fuss. If he succeeds, then we'll make sure that you get all the credit and just commend him for following your guidance. Then offer him some job with a fancy title as a token of gratitude but make sure that it has no substance and appoint your man."

The PM looked at her with admiration and said, "I knew I could trust you. Let's have a glass of wine and then go up to our bedroom."

October 8, Evin Prison, Tehran

The contest between Yonathan (Johnny) Shmaryahu, honorable Member of Knesset, and Zorik for the alpha-male position in the jail cell ended when Johnny broke down in tears, crying about his fate.

Zorik, a natural leader of people in battle and in peacetime, assumed the position of the chief negotiator regarding the interaction with the jailors. He had heard from Johnny and his companion about the meeting with Imam Mourtashef at the airport and the opinion expressed by the Imam on the root cause of the hatred of the Iranian people toward America and Israel—the Great Satan and Little Satan.

Zorik figured that they were all pawns in a much larger game and hoped that a meeting with the Imam could clarify their position. He reckoned that Imam Mourtashef was very close to the religious leadership of Iran, probably even one of the senior leaders, and was in a position of authority. He had no idea of the meeting that took place at the office of the Senior Assistant of the Supreme Leader earlier that afternoon. He certainly had no clue that the Imam oversaw the most sensitive clandestine operation of the Iranian regime that took place in the very same building where the Israelis hostages were held.

When the midday meal was brought to their cell, Zorik asked for permission to talk to guard they had named Fatso, refraining of course from using the derogatory nickname. Half an hour later, Fatso appeared with his whip and cruel smile. "What do you filthy dogs want?"

Zorik stepped away from the far wall of the cell, where all the hostages were squirming, and said, "With all due respect, we wish to speak with Imam Mourtashef."

Fatso was taken by surprise at this request and said, "How do you even dare to mention the name of the Imam?"

Zorik said, "We wish to learn about the true Islam from a senior religious teacher." He saw the look on the faces of his cell mates and understood they were no less astonished than Fatso by this statement.

Fatso growled and walked away without a reply. As soon as he left the cell, the other Israelis asked Zorik if he was out of his mind. Only Inbal understood that Zorik chose the one approach that had any chance of granting them a meeting with someone high enough in Iran's religious hierarchy that had some influence on their destiny. She defended her fiancé and managed to convince all the others that no one was really interested in getting a religious sermon from the Imam.

***

Later in the evening Fatso appeared with his whip and four other jailors that surrounded a man wearing the traditional garb of a senior Iranian cleric. The respectable looking man greeted Johnny and Oded by their names and then asked to be introduced to the other prisoners.

Zorik stepped forward and started by introducing all the cellmates, giving a brief account of where they were captured. He said that overall their treatment was reasonable, and they were all grateful for that. He added that they were innocent civilians and did not know why they were not released.

The Imam took his time, first looking at Zorik for a long moment and then at each of the other Israelis. His glance lingered for a while on Johnny and he noticed the swollen red eyes and realized that he was not the true person in charge, although by all rights he should have been.

He met Zorik's gaze once more and said something in Farsi that caused his bodyguards to leave the cell. Fatso tried to question the instruction, but the Imam gave him a short order, and after bringing a chair for the Imam to sit on, he too left the cell.

The Imam continued in perfect English, "Please sit down, all of you. We are a civilized people and mean you no harm. We know you are innocent bystanders who got caught up in a tough situation due to no fault of your own. We will hold you here until we can contact your government and negotiate the terms for your release."

Zorik looked around and saw that all the other hostages were silent and left with a sense of bewilderment. He spoke up, "Imam Mourtashef, we thank you for your kind words. We also have a keen sense of history and fondly remember that the Great King Cyrus allowed the Jews who were exiled to Babylon by Nebuchadnezzar to return to Judea more than two thousand five hundred years ago. We are sorry that the relations between modern Israel and the Islamic Republic of Iran have deteriorated so far. But all of us here in the cell have had nothing to do with this sad state of affairs. Please let us go and we promise to be the best emissaries that Iran has ever had in Israel and the West."

178 | Charlie Wolfe

The Imam smiled benevolently. "Zorik, is it? I know that you will truthfully report that no harm has been done to you, but you must understand that you are mere pawns in a game that involves political considerations in which individuals don't count. So, you will all just play the role your fate has burdened you with and pray to your God you live to see your families again."

Zorik was put out by this explicit statement, but gathered his wits and said, "Thank you, Imam Mourtashef, for your visit. You have earned our great respect and hopefully one day we'll meet again as free men."

The Imam smiled. "Inshallah, praise God." He called for his bodyguards. Fatso bowed deeply to the Imam but as soon as he was out of earshot, swore and promised the inmates their little ploy would cost them their dinner that would not be served that evening.

Imam Mourtashef left the prison wing in which the hostages were incarcerated and made his way to the laboratory in Basement S, where the work was progressing nicely. He was one of the very few people in Iran who knew that the fate of the hostages was so closely linked to the advancement of the project.

CHAPTER 12

Two Years Earlier, Basement S, Evin Prison, Tehran

The visit of the Supreme Leader was considered by Dr. Muammar Fathi as the pinnacle of his career. Exactly one year earlier he was placed in charge of a small group of scientists that were the elite of the Iranian military-industrial complex.

Each member of this group was vetted by the most feared organ of the Iranian Revolutionary Guards, the department that was in charge of ensuring the loyalty, zealousness, and religious fervor of people in sensitive positions of authority. Fathi's own vetting included a thorough investigation of his personal life and that of his family members, a series of interviews with his close friends and the Mullah of the mosque in which he regularly attended prayers and heard sermons, and the inevitable polygraph test.

The latter was a joke as the interrogator decided to focus on Fathi's ties with foreign scientists, ignoring the fact that most of his training in nuclear physics was in a British university. The interrogator wanted to know if Fathi was still in touch with his thesis advisor and co-students and when Fathi said that they occasionally met in international scientific conferences, he insisted on getting a verbatim account of every conversation.

Fathi seized the opportunity and started a downpour of technical terms, complex theories, and detailed descriptions of sophisticated experimental systems. After ten minutes of this tirade the interrogator held up both his hands and placed them on his ears, begging Fathi to stop.

Fathi remained serious outwardly and said he was only getting started on the subject but inwardly had a big laugh. Finally, he was cleared and received the highest security clearance the Islamic Republic of Iran could install on a person, who was not a religious leader. After all, members of that select group were above the law and accountable only to Allah.

He assembled his group that included a few carefully selected scientists and engineers. During one of the coffee breaks, he hinted at the interrogation and the fun he had with the interrogator in its final stage and was awarded by knowing smiles from his colleagues.

One of them, Dr. Raffsani, a renowned mathematician, went as far as commenting that inferior minds had no chance when trying to ensnare super-intelligent people like him, but before he could develop the subject any further Fathi pointed discreetly at the ceiling.

The "super-intelligent" scientist closed his mouth, but moments later the door opened, and he was "invited" to join the security officer and leave the room. He was not heard from again, despite Fathi's protests that Raffsani was a vital part of the group. He was told to find another mathematician or do without one.

Fathi didn't know that his attempt to ridicule the security vetting and polygraph examination has been reported to

General Aslawi, the head of the IRG, and wasn't aware of the animosity the general now harbored towards him and the uppity scientists and intellectuals in general. Had he been more sensitive to the feeling of other people, especially those with an inferiority complex like General Aslawi, he would have known what to expect at the upcoming meeting.

Had he read any popular psychology textbook or even an article in the popular press, he would have known the difference between "general intelligence" reflected in a high IQ like his own and "interpersonal intelligence" that shows the ability to understand and interact effectively with other people.

Fathi was now going over the presentation he had prepared for the Supreme Leader one last time, as the door to the conference room opened. The first to enter was the General Aslawi, the head of the IRG. He gave Fathi a contemptuous look and scrutinized the room before giving a hand signal that all was safe.

The Supreme Leader walked in and took his place at the head of the table, facing the large screen, and motioned to his entourage to take their seats on both sides of the table. Fathi and his two Senior Assistants, a theoretical physicist and an engineer with a doctorate in material science, stood by his side near the screen. Fathi introduced them and the Supreme Leader acknowledged them with a small smile and a slight nod of his head.

The head of the IRG, General Aslawi opened the meeting. "With the grace of Allah, we have assembled a small elite group to defend our Islamic faith against the infidels. Dr. Fathi has headed this group from the start and devised the action plan to *fulfill the tasks the Supreme Leader has assigned to the group. He has done a relatively reasonable job and he will now present the plan, the progress that has been made, and outline what additional steps are needed to accomplish the aims of the project."*

Fathi began his presentation by reiterating the objectives of his group. His first slide was projected on the screen. "First, let me outline the plan. We have adopted a two-pronged approach. On the one hand, with some assistance from our allies, we have made all the necessary steps for the construction of a nuclear bomb. On the other hand, based on our own expertise we have drawn out the blueprints to build a radiation dispersion device, an RDD in short or what is colloquially called a "dirty bomb." There are three main steps involved with each of these objectives: design the device, get the necessary materials, and construct the device. I am ready to continue with the description of the work, unless there are some questions."

Imam Mourtashef, who was seated next to the Senior Assistant on the right of the Supreme Leader, raised his hand. "Dr. Fathi, when you talk about allies, to whom do you refer?"

Before Fathi could answer, General Aslawi stood up and said, "You know that common enemies make good friends. The North Koreans regard the Americans as their dire enemies, who keep trying to impose on them unacceptable things like democracy, openness, international supervision of their nuclear ambitions, and worst of all, economic sanctions. We view the Great Satan exactly in a similar way. The North Koreans have agreed to supply us with a small amount of fissile material, that the Americans call special nuclear material or SNM for short. This is vital for building an atomic bomb. They are also willing, for a considerable price, of course, to give us their blueprints. However, we think that their design is very primitive and requires a large amount of fissionable materials.

"Our other ally is Pakistan, or more precisely a faction within the Pakistani nuclear community, who is as anti-American as we are. They are working clandestinely as their government's official policy is to adhere to the non-proliferation treaty, the infamous NPT, and not export any prohibited materials, or information that may serve in the construction of nuclear weapons. Both these countries are also no lovers of the Little Satan, Israel. The North Koreans have helped the Syrians, before the troubles started there a few years ago, to build a small nuclear reactor that was designed to produce weapon grade plutonium.

"We all know that this reactor suffered the same fate in 2007 as the damned Iraqi reactor suffered in 1981. You may recall that during our bloody war with Iraq, from 1980 to 1988, our air force tried unsuccessfully to destroy the Iraqi reactor. The Israeli air force did the job for us, unintentionally, of course, because they were concerned that Saddam Hussein would build an atom bomb and use it against them. The Israelis may have saved Tehran from the fate of Hiroshima, but they deserve no laurels for this because they were only worried about Tel Aviv."

The General sat down and the Imam thanked him for the political introduction, refraining from saying political indoctrination. The Supreme Leader motioned for Dr. Fathi to continue his presentation.

Fathi's second slide showed a schematic of a simple gun-type atomic bomb. "This is a schematic of "Little Boy," the atomic bomb that was used in war by the Americans to destroy

Hiroshima. It was constructed with enriched uranium that the Americans manufactured. According to Wikipedia it was very heavy, weighing nine thousand seven hundred pounds, used a lot of fissile material, one hundred forty-one pounds of uranium-235 with an average enrichment of about eighty percent, and had a low efficiency as less than one pound underwent nuclear fission.

"On the next slide you can see a schematic of "Fat Man" that was used to destroy Nagasaki. It weighed slightly more than "Little Boy" and was fueled by fourteen pounds of plutonium. The main difference as you can see is that it had a more sophisticated implosion-type design that, therefore, required less fissile material.

"The next few slides show the more advanced designs that the Pakistanis, through AQ Khan's network, and North Koreans have given us. Our scientists have improved these designs with the help of schematics sold by a former Soviet-Union renegade scientist. As we have a very limited stock of fissile materials, we have devised an innovative design in which plutonium is combined with enriched uranium.

"This is somewhat like the MOX fuel in nuclear power plants where a mixture of plutonium oxide and uranium oxide provides the energy for producing electricity. I must emphasize that this is an original approach to manufacturing atomic bombs, something the Iranian people should be proud of—"

General Aslawi stood up again and interrupted Dr. Fathi, "I must emphasize that these designs have only been calculated numerically with a computer simulation program and to the best of our knowledge have never been actually tested. Dr. Fathi is taking a large risk relying on this unverified design. I demand that his work be examined by a knowledgeable and objective nuclear expert as he himself cannot be completely relied upon."

Fathi was deeply offended by this interruption. His face turned red and he stuttered, "General, please allow me to continue. Before being interrupted, I was just about to say that we have consulted with a leading Chinese bomb designer and he said he would look into this design in depth."

The general became silent and felt humiliated that his thunder was stolen.

The Senior Assistant saw that the debate had become personal and feared that the general would make sure to avenge this offense by making Fathi "disappear," as he had done to some of his real or perceived enemies. So, he raised his voice and said, "Quit quibbling. We are here to update the Supreme Leader and to gain his approval for continuing with our plan. We all know that both of you are patriots, so please work together. Dr. Fathi, continue your presentation."

The shaken Fathi moved on to the next slide. "Even our new design is too large and too heavy to fit into the war-head of a long-range missile. We can adapt it to dimensions that would fit a bomb carried by an aircraft, but we have no suitable planes that can penetrate the anti-aircraft defenses of the Israelis. Probably not even the Iraqi defenses, if for some reason, we decide to use Baghdad for target practice or for a full-scale demonstration. That is why we are also working on the development of a "dirty bomb," shown in the next slide.

"As you can see this is much simpler to design, construct, and test. We need some radioactive materials that are readily available in medical devices used for radio-therapy and even in common commercial products like smoke detectors. The RDD should preferably contain a mixture of short-lived highly radioactive gamma-emitting nuclides with long-lived gamma and alpha-emitting materials to contaminate the area for a long time and make decontamination extremely costly. These materials can easily be dispersed over a large area by conventional explosives, either in open areas or in built-up cities—"

Once again, General Aslawi interrupted, this time without bothering to get up. "Dr. Fathi has failed to mention that these "dirty bombs" are nowhere close to being weapons of mass destruction as a nuclear bomb is. At most, they have a psychological effect as weapons of mass disruption with some economic damage but no real mass casualties. Any kid, who could take apart a medical radiation source and get a few hundred grams of explosives, can make such a bomb. I feel that Dr. Fathi has been wasting our time and money working on this."

The Supreme Leader shifted uncomfortably in his chair. The Senior Assistant sensed that and felt that Fathi was about to have a massive coronary, so he quickly intervened, "General Aslawi, I am asking you for the last time to stop this counterproductive behavior. Dr. Fathi, please conclude your presentation."

Fathi was encouraged by the support he just got and continued, "This is my last slide. If we can get enough fissile material, we can construct what is called an improvised nuclear device or IND that can be transported in a large box or the trunk of a car. We can combine this with a "dirty bomb." Although a nuclear explosion, even a small inefficient one, would disperse enough radioactive materials to irradiate and contaminate everything *within a radius of a few hundred meters or more. This IND can also be placed inside the cargo hold of any commercial aircraft or very easily in a standard shipping container and be disguised as an innocent piece of luggage or equipment.*

"If I can get enough freshly enriched uranium, I can make sure that commonly deployed radiation detectors would not be able to pick it up from a distance. Given some more time and logistical support I can make sure that our Islamic Republic is feared throughout the world and restore the greatness our nation had once enjoyed among the countries of the civilized world."

The Senior Assistant said, "Thank you, Dr. Fathi, for your presentation and for your good work. I wish to remind everyone that this plan is a major component of our insurance policy because once the so called "nuclear deal" between our country and the six members of the other side is signed and enforced the inspectors of the IAEA will be everywhere. They will conduct intrusive inspections of all our declared nuclear sites, they will continue to prevent us from acquiring materials that may serve for production of nuclear weapons and they will impose restrictions on our scientists.

"You all know that this laboratory is located in the basement of Evin Prison in order to circumvent inspections. We assume that no sane person would believe we are about to construct a nuclear bomb in the heart of our largest city. We have realized it is easier to hide this laboratory in a busy place where all kinds of people enter, and some exit, during all hours of the day and where truckloads of supplies and equipment are regularly dropped off. It was Dr. Fathi's suggestion to name this Basement

S—where S stands for the Great Satan and Little Satan that are our dreaded enemies. We are not sure how much longer we can draw out the signing of the agreement, but we must ensure that Dr. Fathi's team is given the resources to complete the job."

The meeting was over, and the entourage left the conference room and was taken on a short tour of the laboratory itself. Dr. Fathi explained that the laboratory was not used to produce the fissile materials—these were to be brought in from other nuclear plants in Iran or provided by its two nuclear allies—but to develop and construct the device.

He showed them the "hot cells," where radioactive materials could be handled safely, the machinery, and equipment that were needed to cast the fissile materials and shape them, the analytical chemical laboratory, and the detectors used for nuclear spectrometry. He gave a brief description of the conventional explosives that were needed to compress the fissile material and the triggering method to achieve a symmetric implosion and cause a nuclear detonation.

Once again, he repeated that their innovative idea of combining the two types of fissile materials, plutonium, and high enriched uranium, in a single device was Iran's latest contribution to the advancement of science. He then took them in to a separate part of the laboratory, where a super-computer was installed and told them that they could run simulations of explosions at a speed that could have only been imagined a decade earlier.

He looked at General Aslawi and said that his organization and the agents of the Iranian Revolutionary Guards were to be thanked for illicitly obtaining the computer. The general smiled at this, but when he heard Fathi cynically adding that since his senior mathematician had "disappeared" the computer was now of little use, he blushed and muttered under his breath that Fathi's day would come soon.

This Arabic idiom "every dog has its day" literally implies that even the lowest members of society will have their day of glory, but in colloquial use it means the opposite that the day of reckoning will come to everyone regardless of how high and mighty they are now.

The Supreme Leader said that he didn't quite follow all the technicalities that Dr. Fathi discussed. He proceeded to nominate Imam Mourtashef as liaison between his office and the laboratory in Basement S and to provide him with periodical progress reports.

The Imam concurred and said that he would pay regular visits to the laboratory and would also start working on a plan to transport the nuclear device, once it was completed, to its target. When the Senior Assistant said that no decision has been made about its target or its use, the Imam nodded and said these decisions were to be made by the Supreme Leader and the Council.

CHAPTER 13

October 10, the present, Moscow

General Koliagin looked at his two guests and smiled broadly—something he didn't often do. "Well, well, well, who would believe that the three of us are sitting together like old friends?"

Imam Mourtashef looked across the table at David Avivi and in a very formal tone said, "General Koliagin, I wish to thank you for arranging this meeting and for keeping it quiet. We all know that strange times precipitate strange events, and this is just one of them."

David acknowledged the Imam and the General and said, "Honorable Imam, I have asked the general to invite a senior representative of the Islamic Republic of Iran in order to avoid an uncalled-for confrontation with Israel. I am glad that you are here because your reputation as a clever and intelligent person and as one of the most powerful people in Iran precedes you and is well known. Especially, among the people who follow the events that are taking place in your country."

The Imam nodded and said, "Mr. Avivi, or is it now Dr. Avivi? Your reputation as a clever and intelligent person is also well known, albeit in limited circles only. We know that you are here with the blessing of your Prime Minister and your boss, Mr. Shimony. Could we please now get down to the business at hand?"

General Koliagin intervened, "It looks as if the Imam doesn't like to beat around the bush. David, please tell Imam what you told me when you asked me to set up this meeting."

David opened, "We were as surprised as everyone else when the news about the assassination of several Iranian nuclear scientists broke. We understood that once the nuclear deal between Iran and Six Powers was signed that there would be no justification to act against your scientists. This, of course, is not an admission that Mossad was involved in any such acts before the deal was signed.

"Israel's policy had always been to refrain from any comment on clandestine operations that were attributed to it. For example, we never confirmed that the Israeli air force was responsible for the destruction of the nuclear reactor that was built by the North Koreans in Syria. Of course, the most notable exception was that we took responsibility for obliterating Saddam Hussein's nuclear reactor for the great benefit to the security of our country and yours.

"So, you must appreciate the statement made by our PM and Mossad Head that Israel was not involved in these recent acts against Iranian scientists. You should take this statement at face value—no tricks were intended. I am here to provide further proof that these actions were not carried out by our government."

The Imam still looked skeptical. "Do you know who did these heinous acts?" When he saw David nodding, he added,

"Can you provide proof?"

General Koliagin looked at David with great interest expecting him to continue but David was obviously unsure about how to proceed. After a couple of moments, when Koliagin was beginning to show signs of impatience, David continued, "You may have heard about the double murder that took place in Berlin three days ago. The two dead people were former Mossad agents, whose real names were Shmuel Jacobs and Rina Rabinov. They were known to their friends as Sam and Ruby. The crime scene was staged to look like a murder and suicide, but our forensics experts have proven it was a double murder and the gun was planted in Sam's hand after his death. Ruby and Sam were dishonorably fired from Mossad three years ago after they were found to be partly responsible for a fiasco that led to a crisis and almost caused a rift between Israel and one of its staunchest allies. Since their discharge from Mossad, they had left Israel and lived in Berlin and worked for a private security agency. I met them shortly before their murder and they admitted that they were guilty of carrying out the acts against your scientists."

Before he could go any further, the Imam spoke up, "Do you expect me to believe that these two Mossad agents did all these murders on their own? You say they were former agents, you disown them and their actions, but can you provide any proof that they were not under deep cover and still working for you?"

David continued, "The firm for which Sam and Ruby worked was owned by a former Deputy Director of Mossad. He is known by his title Segan—meaning deputy in

Hebrew—and I cannot disclose his real name. He was responsible for the debacle that led to the dismissal of Sam and Ruby and he, too, was fired because of this. His firm has earned a reprehensible reputation as a place where you could hire contract killers. We know that some anonymous person, posing as an English gentleman, has contracted Segan's firm to assassinate the scientists, but we have not yet managed to find this person.

"Segan has gone in to hiding and nobody seems to know where he is, but we are concentrating our efforts on finding him and the people that hired him. And, honorable Imam, I don't expect you to believe that Sam and Ruby had operated on their own. Obviously, someone provided them with up to date operational information on the whereabouts of your scientists and where and when they would be most vulnerable. Furthermore, we suspect that someone inside your own establishment has assisted this gentleman, who passed the operational information to Segan."

David had no evidence of this last item but thought that it would be a good opportunity to get the Iranians to start hunting for a non-existent spy in their midst.

The Imam was not a fool, so he skeptically said, "Are you trying to get us to start a witch hunt? Looking for a mole? So far, I have not seen any irrefutable proof that Segan, Sam, and Ruby were not still active Mossad agents working under a guise in Berlin."

David said, "Once we find Segan, hopefully alive, we'll be able to extract a confession from him, and then go after the gentleman who gave him the contract. We doubt that this gentleman was acting on his own and believe that he was a messenger. The real challenge is to find who sent him and why."

General Koliagin commented, "David, I have to agree with the Imam, that you have to offer proof. So far you have presented nothing but words, quite convincing I admit, but without real evidence…" his voice trailed off.

David said, "General, you are correct. I think that the very fact that this meeting is taking place is a sign of good faith on our part. If the FSB is willing to cooperate, I'll provide you with the details on Segan, but you must assure me that once you spot him you will let Mossad take him in."

The general laughed. "Do you think we don't know who Segan is? We have kept track of him, and his firm, but he managed to keep the details of this last contract from us. We'll gladly help finding him, but I cannot promise that we won't keep him for a while before handing him over to you. After all, Iran is our ally and we need to make sure that you don't concoct some false statements that you will attribute to Segan. We have a lot of practice in making people confess and own up to their actions." He paused for a moment and added, "Sometimes, even if they had nothing to confess." Then laughed.

The Imam rose from the table. "Before departing, I must say that I have not been convinced Mossad was not responsible for the dreadful murders of our blameless scientists."

David quickly added, "What about the Israeli hostages you are holding in Evin Prison?"

And the Imam innocently replied, "What hostages?" Stood

up and walked out of the room.

General Koliagin looked at David and in an apologetic tone said, "Well, this didn't go so well..."

David shrugged and said, "Nevertheless, general, I appreciate your help. I believe that some progress was made here. The Imam will at least consider what I said and will be more open to further suggestions for negotiation. We do need to try and release our citizens who are held as hostages and we know where the Iranian regime has its soft spots. A little pressure where it really hurts them, and they will start singing a different tune."

October 11, Office of the Senior Assistant, Tehran

After Imam Mourtashef's return to Tehran, he immediately set up a meeting with the Senior Assistant and General Aslawi to give them a firsthand account of the conference in Moscow. "General Koliagin had arranged the meeting with a representative of Mossad, David Avivi, who was responsible for thwarting at least two attempts by our Muslim brothers to inflict serious damage on the Zionist entity.

"He tried to convince me that the crimes perpetrated against our scientists were not the doing of Mossad. He claimed, without providing any substantiation, that renegade former Mossad agents were behind these deeds. He claimed a private firm in Berlin carried out these murders under a contract with a mysterious English gentleman, who was an emissary of some unmentioned group. Furthermore, he hinted that we probably have a mole within our establishment—either the nuclear agency or the intelligence services."

Both clerics looked at General Aslawi, who waved his hand in a gesture of dismissal. The Imam continued, "Even General Koliagin was not persuaded by these lame excuses and demanded some evidence for the whole story. Avivi said that he had asked for the meeting to prevent a conflict between our country and his, but I believe that he was just seeking immunity from justifiable actions we have taken against Israeli citizens."

The Imam had not yet shared his own grand plan of attacking Israel even with his two esteemed colleagues. In fact, there was no one, in Iran or elsewhere, that knew what was going on in his devious mind. He continued, "As I was leaving the conference room Avivi suddenly raised the issue of the hostages we are holding in Evin. I did not confirm his suspicions that we had them here but then he added that they were ready to negotiate. I didn't respond and left the room."

The Senior Assistant appeared to be staring into space. "I wonder if he was telling the truth. Perhaps Mossad was not involved and the whole operation was a kind of provocation to force us to do something that would be interpreted as an infringement of the nuclear deal. That would give the West, led by the newly elected American President, an excuse to impose new sanctions of us."

General Aslawi also considered the Imam's report from a different angle. "What if there really is a traitor among us. If any foreign intelligence agency finds out about the laboratory in Basement S, then they will for sure renew the sanctions, or even be provoked into a military attack against us."

The Imam said, "I have some sad news from Dr. Fathi. He told me that the loss of our esteemed colleague, Dr. Ali Abdul Abadi, who was murdered in Vienna was a serious setback to our program. Apparently, Dr. Abadi was head of the small section that worked on solid state physics. His replacement is very talented but lacks the experience and brilliance of Dr. Abadi, so we have been seeking more outside help in this area. The problem is that being too inquisitive could raise suspicion that we have not desisted from our weapons program. I don't need to explain what implications could follow."

The Imam felt he could no longer keep his grand plan from them. He asked the Senior Assistant if there were any audio or video recording devices in the room. The Senior Assistant stretched his hand and opened a drawer at the bottom of his desk and flicked a switch that turned off the video camera that was concealed in the frame of the large photograph of the Supreme Leader that hung on the wall behind him right next to a similarly sized photo of Imam Khomeini. None of the participants was surprised, after all they knew that everything said in this office reached the ears of the Supreme Leader.

Imam Mourtashef started presenting his grand plan. "Honorable colleagues, ever since I was put in charge the liaison between the Supreme Leader and Dr. Fathi's laboratory I have been trying to devise a way that will put to good use the products of the laboratory. I was thinking of a way to transport a nuclear device into the heart of the Zionist entity.

"I knew that an overt attack would result in retaliation that could tear the fabric of our Islamic society and destroy our beautiful country. Furthermore, there is no guarantee that we could successfully deliver such a device and penetrate the advanced defensive systems that the enemy has developed against aircraft, short range missiles and even against our latest ballistic long-range missiles. None of our allies are willing, and probably unable, to supply us with offensive weapons that would do the job."

He looked at his two colleagues who seemed to be fascinated by his words, and continued, "So, I thought that we could use the hostages we are holding to deliver the device. Ironically, both hostages and the device are in the same Evin Prison complex within less than three hundred feet of one another."

General Aslawi was considering the practicalities of the idea. He said, "How can you combine the device with the hostages. Do you think it would fit in the pocket of one of them?" And snickered.

The Imam was not in the least amused, and as the Senior Assistant looked at him expectantly, he replied, "Surely you are joking, General Aslawi?" In reference to the title of Richard Feynman's book, "I have given a lot of thought to this crucial stage of my grand plan."

He then explained in detail how he intended to overcome the problem of delivering the nuclear device.

The Senior Assistant was impressed and even the general wiped off the smug expression from his face and nodded appreciatively. The Senior Assistant concluded the meeting by saying, "So far, only the three of us know about this plan. I suggest we tell the Supreme Leader only as much as he needs to know at this stage. I believe we need his consent to proceed but can spare him the details." The other two consented and the meeting was adjourned.

October 11, Mossad Headquarters, Tel Aviv

A deeply frustrated David Avivi sat across the desk from Haim Shimony and gave him a verbatim report of the meeting in Moscow.

Shimony, who had known David well for many years, had never seen him in such a state of anxiety.

David said, "I have totally failed in convincing the Imam, or even General Koliagin, that we had nothing to do with the elimination of the Iranian nuclear scientists. Haim, we need unequivocal proof that the whole operation was carried out by Segan's firm and that he acted without our approval and without our knowledge. Now that Sam and Ruby are dead, there are only two people who can clear us—Segan and the English gentleman, if he even exists. In order to do so, we must find Segan, break him, and have him publicly admit his guilt and exonerate Israel. I am afraid that the Russians may lay their hands on him first or that some other intelligence organization would simply eliminate him before we can get him to do this. Regarding the English gentleman our only link is through Segan, unless we can uncover some other way of contacting him."

Shimony listened patiently and then said, "Let's go back to the basics of criminology—look for the motive. We should go straight to whoever sent this gentleman to Segan in the first place. Surely, he was not acting on his own. Someone was funding the whole operation, someone who stood to benefit directly from the elimination of the scientists or indirectly from the consequences of the operation.

"I believe we should divide our focus. You, David, go after Segan and the English gentleman, while our top analysts will figure out who stands to gain from the removal of these scientists. You can enlist help from Julia, to whom I am told by my sources, you have taken quite a fancy." This last statement was with a small smile, watching David's reaction that caused him to blush.

David responded, "I'll be off to Berlin tomorrow. I would like to meet the analysts this evening and share the information I have on the Iranians, particularly the reaction of the Imam to my presentation. I am sure that he is up to some mischief and had something up his sleeve. The way he ignored my question about the hostages must have been intentional. Yet I believe that they are willing to meet again and negotiate the release of the hostages."

Shimony responded, "I am not sure that they have given up their intentions of developing nuclear weapons. At present they have a lot to lose if the sanctions are renewed but we are all aware that the nuclear deal that they signed has some loopholes they would exploit if the circumstances change. I'll instruct the analysts to focus on scenarios that may drive the Iranian regime to take risks and carry out dangerous steps.

"First and foremost, is the fear of losing control of the country. This is where the interests of the religious leadership coincide with the concerns of the Iranian Revolutionary

Guards for the economic empire they had constructed."

David fully agreed with his boss and said he would go to see the analysts immediately.

CHAPTER 14

October 11th, General Koliagin's office, Moscow

General Koliagin looked at the full ashtray on his desk and then glanced at the antique clock that hung opposite his chair at the head of the large conference table. He was waiting for his top aides and analysts to enter the room but had been wondering how to open the meeting and how much he would tell them about the recent events.

He pressed a button on the intercom and barked an order to summon his personal secretary. The tall girl entered the room without knocking on the door, looked at the general and saw the overflowing ashtray and knew he was in a foul mood. She leaned over allowing her ample breasts to linger on his shoulder and gently picked up the ashtray.

He managed to force a smile and she slowly stroked the back of his neck feeling the tension dissipating. She asked him if he wanted something to drink before the meeting and he just motioned for her to take the ashtray and let them in.

They filed in silently and took their seats according to their rank and importance. Those in uniform sat on both sides near the head of the table, while the advisors and analysts took the chairs at the far end of the table.

The general's adjutant turned on the projector and pressed a button that rolled down the screen and another that closed the curtains. The senior analyst stood up and took the remote control in his hand waiting for the general to open the meeting.

General Koliagin looked around the table, holding the eyes of each participant for a few seconds and reading their expressions. All of them were experts on the political situation in Iran or officers in the Russian military that were familiar with the plans for armed intervention in Iran, if such a case arose.

Some were FSB personnel that were in charge of gathering intelligence for the analysts as well as recruit collaborators inside the Iranian establishment. The older hands displayed no emotion and appeared to be "poker faced," without even a hint of what was going on in their minds, while the junior members were clearly intimidated by the iron stare of the general. They all knew that their careers could rise and prosper or be abruptly terminated by the general.

He spoke so quietly that those at the far end of the table had to strain their ears to hear him. "I would like a candid review of the situation in Iran. I am especially curious about the changes, if any, brought about by the signing of the nuclear deal. We have never fully trusted Iran, even after we supplied them with advance weapon systems like the S-300 aerial defense anti-aircraft missiles, with armament of various kinds and contracted to build more nuclear power plants in addition to the one in Bushehr.

"Their course record in respecting agreements has been

less than perfect, to say the least. They were caught in violation of signed contracts numerous times and always came up with lame excuses to justify these infractions. Who knows what they managed to get away with? We don't know what we don't know but there is no limit to what we suspect. Please speak freely."

The senior analyst, who was considered as the leading expert on Iranian affairs cleared his throat and screened his first slide that showed a schematic of the different government organizations in Iran. "The legislature or Islamic Consultative Assembly (the Majlis for short), consists of two hundred and ninety members, who are elected by popular vote, as is the president, for a four-year term. However, all the candidates must gain approval of the Council of Guardians, whose members are in charge of interpreting the constitution and supervising the elections.

"In addition, there is a Council of Experts that consists of eighty-eight masters of Islamic law, called the Assembly of Experts. They are elected for an eight-year term. This council is controlled by the clerics who wield the real power and they elect the Supreme Leader. The Supreme Leader is also commander-in-chief of the armed forces and controls the intelligence and security agencies. He practically has absolute power over the judiciary system, the media, and appoints all the members of the Council of Guardians who oversee the Majlis. The elected president has some authority but cannot take any significant action without the approval of the Supreme Leader and Council."

The analyst continued to describe the power structure in

Iran highlighting the fact that it is first and foremost a theocratic Islamic government. At the end of his talk he said that there is an ongoing struggle between the conservative elements that wish to retain control by the clerics and religious Islamic establishment and the more liberal factions.

He emphasized that he is using the term "liberals" freely because they are also not against a theocratic regime. Their main objectives are to be more open to the West and reduce unemployment, especially among the educated people who cannot find suitable jobs in Iran.

Finally, he said that in the election that was held in 2016, the ultra-conservatives lost several seats in the Majlis and the Assembly of Experts to the more liberal candidates. This was especially prominent in Tehran and among the more educated voters, while in the rural areas the turn-out of voters was lower but they still gave support to the conservative candidates.

The general was not impressed by this presentation. "You have told us nothing new. Everything can be found in Wikipedia or other websites that are accessible to any ten-year old with a computer and internet access, although I doubt that ten-year old's would bother with the power structure of Iran. I want to know about the Iranian nuclear program after, I repeat after, they signed the nuclear deal. Can you tell us what they are really up to?"

The senior analyst turned pale and managed to say. "Well, I was just getting to this in my next slides." He went on to describe the clandestine Iranian program to develop nuclear weapons that was curtailed by the nuclear deal. He said that the program consisted of three major efforts: first, enrichment of uranium to officially manufacture only low-enriched-uranium (LEU).

This was also approved in the nuclear deal, but the amount was restricted to six hundred and sixty pounds. The Iranians had developed the capability, perhaps even the actual clandestine production, of high-enriched-uranium (HEU) that can be used in nuclear weapons.

Second, to produce weapon-grade plutonium in a specially designed nuclear reactor or by adaptation of legitimate nuclear power plants; and third, to carry out research, and perhaps testing, of nuclear weapon designs.

He added, "The nuclear deal has put an end to most of these programs, or at least imposed severe limitations on them. But we suspect that the Iranians have continued to pursue the acquisition of nuclear weapons at clandestine sites and in secret laboratories."

Before he could continue, General Koliagin spoke, "Have we any proof of this or is it just speculation?"

The senior analyst was dumbfounded. "General, I can base my presentation only on the intelligence provided to me, the rest is just innuendo and speculation. So far, I have not seen any photos, documents, or received reports of actual violations of the nuclear deal. If our esteemed intelligence agencies have anything to the contrary, I'll be glad to get it." He sat back down in his chair and tried to ignore the glaring look that the general gave him.

General Koliagin looked around the table and noted that all the participants kept themselves busy moving their pens around or fiddling with the papers placed in front of them. No one looked up or met his eyes and their expressionless faces could have been carved in stone or wood.

He sighed inwardly and thought that the senior analyst was right, and the fault lay with the lack of up-to-date information on the activities of the Iranians. The FSB had sources within the Iranian scientific community and several collaborators inside the intelligence services and the IRG but none of these had delivered anything that would imply that Iran was in violation of the nuclear deal that it had signed. The general was aware of the motto of all intelligence services regarding getting proof of illicit operations: *absence of evidence is not evidence of absence.*

He decided that in order to maintain his position and to ensure that people continued to fear him, he had to make an example of the senior analyst and to do so then and there. He pressed the intercom button and summoned his secretary.

When she entered the conference room, he told her to arrange an escort for the senior analyst that would take him to his apartment. They were to help him pack his things as he would be transferred to his new job in Irkutsk, where he would serve as the local intelligence coordinator.

The general couldn't help thinking that just a few decades earlier the trip would have been much shorter - only as far as the Lubyanka Building on Bolshaya Lubyanka Street in Moscow.

The senior analyst rose to his feet and all color drained from his face as he followed the tall girl out of the room. The general waited another moment and said that he expected some real information about Iran's nuclear program and then adjourned the meeting.

October 20, Basement S, Evin Prison, Tehran

Dr. Fathi was looking forward to the visit by Imam Mourtashef. At long last he had something tangible to show as proof for the success of his efforts—not computer simulations with strange looking shaded lines and dots moving across a computer screen—but a solid sphere made of a metallic substance.

A broad smile crossed his face, replacing the brooding haunted expression that had become more and more common since some of his leading scientists were mysteriously murdered in Europe less than a year previously.

He still mourned some of them, especially the tragic end of Dr. Abadi, who died alone on a cold street in Vienna, and of Dr. Al-Baida, who fell to his death from a steep cliff in sunny Taormina. He also wondered what had happened to Dr. Raffsani, the brilliant mathematician, who mocked the security officers and was whisked away from the laboratory never to be heard from again.

Despite these setbacks Fathi and his team were on the verge of achieving the goals that were set for them by the Supreme Leader. Fathi was very proud and now was the moment he was ready to reap the honors and recognition he felt were well deserved.

The Imam was unaccompanied when he entered the small office that served Dr. Fathi when he felt that he needed to get away from the test benches and "hot cells" that cluttered the laboratory.

Fathi rose from his seat and welcomed the Imam, bowing his head slightly as a token of respect. The Imam smiled and told Fathi to sit down and give him a brief progress report.

Fathi, brimming with excitement, motioned to the Imam to follow him to the lab and led the way to one of the "hot cells," that at a first glance appeared to be empty. As the Imam approached closer, he saw a small metallic sphere that was only a few inches in diameter. He looked quizzically at the scientist with an unspoken question in his eyes.

Fathi said, "This may not look like much to you but, believe it or not, the energy contained in this small sphere can destroy a whole city and kill all its residents in a flash."

The Imam was a bit skeptical, but also in a flippant mood, and smiled while saying, "Dr. Fathi, surely you are not implying that someone has to take this sphere and hit every resident on the head with it."

Seeing the stunned expression on Fathi's face, he quickly added, "Only joking. Have you calculated the force of explosion of this sphere?"

Relieved a little, Fathi replied, "The yield, or force of explosion, of this little sphere that you can pick up with one hand, is equivalent to that of twenty thousand tons of the common chemical explosive TNT. For comparison, the load a Boeing 747-400 can carry is about two hundred tons, so if you take a hundred Jumbo jets fully loaded with TNT and crash all of them in a city the extent of immediate damage of the blast wave would be similar. But then you have to add the effects of ionizing and thermal radiation and the long-lasting deadly residual radiation and contamination to appreciate the difference between conventional explosives and nuclear bombs."

The Imam was aware of these physical facts but was more concerned with the reliability of the device. "What if it doesn't work as planned?"

Dr. Fathi was now offended. His professional integrity and credibility were challenged. He looked on the verge of a bursting a blood vessel. "This unique design was delivered to us by a Russian defector, tested by our most advanced computer simulation modeling and verified by a Chinese expert of nuclear devices.

"Of course, we couldn't carry out any real full-scale tests. First and foremost, our fissile material is sufficient for just one device—the little sphere you see here represents almost our entire stock. Second, even if we had enough material our chances of getting away with a full-scale test without it being detected are infinitesimally close to zero. Last but not least, is the logistical problem involved in carrying out such a test— the construction of a site, the measurement equipment, and the expenses—in effect, prohibit this. So, Honorable Imam, I can assure you that we did the best we could under the circumstances, and I am confident that it will work as expected."

The Imam was not convinced by this emotional outburst. He said, "Dr. Fathi, you know that if this device is ever deployed and fulfills the expectations of the Supreme Leader and the Iranian people, you will be a national hero. Of course, the scientific and technological success will be usurped by many others from the Supreme Leader, through General Aslawi and many others. If it fails, you alone will be held responsible and I needn't elaborate on the fate that you and your family and your team and their families will suffer. So, make sure that when you declare the mission was accomplished and the nuclear device is ready, that it will perform according to our high expectations."

Dr. Fathi had expected gratitude and appreciation for his accomplishments, not a sermon. He stood there speechless, while some of his senior associates who were within earshot turned pale. Finally, he recovered and said, "Honorable Imam Mourtashef, please follow me to the small conference room and allow me to explain in more detail what we had accomplished in such a short time with such a small group."

Fathi was thinking of Churchill's accolade: *Never was so much owed by so many to so few*, attributed to the fighter pilots that fought and won, *The Battle of Britain* against the Nazi Luftwaffe in 1940. This is what he had expected to hear from the Imam, not the reprimand he had just received.

Once everyone was seated around the conference table, Fathi presented the almost insurmountable problems his team had overcome in less than three years. He kept glancing at the Imam's expression trying to decipher what was going on in his mind. By the time he was through with his presentation, sweat was pouring down the collar of his lab coat and his face was flushed.

The Imam still looked unimpressed and asked, "Dr. Fathi, I think I have gained a better understanding of the problems you faced and solved. What I now need to know, assuming that the device is indeed reliable, is the size and weight of the complete device. I would also like to know if it safe to transport it and if there are any problems involved that may affect its performance. How rugged is it? Is it sensitive to changes of air pressure? Is it sensitive to humidity? Can you assure me that it will work after being shaken? Is it affected by external radiation, radio signals, radar? What about temperature variations?"

Dr. Fathi knew that these questions were really crucial, and he had no way of answering them with certainty. He had no shred of science-based evidence but he was aware that any hesitation on his part now could be his death sentence. So, with all the self-confidence he could muster he said, "Our design was approved by experts, as I have mentioned. The physical and chemical parameters of the device have been meticulously tested by our people. The triggering mechanism was copied from blueprints that were supplied to us by our experienced allies from Pakistan and North Korea. The chemical explosives that produce the implosion that is necessary for initiating the nuclear detonation were manufactured under strict secrecy by our own military industry. They also provided test certificates that show that they worked according to specifications. In short, I am confident that it will work."

The Imam realized that Fathi's long answer evaded his questions. He gave the scientist one of the stares that could turn a full-grown man into a rag doll and motioned for Fathi to continue, but get to the point.

Dr. Fathi was visibly shaken and stuttered, "We have worked out that the device could fit in to a large suitcase or trunk and would weigh a few hundred pounds. You must remember that the atomic bombs that were used in World War

II were much larger and heavier. I can assure you that the device will not be sensitive to changes in air pressure or to exposure to humidity for several days. It will withstand quite vigorous shaking but there can be no guarantee that very severe vibrations would not affect its performance. It will be shielded from external radio signals and electromagnetic radiation—this will add a little to its weight but is a precaution that we have undertaken."

He glanced at the Imam, and for the first time since he entered the laboratory, felt that he was getting through to him.

The Imam rose, nodded briefly, and left the conference room and made his way up from the basement to the street level. He exited Evin Prison and instructed his driver to take him directly to the office of the Senior Assistant to the Supreme Leader.

***

The Senior Assistant was expecting the Imam in order to get an update on the state of affairs in Dr. Fathi's secret laboratory. The Imam said, "I am reasonably satisfied that the nuclear device is almost ready, but I must also express my reservations about its reliability after being transported to the intended target. It would have to be handled with kid gloves and we have to devise a way of minimizing its exposure to electromagnetic radiation, vibrations or extreme temperature variations during transportation."

The Senior Assistant agreed and said, "This means that we have to refine the plan that you have proposed."

The Imam thought about this for a moment and then commented, "I'll have to meet again with the representative of Mossad and "consent" to arrange some kind of hostage exchange."

The Senior Assistant said, "We'd better inform General Aslawi about these new developments. I am sure the general will not be happy about the terms of the hostage release. He would have preferred we make a tough stance and force the Israelis to meet all the demands we had drawn when we started this hostage-taking campaign".

He continued to remind the Imam, not that he needed the reminder, that they had several demands regarding the Israeli nuclear research centers and its nuclear policy.

The Imam, who was a shrewd dealer, said, "The important thing now is to appear to be flexible, just as we did when the nuclear deal was negotiated with the Six Powers. We should start with a long list of negotiation points but slowly relent and agree to terms the Israelis can willingly accept. They are so conceited and sure of their own brilliance that we can easily convince them they had outsmarted us. Then, we must get the hostages on a plane bound to Tel Aviv, and of course have our nuclear device on it as well. When the Prime Minister of Israel, his cabinet ministers, members of the ruling elite of the Zionist state, and the senior officers of the Israeli army, Mossad and ISA come to meet the released hostages the device will go off.

"Not only will the head of the hateful entity be chopped off but the outskirts of Tel Aviv will go up in smoke and the area contaminated for generations will make life there unbearable.

This will be coordinated with our loving friends of Hamas in Gaza and our Hezbollah lackeys in Lebanon who will launch rocket attacks on the south and north of Israel, respectively. We also expect our Palestinian supporters in the Occupied West Bank to start an armed rebellion against the colonialists that live among them and return control over Jerusalem to Islamic rule. Of course, we won't tell them exactly what to expect as this would surely leak to the Israeli Security Agency. We'll just tell them to wait for a signal that will appear to look like an act of Allah."

The Senior Assistant was overjoyed by this detailed plan. He said, "Imam Mourtashef, you'll go down in the history of our nation as the savior of our civilization, perhaps even as the Mahdi. Thanks to you, our New Caliphate would be established in which we, the Shiite followers of the true Islam, will rule the infidels. The Christian crusaders will be once again conquered, the Jews will either pay homage or be eliminated and the misguided Sunnis will either see the true way on earth or see it on their speedy way to hell. This will be nothing like the New Caliphate the terrible ISIS people want."

The Imam said, "Inshallah, with the will of Allah, we shall succeed. Let us now call General Aslawi and tell him what we have agreed to do and put him in charge of making the necessary arrangements with Hezbollah, Hamas, and the Palestinians. You may wish to update the Supreme Leader and receive his blessing. Let's meet again in three days."

CHAPTER 15

October 20, Mossad Headquarters, Tel Aviv

David informed Shimony on the progress in tracking Segan and the English gentleman. "Haim, with Julia's help, I managed to find Segan after he returned to Berlin. He was cooperative and told me about the English gentleman, Alan Ross, and the contract he had accepted. He kept repeating that what he had done was for the benefit of Israel and he acted like a true patriot and expected recognition by the government and redemption of his position as a candidate to head Mossad after your term ends."

Shimony replied, "Doesn't he realize that his actions could get Mossad and the government in trouble. That the days of this type of operation are over and that even during the "cold war," both sides attempted to avoid harming non-combatants. By tacit agreement, scientists were kept out of the conflict and were allowed to continue their work."

David said, "He didn't acknowledge that there were consequences to the elimination of the Iranian scientists and that several Israelis were now held as hostages in Evin Prison in Tehran."

Shimony asked, "Did he mention Ruby and Sam?"

David continued, "He confirmed what we already knew—that Sam and Ruby carried out all the jobs, except the elimination of Mustafa Fahami in London's Chinatown that he did himself. He said the detailed information needed for the operations was supplied by Ross. I asked him about Ross, but he said the name was not his real name and despite his efforts, he hadn't managed to find anything about Ross. I suspect that Ross may have tried to pull a 'double bluff' and actually use his real name that is so common that it is almost impossible to trace. This is like what Segan himself did when he sent Sam to Boston with the name of John Smith."

"What about the double murder of his agents?"

"He denied any connection with the murder of Sam and Ruby and provided me with a rock-solid alibi. At the time of the murders, he was in South America on a cruise to Antarctica and has many witnesses with whom he played bridge during the cruise. He even showed me the receipt for the tickets and several photos of him and his attractive companion on glaciers and with seals. I felt there was no point in asking him for details of the witnesses, but he volunteered some information about his companion. Apparently, she is his third wife and still works for him as his secretary."

"Did you meet her?"

"Haim, our conversation was not a social get-together. It was more like an interrogation and I was careful not to turn him against us. I tried to learn more about the role Ruby and Sam played in his organization and he said they had been his most trusted employees and he considered them as friends. He said he felt responsible for bringing about their downfall and dismissal from Mossad but kept repeating he was a true patriot and whatever he did was for Israel. At some stage I got tired of this imprudent repetition but had to hold myself and continue to listen to his diatribe about his patriotism and the ingratitude of his former country."

"David. Did he say he would agree to make a public statement that he was responsible for the elimination of the Iranian scientists and emphasize that he was acting on his own, without approval or knowledge of Israel?"

"He adamantly refused to do that. He said this type of exposure would ruin his business and put him at a personal risk that was unacceptable to him. I offered him the opportunity to record a video clip with such a statement, but he said it was just as bad."

"Did he show any signs of remorse about the fate of Sam and Ruby or the innocent Israelis that were kidnapped?"

"None whatsoever. He only perceived the elimination of the Iranian nuclear scientists as a great service to Israel. He couldn't care less about the consequences. Haim, this means that we have to make a special effort to keep him alive and out of the hands of other intelligence services."

"On the contrary, if we hand Segan over to the Russians, they will make him confess all and sing like a canary. This may be cruel but Segan deserves to be punished for his irresponsible actions."

"This is very cynical and fraught with problems. The Russians won't stop at probing just these latest actions of Segan and his organization. They will make him spill everything he knows about Mossad's operations in the last two or three decades, ever since he joined Mossad. This could endanger our agents everywhere, could get the present and several past governments in to trouble, this could lead to further deterioration of our relationship with many of our allies. No, Haim, I have to disagree with you."

"Then we'll need to guarantee his silence in the old-fashioned way…"

David was not surprised by this statement but didn't like it. "Suppose we manage to get this gentleman Ross. Find out who sent him and who he is working for."

Shimony considered this for a long moment and said, "Okay. Go after this Ross, or whatever his real name is, and get him to spill everything. Who sent him? Where did he get his funding from? How did he get the operational information he provided to Segan and his firm? And we need a public statement from him that will remove the blame from Israel. Use whatever means you need to track him and persuade him to come clean and confess all. This is now our top priority."

David said, "Segan is our only link to Ross. As far as we know, he is the only contact we have who has spoken to him, and after Sam and Ruby's death, he is also the only one who has seen him. I doubt if anyone in the wine bar will remember him after all this time."

Shimony said, "I think that once you tell Segan about the alternative you'll find him to be very cooperative…"

October 22, Berlin

David and Julia were on their way to meet a reluctant Segan. At first, he refused to meet David again but after a short description of the alternatives, he reluctantly agreed.

When he proposed that they meet at the offices of his firm, David said he suspected it was under surveillance by the Russians and the Iranians. This shook Segan and they agreed to meet in the privacy of Julia's apartment.

Segan arrived fashionably late, just as David had anticipated, and grumbled, "Well, here I am. I already told you everything about the contract and its execution by Sam and Ruby. I had expected that I would be invited to Mossad headquarters to receive some appreciation for my patriotic activities and instead you have come to Berlin with implied threats. This is no way to treat someone who has done so much for Israel—"

David cut him short. "Segan, you are a very clever man and were always an excellent field operative. You must realize that things have gotten out of hand. You are wanted by the Iranians, who want to exact their vengeance on you for eliminating their scientists. The Russians want to "help" us but will make sure to extract every tiny piece of information on Mossad that you may not even remember that you know. The Head of Mossad himself is on the verge of bringing you in alive or taking whatever necessary measures to ensure your silence, including the permanent treatment. I don't think that I can be any clearer than that."

Julia added, "Segan, I know you were treated as a pariah by all the Israeli officials in Berlin. You were regarded as *persona*

MISSION PATRIOT | 221

non grata at the embassy and all personnel were instructed to stay away from you. Now is the last opportunity to redeem yourself and clear your name. Take it!"

Segan said, "What do you want me to do?"

David answered, "Help us find Ross. We'll go on from there. Tell us all you know about him, starting with a detailed description, or better yet try to reconstruct his face with the help of our new facial construction and recognition software."

Segan laughed. "Do you think you are dealing with a rooky? An amateur? I have arranged to take several photos of him during our meetings. These were sent to me from Ruby's cell phone. However, I doubt if this will suffice to find him."

David said, "You'd be surprised what a large database we have gained access to since you left Mossad. Why didn't you provide me with the photos during our last meeting?"

Segan shrugged. "You didn't ask me."

David audibly groaned and said, "What else can you tell us about him? Describe in detail his accent, his vocabulary, his mysterious telephone answering service in London. Divulge everything and anything that will help us to locate him."

Segan replied, "I'll write down the London phone number, but I doubt that it will still be in service. Regarding his accent—I always had a feeling that it was put on. A few times he slipped, and his very British upper-class pronunciation reverted to something with a trace of Middle Eastern accent. I would guess that he was originally from some part of the Middle East, most likely Iran. Undoubtedly, he had attended the best schools in the UK and adopted the right accent, but deep down there were traces of the original Alan Ross beneath the smooth veneer."

David said, "This isn't much to go on, but I'll try to gain assistance from British intelligence and perhaps also from our friends in the CIA. In view of the contract that he offered you and the operational intelligence he provided; he probably still has strong ties in Iran. The hint he gave you about Saudi funding is also helpful. If we combine every piece of information we have on him, we stand a good chance of tracking him down."

Segan rose. "David, I am still a true patriot and glad to help." He nodded and then left the apartment quietly, closing the door behind him.

David wanted to call him back and ask him to sign a testimony, in which everything he said would be documented but Segan was gone. David shrugged and thought that he himself could just print out the conversation and use it even without Segan's real formal signature.

In any case, he surmised, whoever wanted to doubt it, would say that Segan's signature was a forgery and whoever wanted to believe it would not need the signature.

Julia looked at David. "This Segan is a wolf in sheep's clothing if ever I've seen one."

David nodded. "He did give us some useful leads. Let's have a nightcap and go to bed. Tomorrow, I'll fly to London to see what I can learn there."

October 23, Office of the Senior Assistant, Tehran

The Senior Assistant welcomed General Aslawi and Imam Mourtashef and waited for them to take their seats before stating, "The Supreme Leader has approved the plan in principle, but before its implementation we will have to get his final approval. In other words, get everything prepared but do not execute until he says so."

General Aslawi said, "Honorable Imam, I want to congratulate you. You will strike terror in the hearts of the infidels. We must create the impression that we have many more nuclear devices ready to go off in all capitals of the Western World, in Moscow, and in Beijing, or else their retribution will destroy our country.

"Our analysts don't think that any of them really care about the fate of Israel and would not move against us, but we need to be perceived as a real nuclear power with a large arsenal of nuclear weapons to make sure none of them act. Has this been taken into consideration?"

The Imam smiled and said, "Yes, I have reached the same conclusion. If the destruction is contained within the boundaries of Israel then the world will moan and groan a little, perhaps offer asylum to a small number of Zionists, but will not lift a finger to help them. However, our insurance policy is the threat of additional nuclear strikes. So, we will create the illusion that we have many more nuclear devices where this one came from."

The general said, "The Senior Assistant has described your plan to use the release of the hostages as the means of decapitating the elite and destroying the heartland of the Zionist entity. I suggest that we use a ruse to gain their confidence. After you appear to yield in the negotiations and accept their minimalistic offer, you'll propose as a gesture of goodwill to release one of the hostages.

"We'll send the IRG's private jet with the hostage and arrange for its safe landing at Tel Aviv airport. I am sure that the Israeli Security Agency will use a fine comb to go over the plane. Thus, when we send the rest of the hostages with our special delivery package, they will hopefully be careless and less meticulous."

The Imam said, "I like this twist. The Supreme Leader has ordered me to have another round of negotiations in Moscow and has consented to let us appear as retreating from our tough positions. I have requested General Koliagin to host this round and invite the same Mossad agent. This time, I'll pretend to be convinced by his claim that Mossad was not involved in the murders of our scientists but will play hard to get."

The Senior Assistant asked, "When can we expect the completion of the nuclear device's construction? This is the most crucial point of setting our schedule?"

The Imam replied, "According to Dr. Fathi's estimate, he thinks that we will be ready to send the Zionists a special gift for their Hanukkah holidays. In case you don't know, this is another one of history's ironies. The Jews celebrate their victory over the hateful Greeks in their rebellion that ended in 160 BC, almost two hundred years after the forefathers of those same Greeks, led by Alexander the Great, conquered and destroyed our grand Persian Empire and deposed of King Darius III. Then, we and the Jews had common enemies, and now they are the embodiment of the evil enemy. In other words, in less than two months we'll be ready to strike."

The Senior Assistant and General Aslawi smiled and praised the Imam. They wished him success on his upcoming trip to Moscow.

CHAPTER 16

October 23, London

David was greeted by his old friend Colin Thomas after landing at Heathrow airport at noon. Colin told him that he had returned to his old post as head of the counter-terror department at MI6 after his stint at the International Atomic Energy Agency (IAEA) in Vienna.

David said that he was aware of that and they reminisced about their joint project concerning *Mission Alchemist* but soon got down to the business on hand. David told Colin that Mossad was not responsible for the elimination of the Iranian nuclear scientists, which was met by a skeptical look. He said that Segan, a rogue former Mossad deputy director, and his organization carried out the job under contract.

When Colin asked who set up the contract, David took out the photos that Segan gave him in Berlin and added all the bits of information that he knew about Alan Ross.

Colin's skeptical attitude changed when he realized that the repercussions could affect the UK. If indeed the contract was set up by a British national right under the nose of the British intelligence community and the press got wind of that then the Home Office and perhaps the government would be shaken by the scandal. Colin promised David he would do his utmost to identify this Alan Ross person and suggested that they meet for dinner.

***

Later that evening, they had a fine roast beef dinner at Colin's exclusive club and over a glass of Port in the club's cozy study, Colin stated he had a real surprise for David.

David raised his eyebrows and said, "I am waiting…"

Colin laughed and said, "Hold on to your seat. Alan Ross is the name of the former Iranian citizen; whose original name was Ali Rashid."

David just looked at him, so after a dramatic pause Colin continued, "As a matter of fact, he is a member of this gentlemen's club—well, its standards have deteriorated over the years—and he should be here any minute. Believe it or not, but he is a senior civil servant in the Foreign Office. In fact, he is now head of the Iranian desk and played a part in the negotiations that led to the signing of the nuclear deal. One of his tasks was to eavesdrop on the conversations of the members of the Iranian delegation, without revealing that he understood Farsi."

David was stunned. He managed to say, "Do you know if he was acting as a private citizen when he made the contract with Segan or was he on official business for the UK government?"

Colin smiled and refrained from answering. David persisted until Colin relented, "I am still trying to discover that.

I have my doubts whether the exchequer would trust him with millions of American dollars, but stranger things have happened. In our line of business, the improbable happens every day and the incredible at least once a week, and unacceptable and unbelievable things happen every month. Once in a blue moon, the government does its best to undermine itself. I think that Alan Ross has done all of those in one single contract."

David wondered if he could get his hand on Alan Ross and take him to a nice and quiet place, where he would drag the truth out of him. He asked Colin, "I think I need to have a very private talk with him. What do you know about his personal life?"

Colin looked at David for a long moment before responding, "Yes, I am sure that it is a good idea. The Foreign Office has a dubious track record—they always seem to bet on the wrong horse. They failed in preventing the First World War, failed to understand the dangers of Nazism, failed to recognize that the days of the British Empire were over, foolishly participated in the Suez crisis, not to mention the part they played in muddling with affairs of the Middle East countries.

"The rise of ISIS is undoubtedly one of the outcomes of our intervention in Iraq and our participation in crowning a Shiite ruler after the fall of Saddam's regime. Another sign of the anachronistic approach is the very name the Foreign and Commonwealth Office, or FCO for short, that has long lost its past grandeur but has failed to acknowledge that. David, I'll try to provide you with some useful intelligence about Ross. Please contact me tomorrow. Remember this conversation has never taken place."

Colin expected David to say, "What conversation."

David nodded and said, "Thanks for the dinner. It is good to see that there are still clever and honest people in your administration. I'll get back to you tomorrow afternoon after I make some preparations for the warm reception tomorrow night."

***

David contacted Shimony on a secure line and gave him the gist of his meeting with Colin Thomas.

Shimony gave the "go ahead" signal that he had requested and said that a special Mossad team would be sent to London to assist him. David was told to expect them to arrive at noon the next day and meanwhile he called the London station head and arranged to meet him at one of Mossad's safe houses an hour later.

Yehuda Tobias was a veteran Mossad operative, who received the posting in London as a kind of retirement gift. He had risen through the ranks of Mossad as an expert on European affairs and had no field experience. Therefore, he was really excited to have an opportunity to be involved in some real action—of the type he had seen in movies and only heard rumors about the jobs his own organization had carried out. He was also thrilled to work with David Avivi, who was a legend in Mossad thanks to his successful operations.

David was pleased to see Yehuda's enthusiasm and his unabated cooperation. Yehuda said that he had only couple of experienced Mossad operatives at his call but told David that he was informed that three more were on their way from Israel. Mossad had a safe house on the edge of a quiet rural village about twenty miles from London that had a basement and its closest neighbors were a mile away.

He said he would send one of his agents to prepare the house and buy food supplies that would provide meals for half a dozen men for three days. David was very pleased with this and said he needed a good night's sleep in view of what was planned for the next day.

Yehuda would have liked to sit and spin yarns with David for another couple of hours but understood that the time was not right.

October 24, London

Just after noon, the Mossad group gathered at Yehuda's private apartment. In addition to David and Yehuda were the two agents from the London office, Yuval and Iris, who were a married couple in their late twenties with some field experience in Mossad.

Eran and Udi were sent from Israel especially for this mission. Both had served in elite units of the Israeli Defense Forces (IDF) and had been in several fire fights and skirmishes with the Palestinians. They also had been on special operations deep inside Syria and Lebanon, but they had no field record of clandestine operations in friendly countries like the UK.

The pivotal member of the group was a petite, dark-skinned

exotic woman, whose real name was Miriam but nobody called by that name. Everybody in Mossad called her by her nickname Mata, that she had earned because of her resemblance to the legendary and somewhat infamous World War I spy Mata Hari and because of the jobs she carried out.

They had all known the legend about the ploy David had used to extract information from reluctant Greek racists when he was chasing the villains in *Mission Alchemist* and also from an uncooperative Islamist in Germany described in *Mission Renegade.*

Yehuda asked if they would try that again, but David just smiled and said they would use a different technique. He suggested that all familiarize themselves with the target, Alan Ross, and study the venue where he would be captured and the surroundings of the safe house.

In the early afternoon, David met with Colin and got all the operational intelligence he needed for the operation. Apparently Ross was not a hard worker and usually arrived at the office in King Charles Street at eleven in the morning, had tea, and a long lunch, then left the office at five, to have a couple of drinks at a nearby pub and then went off to dinner at his club. Ross had been married three times and divorced twice but was now separated from his third wife as he could not afford another expensive divorce.

Colin said that Ross's two main problems were his drinking and his roving eye that was always searching for good looking women. When the two were combined, that is after a few drinks, the search became intense, almost compulsive. Colin added that all three wives were blondes, who looked like the proverbial English roses with peach skin and blue eyes but most of his extramarital affairs were with exquisite dark women, probably some ingrained heritage from his youth in Iran in the mid-1970s.

Upon hearing this David grinned and said that like a good doctor, he had prepared the best medication for the patient. Colin left wishing David good luck in the enterprise he didn't wish to know anything about.

***

Mata was sitting alone at a small table in the Ross's favorite pub, nursing a glass of red wine and looking sad as if she was stood up by an ungentlemanly gentleman.

Ross had already consumed two or three tumblers of single malt Scotch while sitting at the bar. He kept glancing at the lonely woman using the large mirror in front of him to do so unobtrusively. He ordered another double Scotch and a glass of the finest Bordeaux red wine the bartender recommended and carried the drinks over to the table where Mata was seated. He asked if he could buy her a glass of Bordeaux and join her. Mata looked up at him, appeared to be appraising him for a long moment as if she was deliberating the issue. She pretended to assess his tailor-made suit, leather shoes, and silk tie. She then let her glance linger of his absurdly expensive wristwatch, and finally shrugged and motioned for him to sit down across the table.

Ross asked her, "What is a nice girl like you doing in a place like this?"

Mata almost puked at the cliché that was perhaps the most absurd opening line ever spoken by someone trying to pick up another person. She countered, "I guess I am doing what you are doing here—waiting for someone who didn't show up and looking for some consolation prize."

Ross's smile almost split his face in two, but fortunately his ears stopped it from going all around his skull. "Well, you came to the right place and your timing is perfect. Let's have another round of drinks and then go out and dine somewhere nice."

Mata appeared to be a bit tipsy after consuming her wine and looked as if she hesitated. "I don't even know your name, what you do, and if you are not some kind of pervert or a new embodiment of Jack the Ripper."

Ross was deeply offended. "My name is Alan, I am a senior civil servant in the Home Office, and I can assure you that I am as straight and honest as the members of my club will confirm."

Mata said, "I guess that there is no harm in having dinner together." She excused herself to go to "powder her nose."

Ross rose politely as she left the table and called for the bill. When Mata returned, he was holding her coat and smiling broadly at her. Mata slipped her hands in to the sleeves, making sure to brush against him suggestively. She asked, "So, where are we going for dinner?"

Ross said, his words a bit slurred from the whiskey and anticipation, "This will be a real surprise." He led the way out of the pub. He stood on the sidewalk and signaled to a taxi that had been waiting near the entrance. He opened the door to let Mata in and then got in sitting very close to her and said, "Cabbie, take us to The Delaunay at Covent Gardens."

He turned to Mata, and said, "This is one of the most expensive and best restaurants in London and perhaps in Europe and the World."

Mata snuggled up to and placed her right hand on his knee while with her left hand she opened her handbag and removed a syringe from it. She turned toward him and made as if to hug him with her left hand and quickly injected him in the neck with the contents of the syringe.

Ross was out before she could count to three and collapsed on her. The cabbie turned to her and she saw that it was Yuval from the London branch of Mossad. He said in Hebrew, "Good job. Now we'll drive to the safe house and meet the rest. Do you want to join us there or should I drop you off somewhere?"

Mata said, "I need a shower to wash off all traces of this lecher. But it can wait until we reach the safe house." She moved as far away from Ross as the space permitted.

***

The whole group was already waiting at the safe house. As soon as the commandeered taxi stopped in front of the house, Eran and Udi opened its door and carried the unconscious Ross into the basement.

Ross was slowly coming around and still groggy as they tied him to the dentist's chair that was placed in the middle of the basement. He opened his eyes and squinted at the two figures dressed in black clothes.

David and Udi had their faces covered with black, woolen, balaclava hats that had two round holes for the eyes. The effect was enhanced by the red circles surrounding the eyeholes.

David said, "How are you feeling, Mr. Alan Ross, or should I call you, Ali Rashid?"

Ross tried to move his hands and found that they were tied to the armrests. He tried to move his head and realized that it was held firmly by a special kind of headrest. He vehemently answered, "Do you know who I am? Do you know that the Scotland Yard will turn every stone until they find me? Are you doing this for money? Are you out of your minds messing with me? Do you know who will come after you? Do you—"

David gave a signal and Udi turned on the bright light above the dentist's chair and directed its powerful beam straight to Ross's eyes, blinding him, and making him stop his stream of invectives. He then turned on the drill's motor and the sound of a hundred angry wasps filled the basement.

David said, "This may sound like a bee, but it stings like a scorpion, especially in the clumsy hands of my colleague here. He was thrown out of dentistry school just before graduating because he had drilled some cavities to such a size that there was no filling available and the teeth had to be extracted and replaced by implants. The official letter that was sent to him by the dean of the school was very offensive, so I'll put it in layman's terms: he was considered a menace to the patients and a blemish on the proud profession of dentistry. His grandfather and father were famous dentists in his home country, but he was the black sheep and an embarrassment to his family. Would you like to allow him to improve his skills by practicing on you?"

Udi proudly said, "I have treated some of my patients with anesthesia and they didn't complain until it wore off. Many others simply got out of the chair and ran away. Aha, I see you are tied the chair and your head is held in a static position by this special headrest. So, you won't be going anywhere soon."

He turned off the drill while they waited for Ross's answer.

Ross groaned. "What do you want?" A wet stain was visible on the crotch of his expensive pants.

David said, "Well, Mr. Ross, you have two options. The easy one is to tell us all about the contract you had with Segan's firm in Berlin. Tell us who funded the operation, who supplied the information, what was the true objective of the people who financed it. The other option is to first serve as a dentist's practice dummy and then tell us what we want to know. I solemnly promise that a full confession will set you free unharmed. The choice is yours."

Ross, like most of humanity, didn't like dentists—not on a personal basis—he always claimed, "some of my best friends are dentists"—but as patient. When he was growing up in Iran his father had taken him to a dentist who was not very gentle, had outdated equipment, and drill heads that were worn out due to excessive use. Local anesthesia, like Novocain injections, were unavailable, and children were usually anesthetized with ether that knocked them completely out. When young Ali awoke, he didn't know what was worse—the headache he suffered from the ether or the pain in his jaw from the treatment.

The suave Alan Ross never forgot the painful treatment he received as young Ali Rashid and his worst nightmares revolved around dental treatment. So, his decision to avoid being drilled by the clumsy captor was an easy one. He said, "I'll cooperate but I need a guarantee that you'll keep your promise."

David said, "Your only guarantee is my word. Take it or leave it but you know the alternative, so I advise you to accept this."

He left the basement and a few moments later returned with a video camera, a tripod, and the newspaper that was published that day. Udi untied Ross and took him to a chair that was placed in front of a white bed sheet hung from one of the basement walls.

Ross asked for a glass of water and a couple of aspirins and after getting them, indicated that he was ready to begin.

Meanwhile, Udi asked David quietly, "How did you know that he had a fear of dentists?"

David answered, "You don't have to be a rocket-scientist, as the Americans are fond of saying, to know that many people have dental phobia. Nowadays a more appropriate term is used post-traumatic stress disorder caused by previous traumatic dental experiences. Regardless of the exact term, most people who grew up a few decades ago, or even today in areas where modern dental care is not available, shudder when they hear a dental drill near them. This guy, Alan Ross, grew up in rural Iran as Ali Rashid, so it stands to reason that he has developed dental phobia."

Udi was impressed and then David added, "While he was

still unconscious, I took a look at his teeth and saw that he had not been to the dentist in quite a long time—so from there on it was simple logic…"

***

David was pleased with the video recording. It contained two parts. In the first short part that was filmed with Ross facing the camera, he stated his name and his position in the Foreign Office as well as a few details about his childhood in Iran and his original name. In the second part, Ross was filmed as a dark silhouette on a bright background so he would not be recognized and he gave a full account of his meeting with Segan's organization, without giving his name, and of the actions that were taken to fulfill the contract.

Only after some prompting by David, who remained off camera and his voice was distorted, did he mention the opposition groups in Iran that provided him with operational information. It took some more prompting to get to admit that the funding for the whole operation was given by the Saudis. There were two points he refused to discuss, no matter how much "persuasion" was deployed—whether the action was approved by the Foreign Office and what were the final goals of the project.

David was not very happy with Ross's obstinacy regarding these points but reasoned that even without an explicit answer to these questions, the video was convincing. In his view, every analyst could figure out the second point and no one would be able to prove the involvement, if any, of the

British FCO.

He decided that he would show the second part at his up-coming meeting with the Imam at General Koliagin's office and use the first part only if he had to do so to convince them that it was not a just a bogus video. He considered getting Segan on video to confirm Ross's statement but knew that it was a formidable task, and in any case, it would be difficult to persuade skeptics that it was not another fabricated confession.

October 25, Tel Aviv

David returned to Tel Aviv with the two video clips. He had instructed Yehuda Tobias to release Alan Ross in the afternoon and to make sure that he wouldn't be able to locate the safe house or identify any of the Mossad agents that were involved in his kidnapping.

In fact, the only one Ross got a good look at was Mata and she was already on a plane back to Israel accompanied by David early in the morning. In any case, he doubted if Ross would report the incident to anyone.

He thought that Ross would have to go into hiding and disappear from sight because the Iranian intelligence services would surely place him at the top of their "most wanted" list as soon as they figured that he was behind the elimination of their nuclear scientists.

David wasn't sure what would happen to Segan once his own part in the operation became known. Probably, he reckoned, Segan would be out of business. David felt a little sorry for him—after all, he was a badly misguided patriot. He may have caused a lot of damage to Israel and directly to several Israeli individuals, but his deeds have certainly impacted the Iranian nuclear program and perhaps also the stability of the regime. He may have meant well but didn't consider the consequences.

One thing still troubled David—who was responsible for the murder of Sam and Ruby? He wasn't sure if the Iranians did it, or perhaps Segan or even Ross. At this point he was quite certain that Julia didn't do it, but a shred of doubt still lingered in the back of his mind. He decided that if he could spare the time, he would return to Berlin and try to discover the truth.

David entered Shimony's office and the old man rose from his chair and hugged him warmly. David said, "Here's the video. Ross admitted everything and confessed that he was the one who hired Segan's firm. However, he held back on two points. He refused to say whether the Foreign Office approved the contract and what the final goal of the operation was.

"I am under the impression that the FCO was in the dark and he worked for someone else on his own initiative and that the objective was to destabilize the Mullahs' regime. If the second part is correct then he was probably working, directly or indirectly, for the opposition factions in Iran. From his confession and Segan's disclosure, it looks as if the funding was by the Saudis. I believe that their failure to purchase a nuclear weapon from Pakistan prompted them to make sure that Iran did not possess a nuclear device.

"This coincides with our own policy and that of the rest of the civilized world and even of Russia and China who are not too happy to see a nuclear Iran on their doorstep. So, I think that it is in everybody's best interest to pretend that this never happened."

Shimony was impressed by David's analysis of the situation. "David, you did a great job. Now I have another mission for you. General Koliagin has invited you and the Imam to another meeting in Moscow. He indicated that the Iranians are more flexible—they are probably beginning to have their own doubts about our involvement in the operation against their scientists. You now have more evidence to prove the point. So, go there and do whatever you can to get them to release the hostages. You know the PM has a personal interest in this and has authorized you to act and make far reaching promises if necessary. The meeting is set for the day after tomorrow so try to rest a little and prepare for it."

CHAPTER 17

October 27, Moscow

The meeting in Moscow, hosted again by General Koliagin, started with a much friendlier atmosphere.

Imam Mourtashef even smiled when he entered the conference room and agreed to shake hands with David.

Koliagin looked at his two guests with inbred suspicion and wondered what was going on. The two dire enemies that had previously treated each other with evident animosity now behaved as if they were old friends. He said, "Honorable Imam Mourtashef and admirable Mr. Avivi I am glad to welcome you here once again. I am sure that reaching an agreement between your two countries would serve the interests of your governments as well as those of Russia and the region. I am not so sure that some dictatorial regimes, especially those that benefit from the conflict between your two countries would take a similar view. I can already see that you two have come here today ready to reconcile your differences."

The Imam nodded. "Yes, the democratic government of the Islamic Republic of Iran is ready to listen with an open mind to the representative of the Zionist Entity."

David expected some acerbic rhetoric of this kind and

showed no emotions when he said, "I tried to tell you at our last meeting that Mossad and the Israeli government were not involved in the elimination of the Iranian nuclear scientists. I now have a video testimony from the person who instigated the whole affair and a written testimony from the head of the firm that carried out the contract. I'll screen the former in a few minutes and, meanwhile, you can see copies of the testament I mentioned."

He gave each a document that was based on Segan's account of the contract that his firm received and carried out. It only provided scant details about each of the assassinations but there was no doubt that the essential elements were correct, and even some unpublished details attested to the authenticity of the testimony.

The Imam read it slowly and Koliagin could see that the mention of each scientist and the way he met his fate visibly shook the man. Koliagin himself just glanced at the document and noted, "David, this testimony is not signed. You could have concocted the whole thing."

David had expected this reaction and simply said, "I could have easily forged a signature to please you, but I believe that after seeing the video you will understand why no signature is needed."

The Imam looked up from the document and stated, "This looks convincing as far as the details of the murders of my people are concerned. But again, if Mossad sanctioned these murders then you would obviously know all the details. This document could have been written by anybody who ordered or carried out the heinous murders, not only by a renegade ex-Mossad operative as you claim. Let's see your video and then judge the authenticity of the document you presented as a testimony. I doubt if any court would accept it at face value."

David sighed inwardly, although appeared to be nonchalant. He asked the general's permission to screen the video and General Koliagin responded, "I am now really curious. Please go ahead."

David took hold of the remote controller and turned on the overhead projector. He inserted his thumb drive, manipulated the mouse, and clicked on the icon of his video. Nothing happened at first, so the Koliagin looked at the Imam and David and said, "I guess we have to reboot the computer, just as you both need to do so with the relations between your two countries."

David smiled at the witticism, but the Imam reverted to his poker face and didn't respond.

Finally, the video came on. David tried to read the expressions on the Imam's face and on the general's face. At the beginning, neither had shown any emotion but as Ross, actually his silhouette, continued with his narrative they appeared to be fascinated by the revelation of the contract.

The Imam kept wondering if Ross had a mole inside the IRG or the secret laboratory and feared that its secret existence was compromised. The general was more interested to find out who Ross was and to lay his hands on him and on Segan.

David figured that the body language of both men indicated their skepticism and cold detachment.

David asked them if they wanted to watch the video one

more time and both nodded. When it reached the end, David switched off the projector, and waited to hear their impressions.

General Koliagin spoke first, "Why did you hide the identity of the person in the video and the man who gave the testimony you showed us earlier? This makes your whole story less credible and raises the question if this is just a clever red herring."

The Imam nodded again to indicate that he agreed with Koliagin.

David turned the projector back on and said, "I was afraid that you would want more proof. So, I'll show you the first part of the video and hopefully this will convince you that Mossad was not behind the elimination of the scientists."

He screened the part where Alan Ross gave his name, his former name in Iran, and his position at the British Foreign and Commonwealth Office. David noticed that the body language of the Imam and the general changed and they were now in a receptive posture.

He figured they were now assured that Israel and Mossad had nothing to do with the contract.

The Imam said, "We had always known that the head of the Iranian desk at the FCO was a supporter of the opposition. Of course, we knew he was a former Iranian, but we had never suspected he would be actively mixed up in a dastardly attack on the democratically elected regime. I cannot but wonder if it was possible that his masters at the Foreign Office didn't know what he was up to. If there is any proof of government involvement, this would lead to a major crisis between the

UK and Iran."

The general was still interested in the identity of Segan. He said, "We've also come across this Alan Ross character but thought that he just another of the British civil servants that were self-appointed experts on Iran. I also question the behavior of his bosses at the FCO—is it possible that they knew nothing about his activities? I tend to believe you, and Ross's statement, that Segan's firm operated on purely capitalistic grounds without any moralistic guidelines. I believe that Mossad condones his participation in the contract. I only don't understand why he is still alive after all the trouble he caused."

David looked directly at the Imam and said, "I hope you are convinced that Israel had nothing to do with the deaths of your scientists. We now need to negotiate the release of the hostages you are holding in your prison."

The Imam made a show of deliberating the issue. He said, "I now believe that the Zionist Entity had nothing to do with the murder of our scientists, but there are many other reasons for regarding you as our enemies. Your Prime Minister keeps threatening us that your air force will attack us, he keeps calling us liars, and claims that we are deceiving the world and not following our obligations under the nuclear deal. He keeps trying to turn the American administration and congress against us. He keeps blaming us for supporting terrorists in the Middle East and elsewhere. He keeps inciting the Europeans against buying our oil and trading with us. Why should we be concerned about the fate of a dozen Israelis?"

General Koliagin wanted to make some progress, so he

said, "Honorable Imam, why don't you start negotiations with the Israelis? Your country is ten time bigger than theirs. What are you afraid of?"

The Imam responded, "If the Zionist Entity will stop meddling in our internal affairs and publicly admit it was a former Mossad agent responsible for the murder of our scientists, we would be willing to release one hostage as a gesture of goodwill, and then continue to negotiate."

Koliagin was pleased with this declaration while David suspected that the Iranian had some ulterior motives. He cautiously asked, "Which one will you release first and what more do you want?"

The Imam pretended that he didn't hear the second part of the question and said, "We'll select one of the hostages—probably one with medical problems—and send that person in a private jet directly to Tel Aviv. You will publicly commend the humanitarian behavior of the Islamic Republic of Iran and hold a press conference parading the hostage and praising our regime."

David agreed and left the room after thanking General Koliagin for his hospitality. All three were satisfied with the outcome of the meeting, but the Imam was the happiest. After all, his scheme had made one more step towards completion.

October 28, Moscow, Tel Aviv and Tehran

Three press conferences were held simultaneously in Moscow, Tel Aviv, and Tehran.

In Moscow, General Koliagin announced that an

agreement was reached between the Islamic Republic of Iran and the State of Israel on the release of an Israeli hostage that was held in Evin Prison.

He emphasized it was a gesture of goodwill by the Iranians. The international press that was summoned to the general's office was caught off guard.

They thought the press conference would be another boring propaganda opportunity about Russia's policy in Middle East and that the general would express his country's continuous yearning for world peace. After the announcement, the general's press secretary said that he would take a few questions.

The correspondent for the official Russian television network asked, "Does this mean that there were direct negotiations between Iran and Israel?"

The general replied, "I have personally hosted two unofficial meetings between representatives of both countries. At the first meeting, both sides were suspicious of one another but at the next meeting their attitude had changed, and they demonstrated some flexibility. This does not mean that Iran and Israel are about to resume diplomatic relations, but it is a small step in that direction."

The next question came from CNN. "General Koliagin, can you give more specific details about the negotiations. What exactly did the two sides agree to do?"

The general expected that question. "Naturally, I cannot give the details of the meetings. But the two press conferences that are held at this very moment in Tehran and Tel Aviv will elaborate what each side gave and what it received. Next question."

The CNN correspondent insisted and said, "A follow-up question, general. Why would the Iranians make such a gesture of goodwill? They had publicly and persistently blamed the Israelis for murdering their scientists. What changed their attitude?"

The general was becoming impatient. "This is the last question and my answer is the same. Each side will explain what it received and what it had given at the press conferences that are held at this very moment in Tehran and Tel Aviv. Thank you all for coming here."

***

Imam Mourtashef stood in front of the raised podium in the press room at the Majlis and waited for the small gathering of reporters from the electronic and printed media to focus on him.

He said, "I am glad to announce that the representative of the Zionist Entity acknowledged its indirect responsibility for attacking our brave nuclear scientists. The Supreme Leader and the Council have accepted their apology that these heinous acts were carried out by a former agent of Mossad. As a gesture of our goodwill we have agreed to release two of the secret agents being held as our prisoners. Thank you all for attending."

There were no questions in line with the usual practice in these events. After the press conference, the Imam went straight to Evin Prison. First, he went to laboratory in

Basement S to oversee the activities there. Dr. Fathi was surprised to see him again, just a week after his previous visit.

The Imam went directly to the "hot cell," where he had seen the metallic sphere on his last visit and was disappointed to see that it was in the same position. He looked at Fathi and raised his bushy eyebrows with an unspoken question.

Fathi said, "Honorable Imam, as I told you on your last visit, the core of the nuclear device, the fissile material, is ready. We are now working on the implosion mechanism that includes the conventional explosive that will compress the core to a supercritical mass and the triggering system that will provide the simultaneous and perfectly symmetrical detonation. In addition, we are working on the packaging of the device to ensure it is shielded from external electromagnetic radiation and it withstands the perils involved in its transportation. These things require careful testing to ensure the device works as planned and they cannot be rushed. Before you go, I would like to show you the chemicals from which we have produced the metallic sphere."

Fathi led the Imam to a nearby chemical hood, in which a sealed plastic vessel with a green powder could be seen. He lifted it and said, "This is what is called "green salt" for reasons that are obvious. From this, we produce the fissile metal—plutonium or enriched uranium—from which the sphere you saw there is composed."

As he pointed at the "hot cell" where the sphere was on display, the plastic vessel slipped from his grasp and some very fine green powder escaped. Fathi immediately summoned two of his lab assistants and told the Imam to stand still.

The two men quickly donned protective clothing that included a coverall suit, hoods, gloves, boots, and paraphernalia needed for decontamination. One of them rushed the Imam and Fathi to a shower, while the other one started collecting the precious green powder from the floor.

Fathi kept apologizing until the Imam cut him short and told him to keep quiet. Meanwhile, the lab assistant used a radiation detector to examine them and their clothes and with great relief assured them they were at no risk.

The Imam left the laboratory swearing that Dr. Fathi had crossed the line this time and was determined to punish him immediately after the nuclear device was ready. He made his way to the cell where the Israeli hostages were held.

As he approached "Fatso" stood up and came to attention. The Imam signaled for him to open the cell door. The prisoners were lined up against the wall facing away from the door.

The Imam spoke softly, "Please turn around and look at me. I have some great news for you. We have started negotiations with the Zionist Entity where you all come from and have agreed to release one of you immediately as a gesture of goodwill and good faith. The rest of you will also be released pending the progress of the talks."

He had to stop talking until the excited buzz in the cell ceased. He continued, "I have elected you." He pointed at Vicki Aladgem, but before he could say another word she cried out in Hebrew, "I'll not leave without my husband." The Imam didn't need a translator to understand what was going on.

Morris hugged his wife and whispered something in her

ear. She shook her head and clung to him. He tried to console her, but she would not listen. Zorik saw what was going on and understood that the Aladgems would not be separated without the use of force.

He intervened, "Honorable Imam, I think that after so many years of marriage they cannot bear to be separated. Could you please choose someone else, or better yet, release the two of them together?"

The Imam instinctive reaction was to forcefully remove Vicki from her husband, but then thought about Zorik's suggestion for another moment. He realized that the buzz in the world press that would be created by an even more extensive show of generosity would greatly serve his grand plan. He said, "I am touched by the faithfulness of this old couple. I'll release the two of them, as you proposed, Zorik, but they will have to publicly praise our compassionate treatment of our hostages."

Zorik explained to the Aladgems in Hebrew that they should acknowledge the Imam's generosity. Both got down on their knees and hugged the Imam's feet. Vicki even took off her scarf and dusted the Imam's shoes to remove some tiny green specks that she saw.

The Imam looked down and motioned for them to rise. He told them to pack their meager belongings and follow him out of the cell. The suddenness of the change of the fate of Morris and Vicki affected all the hostages.

Except for Zorik, there was not a dry eye in the prison cell. Even "Fatso" appeared to be moved by the raw emotions. After all, the Aladgems were at his mercy for about two months and he got to know them a little and was impressed by their mutual care and devotion.

The Imam left the prison with the two hostages and made the necessary arrangements to have them taken to the airfield where the private jet was waiting. The Iranian markings were covered temporarily by a sheet of silver paint. The pilot had already filed a flight plan that would take him from Tehran to Tel Aviv—a route that wasn't in use since Khomeini's 1979 Islamic revolution.

The flight plan was cleared by the air controllers in Turkey and had to circumvent the unsafe airspace of Iraq, Syria, and Lebanon. Morris and Vicki were seated in the back of the plane. No shackles or even plastic ties were needed this time. After take-off, a male steward offered them tea and pastries, but they were too excited and just shook their heads.

**

The press conference in Tel Aviv was held at Ben-Gurion airport. The walls of the press room in Terminal 3 had witnessed many press conferences, mainly with officials and dignitaries, but there had never been such an emotional level of expectations. The old terminal had seen Israeli soldiers being returned from captivity in Egypt and Syria after the 1973 Yom Kippur War and of some live hostages and several dead bodies, but that terminal was now almost deserted.

The Minister of Defense hosted the press conference with Shimony as Mossad Head at his side, while David stood in the wings and out of sight. The Minister of Defense opened by saying that the Prime Minister had some prior obligation and could not attend the conference.

A few of the participants knew that the PM's granddaughter was one of the hostages who were still being incarcerated in Evin Prison. Obviously had she been on the plane then no prior obligation in the world would have kept him away.

The Defense Minister continued by reading a formal statement. "The State of Israel gratefully acknowledges the humanitarian gesture of the Islamic Republic of Iran. This could be the beginning of a new phase in the relations between our two countries. We have managed to convince the Iranians that Israel and Mossad had no hand in the tragic fate that befell some of their leading nuclear scientists. Israel apologizes and regretfully acknowledges that these deeds were carried out by a firm located in Berlin that was founded and headed by a former Israeli civil servant in the Prime Minister's office."

He stopped speaking as his adjutant entered the room and handed him a piece of paper. The Minister read the message and a broad smile crossed his face. He said, "I have just been notified that the Iranians have released not one but two of the prisoners—Vicki and Morris Aladgem. They are now well on their way to this airport and we expect their plane to land here shortly."

A spontaneous round of applause broke out and one of the reporters raised his hand and asked, "Will we be able to interview them?"

The Minister gestured to Shimony to answer and he said, "You will be able to see them for a moment but then we will have to take them to have a physical examination and debrief them. In a day or two they will hold a press conference together with the Prime Minister in Jerusalem."

Several more hands were raised, and questions were asked and answered. Most questions focused on the sudden change in the policy of Israel toward Iran and vice versa.

The Minister of Defense summarized. "Israel will no longer threaten the Iranian regime and will not interfere with the ties that it is building with the West and the U.S. after the nuclear deal. Iran has reaffirmed its obligation to refrain from any military nuclear program but insists that it has the right to continue developing its peaceful nuclear infrastructure. Hopefully, the rest of the hostages will be released soon, and the good relations Israel had with Iran will be restored. Thank you, ladies and gentlemen. You'll hear more from the released hostages tomorrow evening or the day after."

October 28, Ben Gurion Airport, Tel Aviv

The unmarked private jet landed at Ben Gurion airport, near Tel Aviv. The control tower directed the Iranian pilot to a large hangar at the edge of the airfield. Before the passengers, in this case the released hostages, were allowed to disembark, four soldiers from the elite unit of the Israeli police approached the plane. Two other soldiers equipped with anti-tank missiles were out of sight from the cockpit but had their weapons trained on the plane. Once the pilot had turned off the engines the hangar was very quiet.

The Israeli officer connected a microphone and earphones to the slot in the plane's fuselage and told the pilot to open the doors slowly. A male steward stood at the door with his bare hands clearly in sight, held away from his body. He let down the staircase and moved aside.

Morris and Vicki now appeared at the door and started to descend the stairs. One of the soldiers led them away, while the officer with the microphone politely asked the pilot's permission to come aboard. Once the permission was granted, two soldiers climbed up the stairs and entered the cabin. The crew consisted of the pilot and co-pilot and two male stewards. They were all smiling at the soldiers.

The officer asked permission to search the plane and it was readily given by the smiling pilot, who in excellent English said, "You are welcome to search the plane but I assure you everything is above board, what you say Kosher."

The soldiers didn't respond and carried out a thorough search of the cabin. In the storage compartment they found a big box that looked like an old-fashioned trunk, favored by rich passengers who went on long steamship cruises a century earlier. The officer motioned to one of the stewards to open the trunk, and after the pilot authorized the request, the steward opened it.

The two Israeli soldiers pointed their weapons at the trunk, prepared for any unpleasant surprise. Indeed, they were surprised to see three expensive looking fine Persian silk rugs. The pilot said, "These are gifts from Imam Mourtashef to your Prime Minister, Minister of Defense, and Mr. David Avivi." He signaled to one of the stewards to take them out of the box and down the stairs.

The Israeli officer sensed the convivial ambience and

asked the pilot if he needed anything. The pilot pointed at the fully stocked kitchenette and thanked the officer for his offer. He said they needed to refuel the jet and the Israeli officer laughed and said, "Imagine that Iran is buying oil from us."

After a couple of minutes, permission was received, and the Iranian jet taxied to the refueling pump following the directions from the control tower. Twenty minutes later it was airborne on its way back to Tehran.

***

In the hangar, there was a small reception committee that included a representative from the Prime Minister's office, another one from the Ministry of Defense, and David Avivi from Mossad. Also present were the children and grandchildren of Morris and Vicki Aladgem, a psychiatrist, and a senior physician from the nearby medical center.

There was only one TV crew from the office of the Israeli Defense Forces spokesman. The edited video would be distributed to all the local and foreign news agencies. After being formally welcomed by the official representatives the excited freed hostages were given fifteen minutes to meet with their family.

They were then were escorted to a small office where they received a thorough medical examination. The psychiatrist was impressed that they were as sane as could be expected after the ordeal of their kidnapping in Turkey and two months in Evin Prison.

The couple were seated on a sofa and drinking tea when

David entered the small office and introduced himself. "I understand that your treatment in the prison was reasonable."

Morris replied, "We, and the rest of the prisoners, were not tortured or harassed. There was one jailor, who at times intimidated us, but overall even he treated us well. We are especially grateful to Imam Mourtashef for choosing us to be sent home. We were so happy when he agreed to send me with Vicki that we kissed his feet." David told them that he had met with the Imam twice and played a modest part in their release.

Vicki was excited to hear this. She said, "I even cleaned his shoes with my scarf. I saw that he had dirtied them with some very fine green powder."

David pricked his ears. As a physicist with some knowledge about nuclear materials, he knew that there were many types of green powders, but there was one type that held a special interest for him.

He asked Vicki if he could have the scarf and she willingly obliged and removed it from her neck and handed it to him. David took a close look and he could see the traces of the powder that she talked about. He then asked, "What is the situation with the other prisoners?"

Morris gave a detailed account about each of his former cell-mates. He said, "There is this young guy, Zorik, who has spoken up for us when it was necessary. He and his girlfriend, Inbal, managed to boost our morale and keep our sanity. I was greatly surprised when he asked for Islamic religious tutoring, but this brought us in touch with the Imam and he made sure that we were not ill-treated. Johnny, the Member of Knesset, was a big disappointed to us."

David told them they would be taken to a five-star hotel in Jerusalem, where they will be guests of the government for a few days until their detailed debriefing ended. They would be allowed to see their family for a couple of hours every afternoon. He informed them that the PM has invited them for dinner and that they would attend a press conference with the PM after dinner.

The date was set two days hence, allowing the Aladgems a little more time to get used to life as free people. Vicki and Morris thanked David for his help in arranging their release and for speaking to them so gently. David shyly shrugged and said that Israel was proud to have senior citizens like the two of them.

***

Meanwhile, the IDF spokesman spread the silk rugs on the floor and the TV crew cameraman was glad to take photos of the beautiful items. The spokesman told the good-looking blonde TV reporter that the rugs were gifts to the Prime Minister, Minister of Defense, and to the senior Mossad agent, who negotiated the deal. She said she wished she had been given such tasteful and precious gifts. This was interrupted by a senior agent from the Israel Security Agency that said the rugs would have to be screened for toxic chemicals, biological agents, and explosive in case they were booby trapped.

The reporter mumbled something about a Trojan horse but then said she had enough footage of the gifts.

***

David placed the scarf in a plastic bag and immediately called one of his colleagues at the Israel Atomic Energy Commission and told him about the fine green powder on the scarf.

Professor Eli Halevy, the chief scientist of the IAEC, told David he would meet him at his laboratory at the Soreq Nuclear Research Center in thirty minutes. When David arrived there, Eli was waiting for him in the nuclear spectroscopy laboratory near the most sensitive detection system.

David handed him the scarf and pointed to the region where the largest amount of green powder was visible. The professor looked at the dust with a large magnifying glass and hummed something unintelligible. He then took a small piece of two-sided adhesive tape and picked up some fine grains and placed the tape under a microscope equipped with a powerful camera, humming some more as he looked at it.

David could see the image of the powder particles on the computer screen. The professor then took the tape and placed it in one of the detectors and the audible clicking indicated the presence of traces of a nuclear material. David instantly understood the significance of what he had seen and heard.

He thanked Eli and said he would get the material fully characterized. When the professor asked where exactly David said that he would send a sample to the most advanced laboratory in Germany. The professor approved the idea and agreed they had diagnostic and analytical capabilities that were beyond those he had access to.

October 28, Tehran Airport

Imam Mourtashef received the report that the jet was on its way back from Tel Aviv to Tehran and everything went as planned. He decided to personally meet the pilot and debrief him. He arrived at Tehran airport just as the plane was landing and waited impatiently for the pilot.

The pilot was not surprised to see the Imam—after all the Imam had personally given him clear instructions. The pilot said, "Honorable Imam, the Israelis behaved exactly as you had predicted. They were very suspicious at first and made me taxi to a side hangar and then a few soldiers surrounded the plane. After I released the hostages they boarded it and searched it. When they saw the big trunk, they became apprehensive and aggressive. When it was opened, they pointed their guns at it and when the Persian silk rugs were taken out and displayed, they didn't know what to do with themselves. Their officer had a sense of humor because when I requested fuel he laughed and said that this is the first time Iran needs to buy oil from Israel."

The Imam said, "Yes, they are misguided Zionists but even I have to admit they are intelligent. Do you know if the rugs were delivered to their intended recipients?"

The pilot replied, "I never got off the plane, so I don't know where the rugs were taken. I must say they were very polite, even friendly after their initial suspicion was allayed."

The Imam thanked the pilot and said, "You did a good job. On the next trip you'll have many more hostages and I expect that the Zionist leadership will show up in force to welcome them. After all, this is an excellent photo-opportunity and their PM never misses a chance to appear as if he really cares for his subjects. I bid you good night and I'll make sure that you receive praise and promotion for a job well done."

CHAPTER 18

October 29, Germany

David placed the scarf in a plastic bag and made sure that it would be in his carry-on luggage when he returned to Berlin the next day.

He had to solve two problems during this visit to Germany. One was mostly personal, there were some aspects that concerned Mossad—to discover who murdered Ruby and Sam.

Although they were fired from Mossad, they had remained members of a select group of excellent field operators who had done a lot for their country. If Segan was responsible for their deaths, he would have to be dealt with and held accountable for his treachery.

If Ross or his sponsors did it, they would have to pay him another visit and make sure he stayed alive just long enough to regret the deed. If it was done by the Iranians, then it would be considered as if they had taken revenge for the elimination of their scientists and that account would be considered as settled.

Julia was the one suspect that bothered David the most. If she had murdered Sam and Ruby, then either she was "turned" and working for some foreign country, or, and

David considered this option as more despicable, someone high up in Mossad had sanctioned the killings. He just had to discover the truth, or the question would haunt him.

His second problem was purely scientific, or more correctly solving a forensic mystery. What did the scarf with the green specks contain? To get an answer he had to travel to Karlsruhe and hand the scarf over to his colleague at the Institute for Trans Uranium elements that was part of the European Joint Research Centers (ITU-JRC).

As its website proclaimed, the role of the ITU was to "provide the scientific foundation for the protection of European citizens against risks associated with the handling and storage of highly radioactive material."

There were several daily flights from Berlin to Karlsruhe that took just under an hour and half. David reckoned that if he took a morning flight, he could have the sample analyzed and return to Berlin in the same evening.

When he landed at Karlsruhe he was met by his friend, Dr. Kurt Myerson, who was in charge of the analytical department that specialized in nuclear forensics. On the way from the airport to the laboratory, David explained the scarf was given to him by one of the prisoners released from Evin Prison in Tehran. Kurt, of course, had seen the press conference and knew the story of the hostages.

The highly skilled scientists and technicians at the nuclear forensics laboratory immediately identified the green specks as a common uranium containing compound. When further analytical characterization was completed it was evident that the uranium was highly enriched meaning that it was suitable for construction of a nuclear weapon. The technicians had another surprise when they detected some minor traces of plutonium—another material that could be used in a nuclear device.

The implications of the analytical results were nothing less than colossal. The presence of nuclear materials in an unlikely site like Evin Prison indicated that the Iranians were violating the nuclear deal they had signed. Furthermore, the existence of these materials in the center of Tehran showed that the Mullahs' regime had no regard for the risk to millions of their own people in the country's largest and most densely populated city.

David wondered what they intended to do with a nuclear device and by putting two and two together, he surmised that the only possible explanation was they plotted to detonate it in Tel Aviv. He thanked Kurt for his help and hurried to catch his flight back to Berlin.

Although he wished that Kurt wouldn't reveal the results and their obvious implications, he knew that even before he set foot on the plane the German government would hear the earth-shattering news. Possibly the information would be shared with all the friendly intelligence services, especially NATO members and the Americans.

***

By the time David's plane landed in Berlin, a mere two hours after he had left Kurt and the laboratory, the secure lines between Berlin and the rest of the Western world were close to collapsing from intensive use.

The commotion was unprecedented: cabinet ministers in a dozen countries were recalled for urgent secret meetings with the chiefs of their intelligence services. Experts on international affairs were summoned to deliver their opinion on the implications. Scientists were consulted, advice was sought from political analysts, and top military authorities were requested to develop operational scenarios.

Politicians of all kinds waited for the news to become public so they could gain some credit, or at least get some time in the media. However, all governments, without exception, swore their members and consultants to secrecy with the threat of prosecution for high treason if a word leaked out. Surprisingly not a word did leak and even the most well-connected journalists and reporters didn't catch on.

***

David decided to cut short his stay in Berlin and return to Israel. However, due to the late hour, the next scheduled flight from Berlin to Tel Aviv was due only in the morning.

Julia met him at the gate and took him straight to her apartment. She had already received word from Mossad headquarters that David had discovered some troubling news about Iran and wanted to know more about it. David was reluctant to share all the details and just said, "There are strong indications that the Iranians had deliberately and blatantly violated the nuclear deal that they had signed. There is some evidence they had been working with fissile materials in a clandestine laboratory in the heart of Tehran."

Julia wanted to get more specific information. "Does this mean that they are trying to build an atomic weapon?"

David replied, "There is not much use for fissile materials of this type for other applications. Yes, we fear they are up to something that goes way beyond conventional warfare."

Julia then hit the nail on the head and said, "Is all this connected to the elimination of the Iranian nuclear scientists that Segan's firm had carried out?"

David hummed. "Possibly, but we have no evidence." He then added, "I wonder if this is related to the murder of Sam and Ruby. Is it likely that they had found out something from the scientists they eliminated?"

Julia said, "I guess we'll have to find Segan and ask him if they said anything about this, but I don't think that they had any type of discussion with their victims."

David said, "I have to return to Israel on the first flight in the morning. Could you try to question Segan with your local people?"

Julia nodded and pulled David to the bedroom. "Let's make the most of the couple of hours you have before going to the airport."

She drove David to the airport, and he boarded his flight. He fell asleep even before the wheels of the plane left the ground. This time he wasn't bothered by the captain's announcement or the cabin attendants' antics—he was much too tired. He woke up just as the plane landed after a dreamless sleep.

268 | CHARLIE WOLFE

October 30, The PM's office, Jerusalem

The Prime Minister of Israel was a great orator and considered as one of the world champions in manipulative public relations. His entrance was announced by the press secretary and he approached the podium with a brisk stride, took a long moment to look at the representatives of the mass media that filled the press-room.

He was pleased to see that all the seats were taken, and more reporters lined up along the walls of the room. He was especially glad to see that behind the last row of chairs, a large bank of TV cameras that represented all the major networks were focused on him. He looked down at the prompter and decided to ignore the statement that had been prepared in advance.

After welcoming the reporters and thanking them for attending he said, "I would like to commend the humanitarian behavior of the Islamic Republic of Iran and its gesture of goodwill. I call upon Vicki and Morris Aladgem to come and stand by my side."

The elderly couple rose from their seats in the front row and stood on both sides of the PM. He continued, "They will answer your questions after my short speech. You all know that ever since the Islamic revolution in Iran that took place in 1979, the relations between Israel and Iran were not good."

Some of the reporters appreciated the gross understatement and barely managed to refrain from laughing. "We were strongly opposed to the nuclear deal between Iran and the Six Powers and to the subsequent lifting of the economic and trade sanctions that were imposed on Iran. But once the deal was signed by all parties and Iran was reinstated as a regular member of the international community, we toned down our opposition. We were glad to see the results of the 2016 election in Iran that indicated things were beginning to change—the ultra-conservative faction in Iran lost some of its power to more moderate representatives of the people."

A round of applause interrupted his speech. The PM paused dramatically, made sure that all eyes and ears were focused on him, and said, "The nuclear deal includes several clauses that impose much closer supervision of the declared nuclear sites and the right to carry out inspections at any suspicious site. In case a violation is found, the economic and trade sanctions may be put back in place, and even more severe measures may be taken if the infringement is considered as a major or gross violation."

The audience fell silent, expecting the PM to announce that something was afoot, but he stepped back from the podium and indicated that Vicki and Morris should take his place.

The senior reporter for Israeli television Channel 12 raised his hand and shouted, "Mr. Prime Minister, will you take some questions, please." The PM ignored him, and the press secretary intervened, "Please direct your questions to Morris and Vicki." And gave the floor to the reporter from Israel's official Channel 11. "Mr. Aladgem, can you tell us how you were captured?"

Morris was a bit uncomfortable by the unaccustomed attention he received. "I have been persuaded by a major publisher to write a book about that and what happened in the prison, so I'll be brief. My wife, Vicki, and I took a hot air balloon flight in Turkey. When we landed, we were taken as prisoners by a group of armed men that threw us into a van and drove across Turkey to Iran. We were placed in Evin Prison and locked up in a large cell with a few other Israelis. I must say that we were treated well from the moment we were captured, until our surprising release a couple of days ago. I wish to thank Imam Mourtashef for allowing me to join my wife or else I wouldn't be here today."

He looked at Vicki and hugged her as she started shedding tears.

A reporter from Channel 13 raised her hand and said, "Vicki, could you tell us about the other hostages?"

Vicki took the microphone. "I can only tell you that they are all well. We were advised not to go into any personal details."

The reporter was disappointed but didn't pursue the matter. She realized that there were probably some sensitive issues involved. She recalled the case of the Air France flight to Paris that was diverted to Uganda by a mixed group of German and Palestinian terrorists in 1976. Among the captives were a man and a woman who had deceived their spouses and connived to travel together to the city of lights. The embarrassment that followed their release superseded the relief of their spouses when they returned home.

The press secretary took the podium. "Morris and Vicki are still recovering from their ordeal. Please respect their privacy."

October 30, Office of the Senior Assistant, Tehran

The television set in the office of the Senior Assistant was turned on to the France-24 channel in English that covered the press conference in Jerusalem. The Senior Assistant and Imam Mourtashef had taken seats on the sofa facing the TV set, while General Aslawi paced to and fro while keeping an eye on the TV.

After hearing the Israeli PM praise the humanitarian gesture, they all smiled, but when he continued his speech they began to feel uncomfortable. They weren't sure if his warning about violation of the nuclear deal was just a continuation of his attempts to intimidate Iran or if he suspected specific foul play. In the back of their minds they worried if he somehow got word about the clandestine laboratory.

The Imam was the first to express this particular concern. "Could the Israelis know something about our plans?"

The general was getting worked up. "Only if there is a traitor among us. I never really trusted the scientists. They may have inadvertently said something, or even worse, are working for a foreign power. I'll have every one of them interrogated."

The Imam held up his hand. "Don't you dare touch them before the device is delivered to my hands. Each one of them is vital for the success of our grand plan. After that, you take them all, parade them through the streets of Tehran and hang them in Meydan a Azadi."

The Senior Assistant just nodded and after some thought said, "Do you think we should continue with our grand plan or abort it?"

Imam said, "If you remember, our original plan was to give them a Hanukkah gift that they will never forget. I checked their calendar and discovered that this year the holiday is particularly early—on 29th of November. This also coincides with the very same date that the United Nations plan for the partition of Palestine was approved. This date is celebrated by the Zionist Entity and mourned by the Arabs. Yes, this would have been ideal, but in view of what's going on we need to implement our plan sooner."

General Aslawi had cooled down a little and said, "What do we have to lose? If IAEA inspectors discover the laboratory, the world will treat us as cheaters and impose the old sanctions on us, anyway. But if we demonstrate our ability to build nuclear weapons and our determination to use them, then we'll be treated like North Korea or Pakistan and no one will dare mess with us. I say—let's go ahead as if nothing has happened."

The Imam wasn't so sure this was the optimal course of action. He said, "I understand the general's point of view, but I believe that we can close down the laboratory, clean it thoroughly. Perhaps we can even fill it with concrete, so even the most accomplished inspectors will find no trace of any nuclear material. Then, general, you can interrogate the scientists and hang them one hundred and fifty feet above ground from Azadi tower, if you wish."

The Senior Assistant said, "I will bring this matter to the Supreme Leader and we shall obey his decision, as always. This may take some time because he will probably wait for some divine guidance. I'll call you back when I hear his verdict."

***

The Imam went directly to Evin Prison. First, he stopped by the cell in which the Israeli hostages were held. He went through the usual routine with Fatso accompanying him. He called the prisoners to turn around and face him and then informed them that Morris and Vicki Aladgem had held a press conference with the Prime Minister.

He only told them about the first part of the PM's speech and the praise the Islamic Republic of Iran had received from the PM himself and from the freed hostages. Zorik was the first to speak, as usual, "Honorable Imam, when will we all be released?"

The Imam looked at them and answered noncommittally, "Soon, Inshallah, with the will of Allah you will all be safe and sound in your country."

Zorik thought it would not be a good idea to pursue the matter and said, "We all wish to thank you once again for letting Morris go with Vicki. We really appreciate this gesture."

The Imam smiled and left that part of the prison and made his way to Basement S. His unannounced visit found the entire staff of the clandestine laboratory in the small conference room, apparently engaged in some technical discussion.

Dr. Fathi was standing at the white drawing board with a red marker in his hand and busy writing down some complicated equation. The Imam identified the black circle that was surrounded by a series of pie-shaped segments that were drawn with a blue marker as the core of the nuclear device and the segments as depicting the explosives used to compress the metallic core. Fathi had completed writing the equation and then added a small red pin-shaped line in the center of each blue segment. When he saw the Imam at the door, he stopped mid-sentence.

The other members of the laboratory staff turned their heads and saw the Imam, and all instinctively stood up as sign of respect. The Imam took a seat and motioned for Fathi to continue with his presentation. Fathi addressed the Imam and explained that the red pin-shaped lines represented the detonators that had to be programmed to explode simultaneously. The Imam nodded and then asked Fathi to conclude his presentation as he needed to discuss something with him in private.

After everyone else left the room, the Imam said, "Dr. Fathi, we are running out of time and have to move ahead quickly. When can you have the device ready and packaged?"

Fathi replied, "We need more time for testing it and verifying its ruggedness. In principle, it can be available for delivery tomorrow but then I cannot guarantee that it won't suffer some damage during transportation."

The Imam considered this and said, "Can you quantify the probability of malfunction?"

Fathi said, "Honorable Imam, as you understand we have never manufactured a nuclear device in this country, and certainly never had the opportunity to do real testing. I cannot give you a solid, verifiable probability. All is in the hands of Allah."

The Imam didn't need a religious sermon from Dr. Fathi. He grimaced at the mention of Allah in this context and walked out of the room, saying, "Dr. Fathi, be prepared to deliver the device as soon as I give the order."

CHAPTER 19

October 30, PM's Office, Jerusalem

As soon as the Prime Minister left the press room he returned to his office. Shimony, David, the Head of the Israeli Atomic Energy Commission (IAEC), as well as the Minister of Defense, Chief of Staff of the IDF, and the Commander of the Air Force (CAF) were already seated around the table in the PM's conference room.

The PM said, "Well, gentlemen, I hope the Iranians got the message. How can we bring their military nuclear program to a standstill? How can we deter them from ever again trying to build a bomb? How serious is the threat?"

Shimony looked at David and gave him a sign to speak. David said, "The green specks that were on Vicki's scarf were identified unequivocally as traces on high enriched uranium. This is the stuff the Iranians were working on clandestinely prior to the implementation of the nuclear deal.

"As far as the IAEA could verify, all the enriched uranium, except a few hundred pounds of low enriched uranium that is unsuitable for nuclear weapons, was removed from Iran. They may have managed to secretly accumulate, or acquire from foreign sources, some weapon grade uranium. The traces found on the scarf are really the first proof of that. The fact that they were collected from the shoes of Imam Mourtashef in Evin Prison probably means that they have a clandestine laboratory there.

"The nuclear forensics laboratory in Germany also found very minute traces of plutonium. As far as we know this must have come from a source outside Iran. These facts point to a gross violation of the nuclear deal and pose a clear and present danger to us if they manage to construct a nuclear bomb."

The Chief of Staff of the IDF asked, "Do we know how advanced they are?"

The PM looked around the room and when he saw that no one volunteered to answer, he addressed Shimony, "Haim, I expect this to be your top priority, although I believe that you have already designated it as such. If they make such a bomb how can they deliver it?"

The Commander of the Israeli Air Force stated, "We have a three-tiered defensive system that enables us to intercept and destroy long-range missiles, medium-range missiles, and tactical rockets as well as short-range rockets. Our defense against aircraft consists of ground-based anti-aircraft missiles, and airborne fighter-jets with the best pilots in the world."

It was commonly accepted by the Israeli public, after five decades of persistent promotion and PR, that their pilots were indeed the best in the world. In fact, Israeli pilots shot down Spitfires flown by British pilots in 1948, British made Hunters flown by Jordanian pilots, Russian made Migs, Sukhois, and a few other planes flown by Egyptian, Iraqi, Syrian, and Russian pilots in the various wars since 1948. Even some Libyan pilots who dared challenge the Israeli air force were "splashed" in 1973.

Shimony allowed everyone to bask in the glory of the Israeli Air Force for a minute or two before saying, "I agree with the Air Force Commander, but I fear that there are other routes through which a nuclear device or bomb can be smuggled into Israel. I am sure that you all remember two such cases from our recent history. They became famous through the not entirely fictional novels of *Mission Alchemist* and *Mission Renegade.*

"I think the Iranians know they have no chance of penetrating our air space in an overt act of war. So, they will try to devise other, less direct ways, by sea, land or air."

This statement gave all the participants of the high-level meeting food for thought.

The PM then directed a question at the Head of the IAEC. "Can you give us an estimate of the power of such a device, if it exists, and assessment of the damage it may cause?"

The Head of the IAEC replied, "With regard to the second question the answer is quite bleak—a nuclear bomb in the Tel Aviv area would devastate the country. Even if the number of immediate casualties is like that from the primitive atomic bombs deployed in the World War, namely on the order of one hundred thousand, the subsequent loss of life would be at least double, considering the population density. The economic consequences are unimaginable as this is the center of commerce and industry.

"I believe that the country would survive but life as we

know it would change dramatically. Your first question, Mr. Prime Minister can perhaps better be answered by Mossad. I can only assume that it would be at least as powerful as the Hiroshima bomb."

Everyone grew quiet, although they had heard these estimates many times before and they were common knowledge, even if not consciously acknowledged by every semi-intelligent citizen of Israel.

The PM realized that a dark mood descended on the conference room. He banged his left hand on the table to get everyone's attention and draw them out of their daydreams or nightmares. He said, "Gentlemen, we have to prevent this from happening with all means at our command. With the physical evidence that David got us, we can try to convince our allies that a preemptive strike is inevitable. Preferably by a combined alliance of all countries that are threatened by a nuclear Iran. I mean not only the Western powers but to enlist the moderate Sunni countries, even the Russians who are not too glad to see another nuclear armed regional power on their doorstep. They may need some prompting and we, too, can use non-diplomatic measures to convince them that stopping Iran now is in their best interests."

As the meeting was coming to its conclusion, the PM summarized, "Shimony, get more information on the clandestine laboratory, its exact location, personnel and status. Use whatever means you see fit. Focus on the delivery methodology—so we can stop it before it reaches our shores. Air Force Commander, make sure your anti-missile and anti-aircraft systems are at a high level of readiness. Conduct exercises, test your systems, train the personnel operating these systems. Minister of Defense, I'll instruct the Minister of the Treasury to turn over the necessary funds for the Air Force and preparation of civil defense. Head of IAEC, I want your experts to interpret the significance of the results brought to us by Mossad. Gentlemen, this is possibly the biggest threat on our country since the 1973 War. It is our responsibility to our children and grandchildren to prevent this catastrophe."

As they were leaving the room, the PM asked Shimony and David to stay behind. "Do you know what is happening with the other hostages? I was pleased that Morris and Vicki didn't know that Inbal is my granddaughter and hope the Iranians don't find this out."

David looked at Shimony and said, "Mr. Prime Minister, one of the scenarios we suspect is that the Iranians will agree to return the hostages and use them to somehow deliver the nuclear bomb. Maybe they will booby-trap the plane with a nuclear device. Perhaps they'll manage to reduce its size and weight so that it will fit in a suitcase and then we'll be almost helpless to prevent its delivery. I need your direct permission to continue to negotiate their release with Imam Mourtashef, because there are risks involved here, as I mentioned."

The PM said, "I had feared that it would come to this—saving my granddaughter from Evin Prison at the cost of putting the country at risk. If it were a direct threat, I would have not hesitated to resign, but in the present situation where the risk is still hypothetical, I prefer to continue to lead this country. I am not sure I can completely trust whoever replaces me if I resign."

Shimony said, "Prime Minister, Mossad will do all in its power to have the hostages back safely and to avert the danger to the country."

November 4, General Koliagin's office, Moscow

General Koliagin was in a foul mood once again. He was looking forward to hosting another meeting with Imam Mourtashef and David Avivi, but something in the back of his mind was bothering him.

He couldn't figure the real motivation of both sides. On the one hand, the Iranians were trying to demonstrate to the world that they were a respectable member of the international community.

Since the 2016 election, the extreme outbursts against America and Israel were toned down—no more "Big Satan" and "Little Satan" banners and chants in "spontaneous" demonstration, no more "Death to America" shouts, even the outbursts and invectives against the Sunni Islamic countries were seldom heard in official speeches and in public gatherings.

On the other hand, there were disturbing rumors that the old guard and extremists were clinging to power and were up to something. He had received a report that several leading scientists and engineers had not been seen in public for some time. Russian agents had reported that collaborators within the Iranian administration hinted that a dramatic move is expected but didn't know in which direction.

One of the agents, who had close ties in the Iranian

Revolutionary Guards was told the IRG was cashing many of its investments and converting their assets into dollars, as if expecting a catastrophic event.

The FSB operators in Germany had heard about a very strange sample that was brought by Mossad for analysis at the ITU nuclear forensics laboratories but had not been able to get any details about the results.

There also seemed to be an increase in the traffic between heads of Western intelligence services. Although these exchanges were either on secure communication lines or in tête-a-tête meetings, the very fact that their intensity grew was an indication something was amiss.

Koliagin also didn't trust the Israelis. He saw the warm welcome the first two released hostages received, and his political analysts spent days dissecting and interpreting every sentence in the Israeli PM's speech at the press conference.

The repeated threats about the dire consequences of Iranian violations of the nuclear deal contrasted with the general atmosphere of rapprochement. He felt the Israelis knew something and this was not an unsubstantiated warning. He understood that the Israelis wanted to wrap up the release of the hostages, in particular the return of the PM's granddaughter, but wondered what they were willing to give the Iranians in return.

No, General Koliagin was not happy. Conspiracy theories were the bread and butter in communist countries, and people of his generation grew up suckling such stories with their mother's milk. He wanted to discover what each side was scheming.

***

David and the Imam arrived at the same time. Koliagin opened the meeting. "This is our third meeting and I hope we'll continue to make progress. I am glad that our last meeting went so well and that the Iranians released two hostages, not just one as agreed, and that the Israeli Prime Minister himself acknowledged that humanitarian gesture and thanked Iran in public. I would like to see how we can help to further resolve the differences between your countries." He looked at David and added, "And of course, expedite the return of the remaining hostages."

David said, "Before we start, I would like to thank the Imam and convey our gratitude for the wonderful silk rugs that he had so kindly sent us."

The Imam adopted a jovial expression. "You are welcome. I hope you make good use of them. The Islamic Republic of Iran is willing to proceed and release the remaining hostages. We have realized that our original demand that Israel dismantle its nuclear research centers and allow IAEA inspector free access would not be acceptable, so we have changed our demands. There are more than fifty political prisoners in Israeli jails that we want released.

"They are mainly Shiite freedom fighters who worked for Hezbollah and we demand that they are to be returned to Lebanon promptly. In addition, we demand all the bodies of dead Shiite freedom fighters also be returned to Lebanon. I have prepared a list of the prisoners. This is not negotiable. We insist that every single one of them will be released, regardless of the allegations against them."

David glanced at the copy of the paper that the Imam handed to him. "I see that there are several terrorists with blood on their hands. They have been involved in the murder of innocent civilians. I need to consult with my government before agreeing to such a deal."

The Imam looked at General Koliagin and said, "General, look at this proposed exchange. For each Israeli, we are demanding only five of our people. Surely you recall other deals where the Israelis released more than one thousand prisoners for just one captive soldier! In the markets of Tehran, this would be an offer no one can refuse."

David asked the general's permission to make a phone call. The general summoned his secretary and she escorted David out of the conference room and pointed at a telephone that was on her desk.

David had his encrypted cell phone but decided to use the telephone she showed him. The call to Shimony was brief and, as the Russian FSB later heard from the recording of the call, the deal was immediately approved. Shimony emphasized that it should be done quickly.

David returned to the conference room and said he received permission to agree to the proposal.

General Koliagin was pleased. "It looks as we have reached an agreement. Honorable Imam, when do you wish to execute this deal?"

The Imam looked at David. "As soon as the Israelis are ready. We have all the hostages in a safe place and can get them aboard the same private jet that delivered the first two hostages at a moment's notice. I propose to carry out the exchange on the day after tomorrow. Our freedom fighters will be brought to the Lebanese border checkpoint and as soon as they cross into Lebanon the hostages will descend the plane's staircase and be reunited with their families. I suggest that both exchanges are simultaneously shown on TV."

He grinned as he looked at them, and added, "A classic split screen event showing the joyous welcome by families and friends on both sides."

General Koliagin's instincts that there was some conspiracy involved were signaling to him that the speed with which this mutual agreement was reached was highly irregular. He decided to pursue the matter later and concluded the meeting stating he would be glad to continue to serve as the middleman.

November 4, Mossad Headquarters, Tel Aviv

David returned from Moscow and made his way directly from the airport to Shimony's office. He was surprised to see that Julia was there but figured that she had some news about the murder of Sam and Ruby.

Indeed, she said, "I have collared Segan and questioned him. He was cooperative but adamantly declared that he had nothing to do with the murder of Sam and Ruby. He is sure that Alan Ross had contracted another firm to do the job in order to prevent them from giving any evidence that would surely implicate him in the elimination of the Iranian scientists. I believe Segan. So, now you have to decide what to do about it."

Shimony thanked her and asked her to leave the office. As soon as the door closed behind her, he said, "David, I believe her. I think you can permanently remove her from your list of suspects. We'll deal with Alan Ross later and make sure that he pays dearly for these murders. Now, tell me exactly what happened in Moscow."

David repeated the conversation, not to say the negotiation that took place in Koliagin's office.

Shimony heard him out and said, "Well, now we have to really suspect the Iranians motives. The deal they offered us is too good to be true, and when something is too good it is probably not true. I couldn't care less about the fifty Hezbollah terrorists and certainly not about returning the bodies, but something smells fishy."

David agreed. "Yes, I think that Koliagin was also suspicious. It is not like the Iranians to acquiesce so easily. I wonder if the private jet is the means for delivery of the device and the return of Morris and Vicky Aladgem was just a "dry run" to test us."

Shimony nodded. "My sentiments exactly. We need to bring this to the PM."

David said, "We should not allow the jet to land at Ben-Gurion airport near Tel Aviv. Air traffic control can direct it to a remote airfield. The best choice would be at Ovda airfield that is mainly a military base that also accepts civilian flights, usually charter flights to Eilat.

"We can take precautions like transferring all our planes away from the base, install a powerful transmitter that will emit strong electromagnetic pulses to interfere with any electronic device on board, and have a very small reception committee for the hostages. We can say that Ben-Gurion airport had to be closed down due to an emergency. So, if indeed there is a nuclear device on the plane and it is not neutralized, its detonation in the middle of nowhere will cause minimal damage."

Shimony nodded. "I like the idea—start working. You have unrestricted authority to do whatever you see fit. I'll update the PM and tell him that the hostages may be at risk, in case the plane is booby-trapped, but the country is safe."

November 4, Office of the Senior Assistant, Tehran

The Imam returned from Moscow and met with the Senior Assistant and General Aslawi to report that their plan was working according to schedule. He told them about the negotiations and Israel's immediate agreement to the new toned-down demands.

He said, "Every customer in the Souk knows that when something is unreasonably cheap it is either broken or stolen. The super-intelligent Mossad agent is probably used to the American way of doing business where the customer can return faulty merchandize and be refunded. This is not how the Middle East works."

The Senior Assistant said, "Honorable Imam, we commend you once again for pulling the wool over the eyes of the Zionists."

General Aslawi was more practical. "So, what is the

schedule and how do we continue?"

The Imam replied, "The exchange is scheduled in two days' time. The fifty Hezbollah prisoners and dead bodies of the fighters will be brought to the border with Lebanon simultaneously with the landing of our jet with the hostages. The nuclear device will be placed in the same locked trunk in which we sent the Persian rugs last time. The pilot will get a key and be told that it opens the trunk, but it will not work because we changed the lock. The device has a double triggering mechanism. It has an electronic trigger that can be set off by an encoded radio message. The message will be transmitted by a radio operator, one of our IRG officers, that we have positioned in a Hezbollah controlled enclave in southern Lebanon and has a range of one hundred and fifty miles—enough to cover Ben-Gurion airport that is about one hundred and twenty-five miles from the border with Lebanon.

"The officer will watch the TV coverage of the exchange and select the appropriate moment to send the signal. The fallback mechanism is mechanical and triggered by a change in air pressure. It is set to automatically go off exactly fifteen minutes after the jet lands and its door is opened. We assume that the timing would be good even if we don't have direct control. This is a new type of device and the Chinese manufacturer assured us that it is foolproof."

The Senior Assistant asked, "Do any of the plane's crew know what they are carrying?"

The Imam smiled. "When they reach Allah, they'll know for sure."

November 4, Moscow

General Koliagin was chain smoking and his ashtray was so full that he used his empty coffee cup for the half-smoked cigarettes and ash. He couldn't rid himself of the feeling that he had all the pieces of the puzzle but didn't know how to arrange them.

He called his secretary and she gave him her usual anti-stress treatment, cuddling his head between her ample breasts and letting them brush his shoulders.

Suddenly, he shouted "Aha, it's the plane with the hostages!"

His secretary smiled and kissed the top of his head and he visibly relaxed.

November 6, Evin Prison, Tehran

The activity in the hostages' cell was like a beehive ever since the previous evening, when they were told they would be released the next day. They all tried to gather their meager belongings in the plastic bags that Fatso had given them.

Each was limited to a single bag, so they had to select what to take back to Israel and what to leave behind.

Zorik wanted to leave everything behind him and to do his best to forget the time he and Inbal had spent in the prison cell. He did a quick mental calculation and realized that he had been incarcerated in Evin Prison since September 20, a little over six weeks. Even if he added the time since his capture on Dal Lake in Srinagar, an event that seemed to be decades earlier, it was less than two months.

He was amazed how much happened and how his life and perspective had changed in such a short time. Like all other prisoners, he was looking forward to being reunited with his family and friends and to announce his wedding date. He and Inbal had quietly discussed this and decided that they would get married as soon as possible, they even considered asking the Imam to perform the ceremony. They would hold a small party for their closest friends and family and have no media coverage when, they refused to think in terms of "if," they were free.

The other hostages were also in euphoria. Jokes, old and new, were exchanged from one end of the cell to the other end. Fatso looked at the captives and thought he would miss bossing them around. He had been told that they would be taken to the airport at ten in the morning and was waiting for the guards as the time was approaching.

A moment later four armed guards entered the corridor and Fatso joined them with the hostages as they marched to a waiting bus. They all boarded the bus with two guards in the back of the bus and two at the front. No one bothered to tie the prisoners or chain them to their seats—they were on their way to freedom and were not about to cause any problems. They started singing and clapping their hands and the guards watched them with benign smiles.

A closed van was driving just ahead of the bus. It had a large trunk in its middle section and half a dozen fully armed guards were seated around it. The trunk was tied firmly to special metal rings that were welded to the floor of the van. Dr. Fathi himself was seated next to the driver.

Unlike the bus, the atmosphere in the van was solemn, although Fathi was the only one who knew that they were literally sitting on a nuclear bomb. The van stopped just short of the private jet and the trunk was loaded on to the plane. Fathi gave an order and everyone got off the plane and left him alone with the trunk.

He unlocked it and set the dual triggering mechanism. The transmitter had been carried by an IRG officer on a direct flight from Tehran to Beirut the previous day and was now on location in southern Lebanon. Fathi took a second look at the mechanical triggering device and shook his head in disgust. This mechanism had not been tested due to the short notice he was given by the Imam a mere thirty-six hours earlier. He had tried to express his reservations about the hasty way the project was unfolding but was told to keep his opinion to himself.

When Fathi finished his preparations, he closed the trunk and locked it. He made sure that it was firmly secured in place with the steel cables. He descended the stairway and was met by the pilot. He gave the pilot a thumbs up and handed him the fake key.

He didn't want to say another word to people he knew were condemned to death in a nuclear blast. At least they would not suffer, he thought, and then wondered how cynical he had become.

The pilot and co-pilot took their seats and the two cabin stewards prepared for take-off, while the hostages boarded the plane and took their seats. They buckled up and tried to relax but the tension and excitement were too great, and they clung to the armrests with both hands.

Zorik looked around him and saw that the crew was watching them calmly, so he loosened up a little. The cockpit door was closed but it looked as if it was not the reinforced type that commercial planes had installed after 9/11. He just speculated what would happen if the hostages decided to overpower their captors and take control of the plane. He knew he could fly it but didn't think this would ever happen.

The twin engines revved up and the plane taxied to its take-off position. The control tower wished flight IRG101, as it was now called, a pleasant and safe journey and within minutes it was airborne and heading west.

CHAPTER 20

November 6, Ovda airfield, Negev, Israel

The large air force base was empty, except for a couple of civil aviation planes, in which David and a dozen elite unit soldiers arrived in and three military helicopters. There was one other helicopter that was chartered by the Israeli TV channel and carried an airborne camera crew. Another camera crew was waiting on the ground right next to the runway. The base personnel were taken by buses to the nearby resort town of Eilat. They were told that they deserved a day off and the government had funded a day of fun and games on the shores of the Red Sea.

The Iranian plane, flight IRG 101, was directed to land at Ovda airfield by the control tower of Ben-Gurion airport. The pilot was informed that an emergency situation had developed, and a Jumbo jet was stranded on the runway, so the field was closed. The pilot reported this to his controller in Tehran and was told to proceed as directed. He asked for assistance and was given a vector by the Ovda control tower.

He was a bit surprised to see that he was escorted by a single F-16 fighter jet. He didn't see that three other F-16's were flying high above him because his radar couldn't see directly upward. He also didn't know that the lead F-16 pilot had been instructed to shoot his plane down if it deviated from its flight path.

The Iranian jet approached the Ovda airfield and given permission to land on runway 02/20. The landing was much rougher than usual, and the plane hit the ground with a thud that sent the hearts racing of everyone on board. The trunk in the hold of the plane was jarred by the impact but remained in place thanks to the steel cables that tied it down.

Zorik didn't appreciate the pilot's skills but he didn't know that the control tower sent him to land downwind, so his ground speed was higher than his airspeed when he touched down.

The airborne and ground-based TV crews filmed the landing of the Iranian plane and it was aired live. The plane taxied to the anxiously awaiting reception committee, but the fuselage door remained closed for a long moment even after it had come to a full stop.

David understood that the Iranian pilot was waiting for permission from Tehran and acknowledgement that the Hezbollah prisoners and bodies were freed and were cross-ing into Lebanon. He wasn't sure what would happen when the Iranians would discover that the flight had been diverted away from Ben-Gurion airport and he thought of giving the soldiers the signal to shoot out the front tires of the plane.

Finally, the door opened, and the staircase was released by one of the stewards. The first to appear at the doorway was Johnny, the Member of Knesset and the rest of the hostages followed him. They were really surprised to see such a small reception party, but they were told the flight had to be diverted from Ben-Gurion airport. The hostages were taken to the two civil aviation planes that were waiting and the planes took off immediately on their way to the official reception at Ben Gurion airport.

David made sure that the electromagnetic signals were jammed and then approached the open door, accompanied by three of the Israeli soldiers and his colleague from the IAEC. He formally asked the pilot for permission to come aboard.

The pilot approved his request and asked whether his plane could be refueled. David said that as soon as he completed a search of the plane's hold, a tanker would come by and refuel the plane. The pilot indicated that it was okay with him. David boarded the plane and went straight to the large trunk. He asked the pilot to open it and both were surprised when the key didn't work.

David called one of the soldiers and told him to force the lock. The soldier took out his commando knife and removed the hinges of trunk without touching the lock. Very carefully, lifting the lid just a fraction, David peered inside, and an uncontrolled cry escaped his lips. "Watch out, there is a bomb in here."

David's colleague pulled out a radiation detector and placed it near the trunk. They all heard it clicking, indicating that radioactive material was present. The pilot said, "Now, I understand what that weird scientist was doing in Tehran and why he locked the trunk and gave me this useless key."

David said, "What are you talking about?"

The pilot told him all about Dr. Fathi and the time he spent alone with the trunk.

David immediately instructed everyone to get as far away from the plane as possible, warning them that the plane may be booby-trapped. He thought that it was a necessary precaution if conventional explosives went off but knew that it would be quite futile in the case of a nuclear detonation. Before he could repeat this warning, everyone had scattered away and there was no one else in sight.

David carefully further lifted the trunk's lid and saw pieces of a mechanical device strewn over the bottom of the trunk. Apparently, the rough landing had broken it, or perhaps it was fragile from the beginning.

The IAEC man pointed at a small antenna and said that it was probably some part of a remotely-operated switch. David took a close look and saw that it was connected to a small box, from which two electric wires led to a larger box. There many very fine wires that came out of this second box and it didn't take a genius to figure that they led to an array of detonators.

David gingerly opened the small box and removed the two AA batteries that powered the receiver ensuring the bomb couldn't be triggered by a radio signal. He looked at his colleague and saw that he was perspiring profusely, and his eyes were tightly shut.

He smiled. "If you can hear me, you are still alive. Okay. From here on, we'll get the bomb-squad experts to dismantle this device." He exited the plane and called everybody back.

He called the Iranian pilot and showed him the dismantled device. He then addressed the entire crew. "You were used by ruthless people, who sent you to your death. Fortunately, you were all saved by some divine intervention. We know that you were sacrificial goats just like those innocent animals that don't know what awaits them. I strongly recommend you don't return to Iran because you'll certainly be accused of sabotage. You will now be the guests of the Israeli government and will soon be sent to any destination of your choice. We don't take innocent hostages."

The jamming device was switched off and David made a few phone calls.

November 6, Tehran

Imam Mourtashef and General Aslawi were watching the live TV broadcast in the Senior Assistant's office. They couldn't believe their eyes. On one part of the screen they watched the Hezbollah people crossing the border into Lebanon and on the other part they saw flight IRG 101 landing on a desert strip in the middle of nowhere.

The Imam turned up the volume and heard the reporter say that the flight was diverted there due to an accident on the main runway of Ben Gurion airport. He checked the map and saw that Ovda airfield was about two hundred and fifty miles from the south of Lebanon and realized it was out of the range of the transmitter that was supposed to send the triggering signal. He kept watching expecting the mechanical trigger to function fifteen minutes after the door of the plane was opened. He looked at his watch and waited. After thirty minutes he realized the nuclear explosion was not going to happen.

He looked at his two colleagues and sadly said, "I think we have reached the end of the road." They nodded but did not say a word.

November 6, Ben-Gurion airport, Tel Aviv

The press conference was held in the largest available room at Terminal 3 of Ben Gurion airport. Despite the late hour, it was standing room only.

The Prime Minister's press secretary said, "Thank you all for coming to this very special event. Israel has many reasons to celebrate today, so we have a busy schedule here. First, the released hostages will be officially welcomed in a small ceremony with the entire government of Israel. Then one of them will tell us all about their plight in the infamous Evin Prison in Tehran. After that, the Prime Minister himself will deliver a special statement to the people of Israel and then will take some questions from the press.

"So, at this time I wish to invite all the released hostages that were freed today to come to the podium. First, I call upon Zorik Shemesh and Inbal Sabatani, who were captured in Srinagar."

The young couple stepped forth holding hands to the applause of the audience. The press secretary continued, "Please wait with your applause until I have presented all the hostages. Please welcome Shulamit and Nate Levy and they are from Haifa and were captured in Tbilisi, Georgia. Then, these two young men, Ari and Avi, who were kidnapped brutally while on vacation in Thailand. This is Yanna and Eyal, who were enjoying the sands of Dahab, in Sinai, and found themselves in prison in Tehran. Finally, here's the man who needs no introduction, Yonathan Shmaryahu our MK, whose disappearance was a major event. You all know him as Johnny and he is accompanied by his bodyguard, Oded."

"Here's Johnny!" he announced but was booed by the more sophisticated members of the media for his tasteless antics.

Zorik stepped to the podium. "I was requested by my fellow hostages to tell you a little about our time in prison. Although we were captured in different countries, by different people, we all ended in the same cell, as well as Vicki and Morris Aladgem, who were released earlier. We were treated quite well by our captors. They didn't torture us or try to extract classified information from us. It quickly became apparent that they were holding us as bargaining chips for some reason. Evin Prison is a formidable place, where for decades, whoever was in power in Iran used it to lock up real or imaginary enemies and members of the opposition. We knew that we would not be rescued by some military operation—it was impossible to do so in the heart of Tehran, but we also knew that our government would do whatever it could to free us."

The loud applause continued for several minutes until the hostages were beginning to get embarrassed. Zorik added, "Thank you, but real thanks are due to our government."

The press secretary held his hand up and when the audience grew quiet, he welcomed the Prime Minister. The PM appeared to be in an extremely good mood. His usual artificial smile was replaced by a genuine smile that grew larger as he stepped up to the podium.

"I am very pleased to welcome the hostages. We have sent medical aid and rescue experts to different points of the globe that suffered from natural disasters, like floods and earthquakes because of moral obligations to help those in times of distress. You know that this government would do everything within reason to help our own people. Inbal and Zorik, please come here."

When the young couple approached, he kissed Inbal and hugged Zorik while patting him on the back. He continued, "This beautiful and clever young lady is my granddaughter and this handsome young man will soon be her husband. Both represent what we want our future generation to be like."

The applause almost brought the roof down as Inbal and Zorik returned to their seats. The PM paused for a moment to signal that he was moving to a more serious subject. "A few days ago, I thanked Iran for releasing Vicki and Morris but warned them that if they were found to be in violation of the nuclear deal they had signed they would be severely punished by the international community. Earlier today they took advantage of the hostage release situation and placed a nuclear device that they had clandestinely constructed on the plane that brought the hostages back home."

He motioned to his press secretary who unfolded two large photographs of the device and the plane. "Thanks to the information our Mossad agents gathered, we were prepared for that. The plane was diverted to an airbase in the Negev and the device was neutralized."

He stopped talking and waited for the astonished audience to calm down. He had to pause for some time while text messages with "stop press" notes were sent by reporters to all the leading news channels. The TV crews were elbowing one another to get a closer view of the PM and the photos of the device and plane.

Finally, he was able to continue, "The international community will not sit still until this fanatical, extremist evil regime is replaced by a sane regime that represents the people of Iran. I will now take a few questions."

No one spoke for a moment and then everyone seemed to be speaking at once. The press secretary tried to gain some control but had to give up. The level of excitement exceeded all previous records. One of the reporters gained the PM's attention and shouted, "Does Israel consider a punitive or preemptive strike against Iran?"

The Prime Minister put on a solemn expression. "Israel retains the right to react against its enemies in the appropriate time and place. I hope this will not be necessary if sanity returns to Iran and the international community. Thank you all, I would like to spend some time with the hostages." The PM walked away from the podium.

EPILOGUE

The counterrevolution in Iran took place a few days after the plot was unveiled. It was not as bloody as the Islamic religious revolution was but several Mullahs and Imams were hanged in Azadi Square and several others were lynched when they tried to escape.

Some nuclear scientists and engineers disappeared, and their families never heard from them again. The Islamic Republic of Iran became simply Iran. Terrorist movements that were supported directly or indirectly by Iran disappeared or lay dormant when their funding and supply of weapons dwindled to a trickle.

Alan Ross passed away in a dentist's chair at the clinic of one of the best dentists on Harley Street in London. No foul play was suspected nor was any responsible. Apparently, Ross suffered a stroke when the dentist's assistant mistakenly focused the powerful lamp on his eyes instead of on his mouth. She had prepared him for a routine check-up, but the bright light triggered some unknown trauma and he had an aneurism that caused the stroke. Not many people mourned him.

Segan died in a freak accident while on vacation with his fiancé at Iguazu Falls in Brazil. For some unknown reason, he plunged to his death from the boat that took tourists to observe the famous Falls from beneath one of the curtains of gushing water. Apparently, he stood up with his camera to take a photo of his fiancé with the Falls in the background and stumbled over the low guardrail to the horror of the other tourists. They could only watch helplessly as he was being pummeled by the tremendous downpour of gushing water.

The investigation did not find any fault with the crew of the boat or with any of the people who were on it. His body was sent for burial in Israel as he had instructed in his will.

One of the tourists on the boat trip, turned out to be an Israeli citizen and he volunteered to escort the body. It looked as if all the arrangements for flying the body had been arranged in advance.

Julia Carmon completed her term as Head of Mossad station in Berlin and upon her return to Tel Aviv, was promoted to head a section that dealt with keeping close tabs on former Mossad agents, a kind of internal security department. She was not too happy with the new assignment but saw it as a steppingstone to a more senior position. She tried to get reunited with her ex-husband, but he had already started a new family with a younger woman, who had given birth to twin daughters.

The Prime Minister's plan to replace Shimony with one of his supporters had to be postponed. The PM had decided to have an early general election as his popularity after the Iranian Nuclear Affair, had skyrocketed. After all, for years he had said that the Mullah regime in Iran couldn't be trusted, that the nuclear deal was a ruse and that Iran continually strived to arm itself with nuclear weapons and become a nuclear power. Now, that he had been proven correct, he believed that he would be able to gain a majority for his party. He didn't want to rock the boat by letting Shimony, who had also gained credit, go without a good reason that could be publicly justified.

David Avivi decided to take a year off his work at Mossad and complete his Ph. D. in physics at the Weizmann Institute of Science. His thesis dealt with the theoretical astrophysical aspects of fusion reactions. He sincerely hoped that the topic would remain theoretical and would never get any closer than the distance between Earth and Sun.

ACKNOWLEDGMENTS

In this book, and my other books **Mission Alchemist** and **Mission Renegade,** I have tried to imagine the unimaginable. Fortunately, these are works of fiction and hopefully they will remain so.

First and foremost, I would like to thank you for reading this book. I hope you enjoyed it despite the scientific jargon that I really tried to minimize.

I dearly appreciate your comments, so please send them to: Charlie.Wolfe.author@gmail.com

I would be especially grateful if you would post a review on the Amazon website.

You may want to read my previous books **Mission Alchemist** and **Mission Renegade** that were first published in ebook format on Amazon in 2015.

Like my other books, this book would not have been possible without the help of Dr. Wikipedia and Professor Google and Magister Google Earth. I also found a wealth of information in scientific articles and books. However, any misinterpretation of the technical and geographical information from those sources is my own responsibility.

It is unnecessary to declare that this book is a work of fiction and any resemblance to real events or people is not to be understood as anything but a coincidence. I apologize in advance in case any person feels offended by the plot.

Special thanks are due to Glenda Sacks Jaffe who meticulously edited this book.

Finally, I am grateful to my family and friends who read the manuscript and enabled me to improve the text thanks to their astute comments.

Please see the Prologue for my next exciting thriller **Mission Rocket Man.**

Printed in Poland
by Amazon Fulfillment
Poland Sp. z o.o., Wrocław